"Jillian Hunter is a n... ...at

—Katherine Sutcliffe, bestselling author of
Hope and Glory

Praise for Jillian Hunter
and her heartwarming novels

INDISCRETION

"A delectab... ...at will
have you lau... ...r repar-
tee. . . . Ms. ... ...adding
wit and pass... ...e clock
and read all ...

—*Romantic Times*

"A sexy, funny, fast-paced read that is sure to please."
—*The Oakland Press*

ABANDON

"Charming characters and perky dialogue."
—*Publishers Weekly*

"Jillian Hunter is a master storyteller. . . . I couldn't
put it down."

—AOL Romance Fiction Forum

"Ms. Hunter has always managed to make a believer
out of her readers."

—*Romantic Times*

DELIGHT

"Funny, touching, sexy, and tender. . . . Jillian Hunter weaves a spell over her audience."

—*Romantic Times*

"Jillian Hunter's *Delight* is just that."

—*Detroit Free Press*

"Hysterically enchanting . . . a 'delightful' take of love, romance, and adventure. A must read!"

—*Old Book Barn Gazette*

"Hilarious from beginning to end."

—*Rendezvous*

DARING

"A winning combination of characters, plot, and quirkiness. . . . You'll be charmed, captivated, and utterly enchanted with . . . the entire plot, setting, and most of all, the special pieces that make a Jillian Hunter romance a rare treat."

—*Romantic Times*

FAIRY TALE

"[A] delightful take of wonderfully warm characters who make you smile and laugh out loud. It's a must read."

—Janet Carroll, Romance Writers of America's 1996 Bookseller of the Year

Books by Jillian Hunter:

Jillian Hunter

Indiscretion

POCKET BOOKS
New York London Toronto Sydney

This book is a work of fiction. Names, characters, places and incidents are products of the author's imagination or are used fictitiously. Any resemblance to actual events or locales or persons, living or dead, is entirely coincidental.

An *Original* Publication of POCKET BOOKS

 A Pocket Book published by
POCKET BOOKS, a division of Simon & Schuster, Inc.
1230 Avenue of the Americas, New York, NY 10020

Copyright © 2000 by Maria Gardner

ISBN-13: 978-0-671-02683-7
ISBN-10: 0-671-02683-6

First Pocket Books printing April 2000

10 9 8 7 6 5 4 3

POCKET BOOKS and colophon are trademarks of Simon & Schuster, Inc.

Illustration by Aleta Rafton; Handlettering by David Gatti

Manufactured in the United States of America

For information regarding special discounts for bulk purchases, please contact Simon & Schuster Special Sales at 1-800-456-6798 or business@simonandschuster.com.

1

Windsor Castle
1843

She hadn't spoken a civil word to him in over two years. But what else could he expect? Patrick Sutherland, fifth Viscount Glengramach, had seduced Anne Kerr seven years ago. Their secret affair aside, she wasn't going to be able to avoid him today, not at a court appearance.

He stared down the corridor of Windsor Castle, wondering what she would say when she saw him. He ought to be wondering why the Queen had summoned both of them into her presence. He couldn't even remember what he had done at the last court affair he'd attended, only that he had felt out of place, a Highlander despite his title. He still remembered, however, exactly what Anne had said to him the single time they had been lovers.

Every poignant detail came back to him.

In his memory he could feel the damp moorland wind blowing through the castle windows, and the mossy stone floor that formed their bed. He could see the heather buds that Anne had woven into her hair, and her frantic race to finish dressing because it was past suppertime, and she was due home hours ago but he had kept her, selfishly. He had loved her so hard they had both fallen asleep on the floor, and only the patter of summer rain on the battlements had awakened them. The hours had passed too fast.

"I don't know what you're grinning about, my lord." She flung his shirt at him. "We have just disgraced ourselves beyond redemption."

"I'm grinning because I'm a verra satisfied man." He bent his head to kiss her bare breasts before she could cover them with her lawn smock.

She wriggled away, shivering, then sat still as he fastened the ties at her shoulders. "If my father finds out about this, we'll both end up dead. Or married."

"Is there a difference?" he murmured.

She scowled at him. "Your father won't be pleased either," she added, "although he probably wouldn't be surprised. But if mine finds out I only spent a half-hour reading to Aunt Mildred, that's the end of me. We must never see each other again, and do not look at me in church again in such an intimate manner."

He plucked a heather bud from her hair. "Never again, Anne? Not even once more before I go off to fight, risking life and limb for my country?"

"Do you take nothing seriously, my lord?"

"Do you take everything so seriously, my wee witch?" he teased back.

"You are a rogue," she whispered.

He kissed her on the nose. "And you're irresistible."

"I'm leaving now. Don't ever talk to me again. I'm supposed to be married by the end of the year."

He sighed. "You might be married before then if a child comes of this. Contact my father should the need arise. He'll take care of you until I come home."

Her eyes widened in horror. "A child?"

He caught her by the shoulders. "You are truly innocent, aren't you? What have I done?"

Well, there had been no child from their foolish indiscretion, and in due time Anne had been married off to Patrick's own cousin, a respectable Englishman her family deemed suitable for their daughter. Patrick had joined the infantry, finding a fit channel in the military for his restless ways.

For years he had guarded the secret of their encounter, only regretting that he had not been mature enough to pursue a serious relationship with her. At first he had been irrationally angry that she had wed another man, even though they had not promised each other anything, but more often he felt simply wistful, wondering what might have happened between them under other circumstances. Most of his friends had settled down and married, and now that Patrick was free from military duty, he realized he wanted a family of his own. His dabblings in trade and charitable work satisfied his intellect but not his heart. The gaming clubs and weekends of golf with friends had grown tiresome. He and his most recent mistress had drifted apart;

clearly he did not care for her deeply enough to attend the parties she enjoyed. They had nothing in common outside the bedchamber.

The sound of Anne's slippered footsteps on the carpet brought him back to the present. He caught a glimpse of blue-black hair, a curvaceous figure sheathed in pewter-gray silk, and his heart contracted in his chest. She had always been too beautiful for her own good.

She looked up; she was still too far away to see his face, to read whatever emotions would register when she realized who he was. Shock, outrage, embarrassment. She probably remembered him only as a rakehell. Life, however, had been kind enough to him in the intervening years. He had reconciled with his father before he died, inheriting a modest fortune and viscountship. He'd become an officer in the 71st Light Highland Infantry, recently fighting for the British Empire in Bermuda. Yet he had never forgotten her. Would that old attraction flare up between them again? Anticipation built inside him. It was pleasant to contemplate resuming an affair that had never had a chance to deepen into something meaningful.

She had stopped midstride—did she see him standing in the alcove? No, she was covertly adjusting her collar. His mouth flattened into a line of amusement as he watched her. He'd come back to Scotland barely alive, a hero of sorts in his regiment. He was well-off and well-enough liked in London, but no one could call him a social tulip.

She hesitated again, not to look at him, but to stare uncertainly at a door. He studied her elegant profile in appreciation. The Widow of Whitehaven, they called her. A virtuous woman who avoided court and stayed in seclusion on her Hampshire estate with her beloved horses. To see her now, dressed so primly in that pearl-buttoned bodice, her raven curls so artfully tamed, no one would ever guess what a hellion Anne Kerr had been.

No one would ever dream she and Patrick had stood together, naked and shivering with as much lust as cold, in their own private waterfall behind their ruined Highland castle, and that he had washed away her virgin's blood with his bare hands, or that for a few hours they had found solace from their mutual unhappiness in their unwise mating.

"I know I hurt you, Anne. I'm a clumsy bear."

"Aye, but it doesn't matter. I'm as much to blame as you."

A wave of longing swept over him, and a cynical smile curved his mouth; what remained a pleasant memory for him might have become a nightmare in Anne's mind. Perhaps he ought to pretend they were nothing more to each other than distant relatives.

She was coming straight toward him now, as blithe as a dove flitting under the shadow of a waiting hawk. But Anne carried steel beneath her wings, not so much a dove at all but rather a full-fledged phoenix who had risen from the ashes of her shame and made quite a life for herself. She was admired by the society she shunned, praised for her virtue—once married to his respectable English cousin, David Crafton, sixth Baron of Whitehaven.

Yet Patrick would always think of her as his Anne, a little wild at heart, more of a hoyden than her Bible-quoting mother or emotionally aloof father could control; ironically, Patrick had met her at church where their guardians had dragged the two youngsters for moral guidance. His incendiary affair with Anne had been sparked by a single bored look exchanged across a pew.

"Excuse me."

At the sound of her voice, his courage suddenly deserted him, and all the clever lines, all the quips and witty greetings he had planned seemed hollow and inadequate, considering he had stolen her innocence. She hadn't spoken to him since her husband's funeral.

He turned his back on her, rudely, and stared at the picture of a hunting scene hanging on the wall. The glass revealed the tension in his face, not a gently hewn face by any means, and it seemed stupid to delay the inevitable.

He hoped she wouldn't shout—no, she had become the antithesis of the hoyden he adored, the essence of refined decorum. She wouldn't shout. She would cut him dead with a look and that would be the end of that.

"Excuse me," she said again, her voice so amazingly polite and well-bred he might have dreamed they had spent an entire day making love in their abandoned castle. He might have dreamed there wasn't an inch of her body he hadn't explored, tasted, touched and plundered.

"Could you help me, sir? I appear to be hopelessly lost—I'm looking for the waiting room." She allowed the slightest catch of anxiety to creep into her voice as she confided, "I have an appointment with Her Majesty. I cannot be late."

It seemed she too wondered what lay behind the summons, and presumably did not know that he had also been invited.

"It's to your right," he said, his Scottish burr distinct in the silence.

"To my—"

He turned and looked down into her perfectly oval face, drinking in every detail, the aquiline nose, the gray eyes like morning mist, the mouth that had always smiled too easily, the abundance of black curls that she had swept back onto her shoulders.

The sight of her affected him on a dozen different levels: emotionally, he was on a pendulum, swinging from pleasure to uncertainty; sexually, she struck him with the impact of a thunderbolt as she had when he had first seen her riding bareback across the moor to meet him.

"Anne," he said, experience coming to his rescue. "You haven't changed at all."

For a moment she did not react; she didn't even blink. Her face remained a polite blank, but the illusion did not last long. It didn't even last long enough for Patrick to hope she had considered forgiving him for what he'd done when they were both so young and instinctual and tomorrow didn't exist.

"*You.*" Ice crystals hardened in the eyes he'd once found guileless and enchanting. Renewing their association did not loom as a distinct possibility. She looked as if she'd rather cleave his head open with her grandfather's claymore.

He braved a grin, not unaware of his own appeal. "It's been too long."

"Not long enough for me, you weasel, you wolf, you— What are you doing at Windsor Castle?"

He took a breath. He'd caught her off guard, and it wasn't going well. "I'm here to see the Queen."

"Is that right? For an assassination attempt, I suppose?"

"Lower your voice, Anne," he said, frowning in the direction of the two footmen in blue livery who had just appeared at the other end of the corridor. "I have no intention of hurting the Queen."

"Then why—Oh, of course not. Murder isn't your style, is it? Seduction and drunkenness are, and since I think I can safely assume you aren't here to seduce Her Majesty—"

"Thank you," he said, giving a sigh.

"—I can only assume you're here to steal something. The Hanoverian Crown Jewels, or does she keep them in a safer place?"

He rubbed the bridge of his nose, considering his options. He could kiss her and hope to shock her into utter silence. He could beg, point out that he'd changed, inherited a title, lived an exemplary life.

"Obviously you didn't read the letter I sent you after David's funeral," he said dryly.

"It burned into lovely ashes," she retorted.

He paused. He had spent a week on that bloody stupid letter, striving to affect a suitable tone. "Did you hear my stallion took a trophy at the St. Leger?"

She edged around a hideous tiger's head mounted on a marble pedestal. "I don't particularly care if your stallion sprouted wings and flew you to Olympus. I don't want to know one single thing about your life."

That hurt; he knew he had misbehaved a wee bit in the past, but he was willing to make amends. "I am not here to steal anything." His gaze flickered over her, and unconsciously, he had maneuvered his muscular body to block her way. Queen or not, she wasn't going anywhere until he'd at least made her agree to meet him again. "Believe it or not, I was invited."

"Invited?" She took a theatrical step backward. "To interview for the position of royal rat killer?"

He looked intrigued. "Is it still open?" He brought his hand up to his cravat. "Actually, I think the Queen has something a little more important in store. I've met her before, you know. Obviously I made an impression."

"Oh, really? Well, I've met her too, and from what I know of her, she'd be more likely to invite Genghis Khan to court than you."

He put his hands on her small shoulders and gently steered her toward the wall, trying not to laugh. "Watch out."

"What on earth do you think you're doing?"

"Moving you out of the way of the Mongol warriors," he said in a droll voice. "The very mighty ruler Genghis Khan would never have traveled to a foreign land without them."

She leaned against the wall. "Well, you've read a history book since I knew you. I'm amazed. I didn't realize you were literate, or that you could stay sober for the time it took to finish a page."

He gave her an engaging grin. "Would you like to hear me recite the alphabet?"

She grinned back. "It might not be a good idea to strain your mental processes with such a demanding task."

"Are you still that angry at me, Anne?"

"No, Patrick. I appreciate your part in my ruination. Now kindly move out of the way. You've done enough damage to my reputation, thank you."

"I couldn't have done that much damage," he pointed out, "or you'd never have been invited to court."

"Perhaps that's why I've been invited." A note of panic crept into her voice. "Perhaps the Queen found out about us and is going to banish me from her presence forevermore."

"That is entirely unlikely, sweetheart. Ever since her visit to Scotland last year, we Highlanders are all the rage. I suspect we're about to be invited to be part of some Gaelic spectacle."

She narrowed her eyes. "Are you behind this?"

"Don't be insulting, woman." He held out his arm. "Come on. We'll present a united and dignified Highland front if only for appearances. You can thrust the ancestral dirk into my heart afterward."

"Dignified, I agree to." She stepped toward the antechamber door, refusing his arm. "But I have a feeling I'd be safer united with Mephistopheles than with you again."

He laughed quietly. "Oh, Anne."

She arched her brow. "Oh, Anne, what? Or shouldn't I ask?"

"It is good to see you again."

She sighed. "I cannot say I return the sentiment."

2

She buried her hands in her skirts so he wouldn't know how badly they were shaking, but perhaps it was a futile gesture. Tiny shudders of reaction coursed through her body like electrical impulses. *Him.* Him. It was too much to believe they had both been brought here by coincidence. What could it possibly mean?

She caught a glimpse of herself in the beveled mirror on the antechamber wall, her face as white as a shroud, and Patrick, on a furlough from Hades, directly behind her. The image of him should have shocked her, the straight black hair and blue eyes, the clefted chin, but strangely it did not. He had always been a shadow at her side, part of her that would not go away, despite all her efforts to pretend that that episode in her life, that impulsive, poignant, sexual interlude, had not existed.

The last time she had seen their joined reflections had been in a crystal pool below a Highland waterfall where they had washed after making love. But even then they hadn't been able to keep their hands off each other, and she could still see his strong nude body; she could remember the power in his arms and the heat that flooded her belly as he took her where they stood.

She had been so shameless, so enamored with him, submitting to his seduction. Every time he thrust into her, she had surrendered a tiny piece of herself. There hadn't been much left to give to her husband on her wedding night, although David had been so happy to have her, he had pretended not to notice his wife's unmaidenly state.

"Sit down, Anne," Patrick murmured. "You're about to face the Queen, not the firing squad."

It was his voice that brought her back to the present, that lulling voice, that jolted her out of her thoughts. And what had she been thinking about—her affair with the scoundrel, of all things. Less than three minutes in his company, and she'd opened up a Pandora's box of sin, desire, and heaven only new what else would fly out in her face before she could slam the lid shut.

She wasn't thinking of how to please her morally minded sovereign. She was remembering the pleasure she had shared with the most shameless man in Scotland.

"What is the matter with you, Anne?"

His voice again. She tried to focus on his face—no, that wasn't a good idea. She was embarrassed, flustered, remembering what they had shared, and despite what she pretended, she could not find it in her heart to blame him entirely for their bittersweet encounter. Still, the sight of him reminded her of a time when she had been so confused and unhappy.

"What do you think is the matter with me?"

"I don't know." There was genuine concern in his tone. "You look deathly pale—you aren't going faint on me, are you?"

"Not if the floor is available." She released a sigh. "Why has she summoned us all the way here? It can't be for any good purpose."

"Why not?" he asked, starting to feel dizzy from watching her walk back and forth in front of the door.

"Because you're involved, that's why."

"I wish you'd stop giving me so many compliments," he said wryly. "I might get the impression you harbor a certain tenderness for me."

"Where on earth would you get an idea like that?"

He leaned up against the mantelpiece, arms folded across the hard plane of his chest. He was a well-built man, lean and powerful. That much hadn't changed, and for a moment she was so awed by his physical presence, of how incongruous he looked in a royal antechamber, that she almost missed his next outrageous remark.

"I will not be dishonest with you, Anne. I find you more attractive then I did seven years ago."

The words barely sank in before she could feel herself start to shake again. "Are you—" she gave an incredulous hoot of laughter, "—you're actually trying to lure me back into your bed with the Queen about to be announced at any instant?"

He gave her an indulgent look. "Actually, I had something more involved in mind than a few feverish moments."

"Indeed." She froze, her hands tightening into fists at her sides. "Oh, that is so amusing, but at least it answers one question."

"What question is that, my wee witch?" he asked quietly, his blue eyes brooding.

She gritted her teeth, refusing to respond to the nickname he had whispered in her ear when they had made love. Witchcraft, aye, that's what it had been.

Sometimes when she looked back on her mistake with Patrick, she thought she must have been under a spell. There was no other explanation for her behavior and willful disobedience that entire summer. Her parents had pulled their hair in frustration at her strange moods and wild rides across the moor before marrying her off in exasperation. Her aunt had prayed aloud for her salvation. Everyone said she was possessed, doomed, and on the path to hell when in reality she had been only an unhappy girl with a mind of her own. In the Highlands, some people would say Patrick had cast a glamour over her, a bewitchment, and even now she could believe it. She hadn't met anyone like him since.

But she had broken the spell, hadn't she? She had married a sweet, upstanding man and had settled into respectability. She had paid penance with wifely obedience and the suppression of her true self. The glamour couldn't last forever, could it? It was just that he had caught her off guard again. She was shaking from head to toe because he had surprised her, appearing unexpectedly at Windsor Castle. She had always managed to maintain a semblance of control at their other accidental meetings.

But then David had always been at her side, the dependable husband, a charm against evil, an unknowing talisman against temptation.

Temptation.

She closed her eyes. If Patrick so much as breathed on her, if she even looked too deeply into his eyes . . . if he touched her, well, she didn't know what she would do. He might possibly stir up the settled ashes and find a few embers still smoldering from their affair, and all hell would break loose.

"What question, Anne?" he said again.

"Where you spent the last year," she said, shaking off the unwelcome memories. "It was obviously in a lunatic asylum."

"How did you guess?"

"They probably have your cage waiting for you in the institution," she said.

"Do you still like to be kissed behind the knees?" he countered, teasing her back.

Before she could react, an interior door painted in gold opened and two footmen appeared, oblivious to the thunderstorm brewing under their very noses. "Her Majesty will see you now. Come this way, please."

"I don't trust you," Anne whispered as Patrick waited politely for her to proceed him. "I think you're nothing but trouble, and I shall do my utmost to avoid you."

3

She was too upset to appreciate the significance of being ushered into the Queen's private sitting room. She caught a dazzling impression of gilt everywhere, and a case of Sèvres ornaments opposite a carved fairy-tale cradle that sat beside the Queen's armchair. Her Majesty had given birth to a princess only a few months earlier.

Anne had not been to court since David had died. Even before then her appearances had been sporadic. She and David had preferred their quiet life in Hampshire, far away from London or from the Highlands where a handsome rogue had seduced her. She had needed solitude to ponder her life, her wild impulses, and solitude had suited her well.

She had never felt for Patrick's very proper, very British cousin, the Baron of Whitehaven, the same reckless passion she had felt for him. She would never abandon herself so foolishly like that again, but she had come to feel a kind of love for David, and they had enjoyed a peaceful life together. At the least she would always be grateful to him for rescuing her from her parents and the odious assortment of suitors they had considered to take her off their hands. David had given her shelter and security, and the freedom she needed to indulge her passion for horses.

"Lady Whitehaven," she heard the Queen say, "how good it is to see you again."

She felt herself go through the motions of a curtsy and a proper response; one did not initiate conversation, the Queen did. She followed protocol, but her mind was focused on something else.

The Queen turned her attention to Patrick, and Anne stared at the cradle, thinking of the child she had lost to a miscarriage early in her marriage. It was for David that she had kept up her connections at court. Appearances had meant so much to him, and he had been kind, but he hadn't exactly left his widow financially prepared. Money had trickled out of his hands like water. He'd lent to anyone who asked him, and Anne found she would have to struggle to afford a modest lifestyle. Family obligations also had their price. The cost to keep her ailing aunt sheltered and to maintain her own small stables rose every year. She hoped to sell her Berkeley Square residence before winter.

The low murmur of Patrick's voice sent a shiver of anxiety down her spine. Sometimes she still dreamed of him. Sometimes she still woke up with a pounding heart, reliving the moment when she had cast propriety aside to be with him. All her upbringing, all common sense had abandoned her, and she was shocked at what they had done. For months afterward she had been so numb, pretending she felt nothing but resentment for him; in fact, he was the only man she had ever been attracted to in her life. And marrying him had been out of the question—her parents would flay her alive before giving her to such a rogue.

She took a slow breath. By the time Patrick had left Scotland, she had resigned herself to her mistake and married another man, her short-lived affair swept under the carpet and her heart so bruised, she could barely smile.

His reappearance in her life could only signify the worst sort of trouble.

Queen Victoria had not summoned them here to exchange pleasantries. Had the scandal of their fleeting association become known? Would they be censured, banished, forced to explain? As far as Anne knew, no other living soul was aware of what they had done.

She stared at the cradle and thought of all the children she would never have; she had no wish to be entrapped in marriage in the near future. She thought of the man standing next to her, and she could feel the heat of his body stealing into her skin. Seven years had carved interesting lines in his face. His complexion was dark, from recent travels to some exotic land, and Anne remembered David mentioning that Patrick had entered some kind of foreign trade, but Anne had not questioned him on the subject. She had not dared give her secret away by revealing any interest whatsoever in Patrick.

"Lord Glengramach," the Queen said warmly. "The trade winds obviously agree with you. Does your fellow Highlander not cut a dashing figure, Anne?"

She fought a wave of light-headedness. She *doesn't know*—she caught the look Patrick threw her. "I . . . I really hadn't noticed, Your Royal Highness."

"Not noticed?" The Queen's round face took on a faintly surprised expression. Victoria might be high-minded, but she was young, and it was a well-known fact that she appreciated a fine specimen of manliness, especially if that specimen was a Scot, a people she had recently come to admire for their wry humor and honesty.

"But he is a hero, Anne. Have you not heard that he almost gave his life in our defense in Bermuda?"

Anne had heard, all right. In fact, three years ago, when Patrick had returned from Bermuda suffering from a fever, she had rushed to his side at his father's house, abandoning her husband and friends. It had been the height of madness to visit him, but she'd thought he was dying, and she had wanted to see him one last time, perhaps to prove to herself that what they had shared was well and truly dead. It had been her only foolish lapse since their indiscretion; she'd barely spoken to him after that, and her unsuspecting husband had actually commended her kindness. Yet in an odd way Patrick was family. By marrying his cousin, she had made them both a part of her life.

"I have heard of his bravery, ma'am," she said in a polite but detached voice.

The Queen motioned them both to sit before her, leaning forward to speak. "I have embarrassed her, Lord Glengramach, and that is perfectly proper. You are distantly related to each other, are you not?"

"Lady Whitehaven was married to my second cousin, who died two years ago, Your Royal Highness," Patrick answered, arching his brow at the way Anne sat on the opposite end of the gilt sofa to avoid touching him.

"You have the most unusual blue eyes," the Queen told him unexpectedly. "So like my dear husband's, the eyes of an angel."

An angel? Anne all but let out a roar of outrage. If only the Queen knew—but Anne could never reveal his true nature without revealing her own. Patrick was the darkest angel to disgrace heaven's door.

He turned to look at her. "Are you choking, Lady Whitehaven?" he inquired, so concerned she could have killed him.

"Perhaps she needs a light tap on the back," the Queen suggested.

A devilish light glowed in his eyes. "Shall I tap you, Lady Whitehaven? I'm good with my hands."

"I . . . I—"

I'm good with my hands, Anne.

You're good with everything, you devil.

Aye, I know. Open your legs wider. I don't think you screamed loud enough when you came the first time.

"Keep your hands to yourself," she blurted out.

The Queen gave her a quizzical look. "Is something amiss?"

Anne felt Patrick gazing at her in amusement. The man had seen her naked. She swore that even now those blue eyes of his could look through not only her clothes but through seven years of propriety and hiding secrets and overcoming. He saw straight inside her as if taunting that reckless girl he had ruined to respond to him.

The reckless girl in Anne had been brought under control a long time ago.

"I had a . . . cramp in my back, ma'am," she said, pressing against the hard-backed sofa.

The Queen was full of sympathy. "It's the furniture, so undersprung, and the plumbing system is even worse. I vow I cannot wait until work is begun on the new residence. You must visit, and perhaps return the favor by having us at Balgeldie House some autumn for a shooting party."

A servant in livery brought in tea with creamcakes on a silver platter. Anne should have been honored by the gesture, but she braced herself for the worst. Perhaps the Queen was going to suggest that she retire permanently to her isolated Scottish lodge where her sinful character could die a natural death.

"The hunting lodge does still belong to you?" the Queen asked.

"Well, yes. The family uses it infrequently." She cast a sidelong glance at Patrick, who looked uncomfortable on the delicate sofa. Uncomfortable, but not particularly worried, as he followed the Queen's example by helping himself to a cake. Anne took a tiny nibble of her own pastry, swallowing without tasting it.

Devil that he was, he would never have revealed their past indiscretion, or would he? The cruel fact was that even if the Queen had learned the two of them had been lovers, it was only Anne, the woman, who would bear the stigma.

Patrick, on the other hand, would receive a half-hearted scolding in this age of double standards. Then he would go on his merry way ruining maidens in private, or whatever he set his dark heart to these days.

"My friends inform me you have sponsored the building of another grammar school in the Highlands," the Queen said to Patrick. "How proud you must be."

"It was the least I could do with the profits from my investments," he said modestly.

Anne rolled her eyes.

The Queen put down her plate. She regarded them both in absolute silence. "I am afraid I have misled you. I have not called you here to discuss something as pleasant as a holiday in the Highlands or the construction of a grammar school. A far more serious affair brings us together."

"Oh," Anne said, her voice breaking. "Oh, dear."

Patrick stretched forward on the pretense of putting his plate on the table. "Straight face, Anne," he said to her in an undertone.

The Queen released a sigh. "You are aware that the husband of one of my former ladies-in-waiting has met a rather strange death in the Highlands?"

Anne frowned. "Strange death?"

"I am referring to Lord Kingairn," the Queen said,

frowning back at Anne. "Surely you remember your own uncle's death in your lodge?"

"My uncle?" Anne said, feeling like an idiot.

Patrick cleared his throat. "Uncle Edgar."

"Isn't he *your* uncle?" Anne said under her breath.

"I don't think so," Patrick answered. "I thought he was David's uncle."

"Perhaps he is," Anne said. "Or at least his great-uncle, ma'am."

The Queen arched her brow. "At any rate, he was a member of your family, and his death has plunged poor Lady Kingairn into the depths of unhappiness."

"I do remember now, ma'am," Anne said, suddenly able to breathe again. "I was not in Scotland at the time of the sad incident."

"The circumstances of Lord Kingairn's death have raised certain unfortunate questions," the Queen continued. "Certain . . . rumors, which I shall not repeat."

"Do you mean the rumor that he was found nude and spread-eagled on a burial cairn with strange markings on his body, ma'am?" Patrick said.

Anne gasped.

The Queen gave him a look. "Thank you for your blunt honesty. It is what I admire most about the Scottish temperament. I am happy to report, however, that such an atrocious rumor is entirely unfounded. There is not a whit of truth to it."

"I should hope so," Anne said in a choked voice.

"Lord Kingairn died of an apparent heart seizure," the Queen added. "It saddens me to say that a few disturbing questions continue to circulate about the events of that tragic evening."

"I had not heard the details of his death," Anne said worriedly.

"Your good husband understandably did not wish to upset you," the Queen said. "However, gossip is a most dangerous thing. I cannot allow these rumors to continue upsetting my friends."

"Of course not, ma'am," Anne said.

Patrick nodded. "Nip 'em right in the bud, I always say."

"And that is why I have summoned you here," the Queen said.

Anne could barely contain her relief. "I shall immediately begin a correspondence to Balgeldie House instructing all of my staff and neighbors to stop discussing the subject."

Patrick hadn't moved; Anne sensed he might not be completely satisfied with the Queen's explanation. If she hadn't been so giddy with relief, she might also have questioned the frown that marred Victoria's broad forehead.

"There is a little more to the matter, I am afraid," the Queen said delicately. "I wish you to travel to the very source of our trouble and put out these flames of scandal in person."

"Together?" Patrick said, leaning forward so abruptly he almost overturned the tea table.

"The details I will leave to my dear friend and adviser," Victoria said, purposely not elaborating.

"But, ma'am, surely it is not necessary that I take

Lord Glengramach from his charitable duties to accompany me?" Anne asked.

Victoria hesitated. "Perhaps I have not made myself clear. The suggestion of foul play has been raised in your uncle's death."

"Murder?" Patrick said, his knee jarring the table.

"I can certainly manage to squelch a few rumors myself," Anne said, struggling to sit forward. "After all, Uncle Edgar expired on my estate, and the suggestion of foul play seems so unlikely."

"But he was my uncle," Patrick insisted. "I should be the one to get to the heart of the matter."

"We could hardly ask an unprotected woman to place herself in possible danger," the Queen said to Anne. "It has been suggested to me by a trustworthy source that Lord Glengramach is the best choice to accompany you on this mission."

"Suggested by whom, ma'am?" Anne said, tempted to empty the teapot on the scoundrel's head because she knew it had to be him.

"It is a most excellent suggestion," Patrick said before the Queen could open her mouth. "Your adviser is a man of remarkable insight and sensitivity."

"But I cannot travel unchaperoned with a strange man all the way to Balgeldie House," Anne protested.

The Queen pursed her lips. "It is my intention that Lord Glengramach serve as your protector, and naturally you will be properly chaperoned. As to being a stranger, is he not a member of your family?"

Anne could feel the devil gloating beside her; she could feel the flames of another bonfire ignited in Hades on his behalf. She smiled wanly. "I understand your wish to keep this inside my family, ma'am, but perhaps I could select another protector to assist me in my inquiry?"

"Who?" Patrick asked indolently, crossing his legs. "All the men on your side of the family have gone on to their heavenly rewards."

Anne imagined the ornamented room closing in around her like a trap. *This was planned. A conspiracy. But why?* A man like Patrick did not need to conspire to find a woman. "I meant the men on David's side of the family," she said firmly. "Lord Ethelwere, perhaps."

"A trifle difficult to be of any help from Madagascar," Patrick said.

"Then there is Uncle Bran in Yorkshire," she said in a tight voice.

"An excellent choice," he said. "Except for the train accident that left Bran with two broken legs."

The jaws of the trap were snapping shut. Like a cornered fox, she made a final effort to extricate herself. "Lord Anthony," she said triumphantly. "I received a letter, a *healthy* letter, from him only last month."

"Gambling problem," Patrick murmured, making an embarrassed face at the Queen. "Did he ask you for money in his letter, Anne?"

Anne stared mutely at the cradle, wondering why on earth the image of a bad fairy casting a malicious spell kept sneaking into her mind. "Why, yes, but—"

"Creamcake, Lady Whitehaven?" he said, propping another plate on her lap.

The Queen rose from her chair, indicating the interview had ended. "I will leave the details of the investigation to my adviser. I doubt I need to remind either of you how much I value discretion."

Anne pushed aside the plate and surged to her feet. "Please, ma'am, do not leave us hanging in suspense. Who is this mysterious adviser we are asked to obey?"

The Queen gave a little laugh that made her blue velvet lappets bounce around her plump cheeks. "It was to be a surprise, but was I referring, of course, to one of the Crown's staunchest supporters, to none other than your beloved aunt."

4

$\mathcal{T}$he interview was over. The footmen had escorted Anne and Patrick back into the antechamber where they sank onto the sofa in a state of shock, as stiff and gray as a pair of gravestones in a cemetery.

Anne noted that Patrick looked only a little less shaken than she, but she ignored that fact. She still wanted to blame him; she still suspected he had a hand in this.

"Beloved aunt, is it? My only aunt is infirm and has never set foot at court in her life."

He lowered his hand from his eyes. "I've just had a horrible thought."

"You realized you were going to hell?" she said sweetly.

A muscle ticked in his jaw. "I know who the beloved aunt is."

She sat forward. "Please tell me you mean your darling, ancient Aunt Meredith with all the lap dogs."

He shook his head. "I'm afraid not."

They stared at each other in terror. "You don't mean—"

"Aye," he said grimly. "I do. I'd heard Auntie Nellwyn had moved back to London, but it didn't strike me as suspicious until now."

Anne could not speak for several moments. "Then I'm in far worse trouble than I realized. No wonder the image of a bad fairy kept flashing before my eyes. And you—you are a dark prince if ever there was one."

"Dark prince?" he said in confusion.

"I think I'm beginning to understand. For reasons I could never fathom, you were Nellwyn's favorite nephew," she said. "At least that's what David always thought, and I believe he was a little jealous of that old woman's favors."

He looked annoyed. As irrational as it was, he hated it whenever she mentioned her husband. There had always been a lingering regret in his life that she had not belonged to him. "What is your point?"

"That you and Nellwyn concocted this scheme together."

Amusement relaxed the lines of his chiseled face. "I see. The wicked prince and a bad fairy lure the innocent wee princess to the castle to—? Would you care to enlighten me as to our evil purpose? I appear to be a bit in the dark."

"That part should be obvious," she said.

"Prick your finger?" he guessed, grinning.

Her voice was droll. "My finger was pricked a

long time ago, and I fell under a very dangerous spell. But hear me, Patrick, I've been wide awake for years now. I stay away from spindles and dark princes."

He studied her for several moments. It was too hard not to tease her; in fact, he could not resist, loving the way she flared like a candle. For so many years she had ignored him; at least now he had found the means to elicit a response. He narrowed his eyes in concentration.

"A possibility has occurred to me. When did *you* last have contact with Nellwyn?"

Her shoulders tensed; she knew something menacing lurked behind that half-smile. "I don't know. Three months ago, or four, I suppose. What does that matter?"

"Aha." He scooted across the sofa toward her, forcing her into her little corner again. He took up half the space anyway, and he wasn't above using his physical presence to intimidate her. "Then that explains it."

"Explains what?"

"Perhaps this whole thing was your idea. Perhaps you and Nellwyn hatched a plot to make me pay for my youthful mistake."

"A mistake that ruined my self-respect."

"You do not look ruined, Anne. You look ripe and lovely, my wee witch. Do you know what I regret most?"

"Don't tell me."

"I regret not what we did, but that I did not find a way to make you wait for me."

"It obviously wasn't meant to happen."

"Perhaps not then."

"But . . . you were David's cousin."

"Aye," he said softly, "and you were mine first."

She closed her eyes to compose herself, which turned out to be a mistake. He took advantage of her inattention to slide even closer, and the familiarity of his body, the clean scent of his skin, penetrated her shield, reminding her of how easily she could weaken.

Three times isn't enough with you, Anne.

Let me go, Patrick. I have to wash before I go home.

Why? I'll lick you all over, and you know you're not going to make it to that door before I have you on your back again.

Have you no shame?

None. Now lift your legs over my shoulders. Aye, that's right. I'm going to bolt you to the floor. . . .

"Anne," he said softly, his arm curling around her shoulder. "What are you thinking, lass? Is it possible that you put Nellwyn up to this because your pride would not allow you to come to me in person?"

Her eyes opened. "Tell me that isn't your arm around my shoulder."

His thigh pressed against hers, his tone seductively tender. "If you'd read my letters, you'd know there was no need to involve my old battle-ax of an aunt in order to renew our affair. I'm yours for the asking, woman. Go on. Ask."

"Tell me that I do not feel your thigh against mine."

He leaned over her. His warm breath brushed her cheek, stirring dangerous sensations. "One word from you is all I need."

"Bastard." She gave him an evil smile. "Good enough?"

He grinned, the sensual warmth in his blue eyes more devastating than she remembered. "One *encouraging* word."

"Need I remind you that we are in the royal antechamber awaiting your beloved aunt?"

His face registered no reaction; he was focused entirely on her. "There was always that unholy attraction between us, wasn't there? Time and place didn't matter."

She looked around in alarm. "They matter now."

"Attraction like that can grow into the deepest kind of love," he said quietly.

"Or, in our case, into hatred."

He laughed at that, undeterred. His face grew even more intense. His voice deepened to the velvety Scottish burr that turned her insides into burnished honey. "Hold verra still."

A quiver went through her. He framed her face into his large hands. "What are you doing?" she said in horror.

"Just hold still." He sculpted her fine jaw and cheekbones with his long fingers as if relearning the symmetry of her face, as if touching the most precious treasure in the world.

"*Patrick.*"

He slid his left hand down the base of her skull to anchor her slender nape. "Don't move."

His blue eyes impaled her like a butterfly beneath a sword. There had always been a sense of power about Patrick that overwhelmed her. Obviously seven years had only enhanced his skills as a seducer, and she was beginning to suspect it hadn't exactly strengthened her immunity to his charm.

"There is something on your lip, Anne," he said in that gentle voice she should have known better than to trust.

"What is it?" she said in embarrassment. She felt stupid for imagining a seduction. "A spot of cream-cake?"

"No." He grinned wickedly before closing in for the kill. "My mouth."

A rush of poignant memories engulfed her as his lips brushed hers in the briefest of kisses. "No, Patrick," she whispered, turning her head. "No."

"No?"

"No."

He drew away, his voice uneven. "I've waited too long to tell you I'm sorry. Forgive me if I've come at you with all the grace of a warlord. Delicate words have never been my style."

"Neither has discretion. Good Lord, Patrick."

He smiled knowingly. "It's going to be different this time, Anne."

She closed her eyes. "It certainly is."

"We're going to be together again."

"Not if I can help it."

"By royal decree. Do you never think about that day?"

"No," she said, with such vehemence that he

blinked in surprise. "And neither do you—it didn't happen. Please, Patrick, if there is any decency in you at all, let the past be dead."

"To our future, then." He lowered his voice. "Tell me you felt nothing when I kissed you."

"I felt nothing."

"Liar."

"Look who's talking. You were the most wicked boy in the world."

He regarded her intently. "People change."

"Sometimes for the worse."

"Are you going to resist me the whole time we're together?"

"Count on it," she said coldly.

He snorted. "Well, that ought make my job as your protector verra challenging."

"I do not need a protector."

"Aye," he said, infuriating her with his smugness. "You do."

"There are plenty of men the Queen could have asked in your place," she said indignantly.

He sat back, took a deep breath, not as composed as he would like. "There are no reliable men in your life—don't tell me otherwise. I've made a few inquiries here and there. The Widow of Whitehaven fends off all attempts at courtship, and for those who have half a chance, well, let's just say I'll be giving them some friendly advice to seek a partner elsewhere."

She shook her head, stunned. "You wouldn't."

"Aye, I would. You see, you gave something more to me than your innocence that day at the castle.

Aside from my disreputable friends, no one except you and Nellwyn wanted anything to do with me. Everyone thought I was bad, and I guess I set out to prove them right. But you were different. You didn't treat me like I was poison. You were sweet to me, and after we parted I began to think perhaps I wasn't all that hopeless."

"Oh, Patrick. We were so young."

The bruised look in her eyes disturbed him, and he wondered guiltily if had he ruined her for anyone else, even her own husband, and if so he would make it his goal to heal her.

He imprisoned her hands in his, surprised at how fragile the bones felt. "Can you not accept that fortune has brought us back together?"

"Fortune, my foot. Nellwyn is the devil's handmaiden."

"Aye." He nodded agreeably. "That she is. And I'm finding it hard myself to believe that someone would have snuffed out harmless old Uncle Edgar. Especially in a remote Highland lodge where wellbred people meet to enjoy life, not to kill one another."

"It isn't possible," she said in a low voice.

"But if there is a killer running free," he continued, lacing their fingers together, "if there is the least chance that you are in any danger, then it is my duty to take the Queen's request to heart."

"Compassionate to the core, aren't we?"

He chuckled. "I don't need a royal decree to obey the protective instincts that come naturally."

"And the predatory instincts?"

He smiled slowly. "A little more under control than in the past."

"I won't go to Scotland with you, Patrick. I refuse to place myself again in such an embarrassing position. I believe I might even hate you."

"Then why did you visit me when you thought I was dying?"

"Perhaps I wanted to gloat at your grave."

He shook his head, amused and sad. "Not you, Anne. There isn't a mean bone in your body, and I remember your body verra well."

She snatched her hands back into her lap. "There's someone outside the door, and it's probably Nellwyn, listening to every incriminating word. She doesn't know about us, but the woman isn't stupid. She'll soon catch on if you don't behave."

He scratched his cheek and leaned back against the cushions, examining her in detail. When he'd returned with his regiment from Bermuda to Scotland, he had been seriously ill, suffering from a systemic infection and fever. At one point everyone, including him, had thought he would die.

He may have called out for Anne, he couldn't remember what he'd said in his delirium, but one night his father had ushered a woman dressed in black into his room. He hadn't realized it then, but at the time Anne had been in mourning for her father.

Patrick had wondered if she was the Angel of Death. She was so pale and beautiful and her eyes held sadness and a sense of finality that penetrated his feverish haze. She'd touched his face with her delicate pale fingers. She'd laid her head on his chest and wept, saying she had resented him for so long, but she hadn't wanted him to die.

He sighed. "Do you remember what you told me when you thought I was dying?"

"Hurry to hell?" she said.

"You said you had never forgotten me, that your husband didn't understand you, and you were crying."

"I don't remember," she said, her face hot.

"I do."

In fact, however, Patrick himself had been left wondering how much of the conversation he'd imagined, if he had put more meaning to her visit than she had intended. Still, not one of his past lovers or friends had shown up to stand watch at his death bed. They had been too afraid of catching his mysterious malady.

"I never did thank you for that visit, Anne," he said. "It meant more to me than you know." He couldn't resist teasing her again. "Even if it was only to wish me a speedy voyage to hell."

She looked him straight in the eye. "My pleasure."

He gave a wry chuckle, appreciating the prickly side of her personality. It was only after her visit that he had admitted to himself how much he'd regretted losing her. He suspected she had more depth and capacity for emotion than any woman he'd met since, and it had taken almost dying to make him realize he wanted someone like her in his life.

"Your visit seemed to spur my recovery," he added.

She sighed.

"I came to visit you in Hampshire afterward, but your maid claimed you were unwell," he said. "David showed me around your stables, the perfect host, even if his wife was obviously avoiding me. Of course I didn't betray anything. I left without a word."

She softened at the mention of her husband. "He always liked you. I never understood why."

The door behind them rattled, and the refined tones of a woman's voice echoed thinly outside in the corridor.

"It *is* her," Anne said in dread. "I'd know Nellwyn's voice anywhere. Oh, I could die."

Patrick sat forward, taking advantage of their last moment alone. There were so many things he wanted to talk about. "David admitted something to me that day in the stables. He said you were genuinely worried when I was ill. He said that your concern for a member of his family had touched him."

He was almost sorry he'd shared this when he saw the guilt-stricken look on her face; David himself had died of a chest inflammation less than a year later; but the truth was, her official period of mourning was over, and it was the conversation with David that had made Patrick wonder if she still felt a spark of something for him, even if she had buried it beneath layers of embarrassment and regret.

"My two favorite people in the world," a distinctive voice said in the doorway. "And look at the pair of you, what a handsome picture you make together."

He lifted his head from Anne's face, wishing his aunt had allowed them a few more moments alone. Most of all he had intended to tell Anne that their long-ago liaison had meant more to him than he'd ever been able to admit.

5

For a woman who stood barely five feet tall in a pair of high-heeled pumps, Nellwyn Munro, the Marchioness of Invermont, certainly knew how to command a room. In a similar fashion she had commanded all five of the husbands she had outlived. Yet at first glance few people noticed the spine of iron that supported her frail frame, or the glitter of wickedness in her hazel eyes. Age approaching seventy might have turned her hair to silver, but she hadn't been called Naughty Nellwyn, or Nellwyn the Hellion, for nothing.

The current court favorites knew little of Lady Invermont's colorful past, and those who did pretended to have forgotten, having their own secrets to hide. Patrick's paternal uncle, the Earl of Rossmuir, had published a book of verse in her honor.

She entered the room wearing a hideous mustard-yellow taffeta gown embroidered with black velvet stripes. Her silver hair was parted in the middle to accentuate her deceptively sweet face. She was retired from politics now, having served a stint as Mistress of the Robes, but Society still sought her opinions, and she was popular at parties.

"The bad fairy has arrived," Anne murmured, rising dutifully to kiss the woman's wrinkled cheek. "Auntie Nellwyn, you look spectacular, as usual."

"Aye," Patrick agreed, enveloping her in a powerful hug. "Like a big bumblebee."

She laughed, looking past him to Anne. "She's gone as gray as a ghost, Patrick. What have you done to her? Has he been bad, Anne?"

"What do you think?" she said as the woman settled between them on the sofa.

"She was a wee bit surprised to see me at court," Patrick explained.

"I thought I'd interrupted him in an assassination attempt," Anne said. "I almost called the guards."

"I tried to convince her that I'd changed," Patrick said.

Anne's temper boiled over. "And then he did something to prove he was worse than ever."

Nellwyn directed a frown at her nephew. "Just what exactly did you do?"

"Nothing." He shrugged, a pillar of wounded innocence. "Oh, all right. I gave her a wee kiss."

"In the Queen's sitting room?" Nellwyn asked, sounding more pleased than shocked.

"A friendly kiss." His guileless stare made him manage to look like the injured party.

"It felt more feral than friendly," Anne retorted, her back arched in anger. "By some miracle, he appeared to charm the Queen. I don't know how."

Nellwyn shook her head. "Her Majesty made her first visit to Scotland last year and has been enamored of the land ever since. Patrick has made a favorable impression on the court. The Queen likes the primitive life."

"Primitive," Anne said. "That describes him."

"I think," Nellwyn said, her tone brisk, "that this conversation needs to be continued in my townhouse. We shall meet for supper three days hence, and I will expect you to be on your best behavior. Patrick, tell the footman you will be leaving. Anne, follow him to see he stays out of trouble. We will make our plans in the privacy of my home."

Nellwyn stood with the Queen on the terrace of Windsor Castle. "It was good of you to help me, Your Royal Highness. We shall all be leaving for the Highlands within a week. The arrangements have already been made."

The Queen nodded; she was distracted by a warning that a reporter from the *Morning Post* had found his way onto the palace grounds. She thought of the thwarted assassination attempt three years before, and there had been as many break-ins last year alone.

"I am happy to help," she said at last, her blue velvet skirt rustling as she resumed her walk. "Indeed, Albert and I long for the mountain life ourselves. Is there a better tonic to the nerves to be found anywhere in the world? Are there any people more at peace with themselves than our Highlanders?"

Nellwyn compressed her lips. Peaceful was not

the word she would use to describe the atmosphere between Anne and Patrick. Volatile or explosive seemed more apt. Indeed, she would have need of a nerve tonic herself before she had achieved her goal with that pair.

"Lady Kingairn suffered another fall, ma'am," she said. "I am all the more determined to quash any evidence of scandal concerning her husband's death at its source. Patrick is discreet if nothing else."

The Queen nodded again. "Nobility of character is what comes to mind when one meets such a man."

Rakehell and rogue were what came to Nellwyn's mind, but she merely smiled in agreement.

"Chivalry is not dead, ma'am."

"Nor is danger." Victoria shook her head. "How sad to think of our beautiful Highlands as a place where a murder plot might be hatched, but one must remember its violent history. I am fiercely glad Lord Glengramach will be your protector."

Anne stared across the table at the tall man whose face took on a sculptured hardness in the candlelight. The lobster salad they had been served was untouched. They had finished a bottle of madeira between them and were working on another. Since their encounter at Windsor, she had dreaded this meeting, thinking of every excuse imaginable to avoid it.

"Don't you have somewhere else to go?" she asked rudely. "Isn't there a mistress waiting for you in a parked carriage?"

He took a sip of wine, unruffled by the insult. "I

prefer the company in this room. I've never been much of a womanizer."

She snorted in disbelief.

He smiled. "It's true. Not before and certainly not after I met you, although I do admit to a string of meaningless liaisons the year following your marriage."

"What stopped you?"

"I was only making myself and those other women miserable," he said in amusement. "Who wants a lover who wants someone else? Perhaps I was hoping to find another girl like you."

The ormolu clock on the mantelpiece chimed the hour. Anne wriggled in her chair. "Where is she?"

"I don't know. I hope she doesn't come." He leaned back in his chair, his lanky frame relaxed. "I could look at you for hours."

"Well, don't. It reminds me of things I don't want to remember."

He stroked the stem of his glass with his thumb. "It pleases me to remember you."

She frowned. "Don't."

"I can't help it. Our affair was the highlight of a verra unhappy period in my life. I had lost my mother to cancer two years before I met you. I look back now and realize that her death was when my hell-raising began. For my father it was the opposite. He withdrew to grieve. I misbehaved, and if I'd been in my right mind or possibly more mature, I would have pursued you, your parents be damned."

She heard the clip-clop of a horse-drawn carriage

outside. "That was sex," she said quietly, not daring to move. "That was madness."

"Was it?"

Anne swallowed, remembering against her will. He had practically torn her clothes off the instant she walked into the ruins of the medieval keep, and she hadn't done a thing to stop him. Reckless idiot that she was, she had submitted to everything he demanded.

He hadn't been satisfied with merely kissing her. He had devoured her. He had eaten her up from head to toe. They'd made love in the sun and in the rain, and he'd introduced her to positions that would have made Lucifer blush. Their desire was so intense they didn't feel the chill of autumn in the air or the inevitability of their parting, that like a long winter shadow, loomed just around the corner. They had never stopped once, in their delirium of lust, to consider the consequences of their behavior.

"You have no children," he said gently, a statement of fact more than a question.

"No." And she should have left it at that, preferring him to think her barren rather than reveal that she and David had barely shared a bed in their years of marriage. "I was only pregnant that one time," she added quietly. "I never conceived again."

"That is a shame, Anne." He hesitated. "I suppose it is a blessing I did not get you pregnant. If I had gone off with the infantry and you had married David, I would have been in the unpalatable position of having to kill my own cousin to claim my bairn and woman."

"Dear God," she exclaimed.

He rose from the table to refill her glass. The clatter of traffic drifted from the street, a carriage driver shouting on the corner.

"I'll wait," he said, brimming with male bravado. "I'll find a way to prove I am not the man you remember. You'll see."

She smiled at him over her shoulder. "The only problem with your plan is that I cannot tolerate the sight of you."

He leaned over her, his voice deepening with laughter as his arms imprisoned her in the chair. "And even that doesn't have to be a problem, depending on one's perspective."

6

They were playing cards on an overstuffed poplin sofa when Nellwyn joined them. Anne threw down her hand in relief. "Auntie Nellwyn, at last. Do you know what time it is?"

Nellwyn peeled off her gloves in irritation. "Have I not kept you fed and entertained?"

Anne stood up, looking for her own mantle. "I have thought this over, and I've decided you will have to investigate Uncle Edgar's death alone. I refuse to associate with your nephew."

"Sit down, Anne," Nellwyn said sternly. "You have not heard me out."

Anne frowned. Then she obeyed.

"Lady Kingairn has suffered a second fall," Nellwyn explained, looking her age in the candlelight. "She has been confined to a wheelchair. If this tragedy is not unfortunate enough, my solicitor has just discovered that Edgar withdrew a major part of his wealth from their Lombard Street bank before his death."

"Blackmail, do you think?" Patrick asked.

Nellwyn sank down into her chair. "I have no idea, but we cannot allow her to die destitute, can we?"

"Indeed, we cannot," he said heartily, rubbing his big hands together. "When do we leave?"

"Anne?" Nellwyn said, cocking her head. "Are you in agreement with me? Could you live with yourself knowing you had done nothing to right a possible injustice against an invalid, if not a crime?"

"Verra well phrased, Auntie Nellwyn," Patrick said. "Of course our Anne is in agreement. How could anyone refuse to help a defenseless widow?"

Anne glared at him. "I can speak for myself, thank you, Patrick. Nellwyn, you know you can depend on me, but I simply have no wish to return to the Highlands, or to stay at Balgeldie House with *him.*"

"He is a part of the plan," Nellwyn said, unperturbed.

"What plan am I a part of?" Patrick asked, eager to be on his aunt's side if it meant staying with Anne.

"The plan to unmask Edgar's murderer while we pretend to host the annual shooting party," Nellwyn explained. "Anne and David held a yearly ball and house party at harvest end for their neighbors and friends. In the past two years, Anne has been gracious enough to continue the tradition in absentia."

"I was in mourning," Anne said. "I knew David would have wanted the tradition to go on. He loved the Burning of the Water best when everyone went fishing at midnight on the loch."

"Which was precisely when the murderer struck last year," Nellwyn said.

Anne rubbed the gooseflesh that rose on her forearms. "We don't even know there is a murderer, do we?"

"The doctor's report of autopsy claims Edgar died of a heart seizure," Nellwyn admitted. "But that does not explain the rumors that have circulated in the village ever since."

Patrick laid his head back on the sofa. "Such as?"

"Such as Edgar never appeared at the ball before he went fishing." Nellwyn paused for effect. "Such as one of the gillies in attendance swore he saw a body being dragged by two people into a boat a few hours earlier. Of course, later he admitted it could have been a group of drunken guests in high spirits."

Anne sighed. "I don't know that that signifies anything of a suspicious nature. David had to drag me into our boat once."

"Were you drunk?" Patrick asked curiously.

"Indeed, I was not. I was pregnant. The rocking motion of the boat made me sick to my stomach, and I could not bear the smell of fish."

"I guarantee that Edgar was not pregnant," Nellwyn said. "And what of his missing money? It may not seem a large sum to you or me, but it is to a helpless invalid, and the man was a known spendthrift."

"I say we leave immediately to investigate," Patrick said. "We cannot solve anything on a sofa."

Nellwyn nodded. "I have already reserved our passage on a pleasure steamer."

"Let us not act in haste," Anne said. "In the first place, why should we assume the murderer will be waiting conveniently for us to catch him? Has he killed again?"

"Who knows?" Nellwyn said.

Anne frowned. "What if he has fled the country?"

"What if he is deciding to make you his next victim at this very moment?" Nellwyn countered.

"Me?" Anne said, turning pale. "Why me?"

Patrick raised his head. "I shall take care of you, Anne, should the need arise. Don't worry. That is precisely what I'm here for."

"Quite possibly there is not a murderer at all," Nellwyn conceded. "This entire affair might be nothing but idle gossip. However, it is our duty to stop the taint of scandal from spreading. I have promised the Queen discretion."

"Then Patrick definitely needs to stay home," Anne said.

"Patrick does not need to stay home," Nellwyn said crossly. "He is the most important part of my plan."

"And what exactly is this brilliant plan?" Anne asked.

Nellwyn's eyes twinkled with anticipation. "At first I thought he should go in disguise as a coachman or gamekeeper to conduct the investigation. And then I realized such a masquerade would not suit our purposes."

"Well, thank God," Patrick said.

"So," Nellwyn went on, positively bubbling, "I decided he should pose as your butler."

Silence fell; when Patrick finally found his voice, it emerged as a raw croak.

"Me, posing as—a butler?"

Anne all but fell off the sofa in a paroxysm of laughter.

"Yes," Nellwyn said delightedly. "Isn't it the most ingenious scheme in the world? You see, there are two positions of power in every proper household. The lady and her butler."

"What happened to the man being master of his domain?" Patrick asked.

"It is a myth," Nellwyn retorted.

Anne smiled. "Everyone knows that."

"Bloody hell," Patrick said. "No one told me I was to pose as a domestic. This is damned humiliating."

Anne attempted to look serious. "Oh, but it is so clever, Auntie Nellwyn. He shall be our personal belowstairs spy."

"Exactly." Nellwyn scooted her chair toward the sofa where Patrick sat, as enthusiastic as a stone. "We need someone to move around the substrata of society to pry. A butler has access to secrets that would never be divulged to a gentleman—the gossip of tradesmen, servants, guests. Such a masquerade will also serve to protect your reputation, Anne. It will explain why you and Patrick spend time together."

"And I'm supposed to protect Anne between polishing the silver and listening at keyholes, am I?" he said distastefully.

Nellwyn chuckled. "Precisely. You'll barely have to leave her side."

"Except at night," Anne added.

"No one in the parish knows you, Patrick," Nellwyn said. "You have never attended one of Anne's famous shooting parties before."

He folded his arms across his huge chest. "This isn't what I had in mind."

Anne arched her brow. "But you couldn't live with yourself, knowing you had failed to help an invalid in her last months, could you? You would never let pride stand in the way of protecting Edgar's name, would you?"

He stared at her in dead silence.

"Excuse me a for moment," Nellwyn said, rising from her chair. "I must pop outside to make sure the coachman isn't still waiting in the rain. I can see we'll be talking into the wee small hours. You'll both stay the night, of course."

Anne waited until the door closed before she broke into a devilish grin. "Remember, you've received a royal order."

He drew a breath. "The Queen didn't order me to be your damned butler. My featherbrained auntie did."

"Well, it amounts to the same thing," she said. "You were told to follow Nellwyn's instructions."

"But she's insane."

"You'll have to learn to curb that tongue if you expect to be in my employ," she said mischievously.

He shoved his rawboned body to the edge of the sofa. "You're taking pleasure in this, aren't you?"

"Do you blame me?"

He didn't answer, and she knew she shouldn't

gloat, but wasn't it just perfect? This was the setting-down the arrogant devil deserved.

"What have I done to merit this?" he asked at last. "Oh, aye, I know the obvious, but I *didn't* know you concealed such a capacity for vengeance in your heart."

She stared at him. "Do you really think a girl gives herself to a charming man and then forgets him? I was devastated at what we had done, Patrick. My parents thought I was possessed of demons. I never had a chance at making a happy marriage afterward. I could not stop thinking of you for ages."

"Could you not have waited for me, then?"

"No. I'd have married anyone my parents chose to escape them. David took care of me, but I put him through an entire year of misery before I accepted my life. I came to him as damaged goods."

He looked tortured. "I thought you loved each other. If I'd known you were unhappy, I'd have—"

"What? Murdered him in a duel and caused the scandal of the century? We *did* love each other. In any case, he's gone now and I'll never know how much he understood about my past, but is it any wonder I should enjoy seeing you suffer your share of humiliation?"

"Is that what you want? To humiliate me?"

She gave him a smile reminiscent of her old hellion self. "It isn't really such a horrible punishment, is it? Are you at all surprised that I would want to savor a small measure of revenge?"

* * *

Patrick didn't know if foul play had been involved in Edgar's death. He didn't know if he believed Nellwyn's intentions were entirely unselfish. The silly woman had sought dangerous thrills all her life, including an excursion into the head-hunting jungles of Kali Simpang with the island's white rajah.

But he did know he couldn't give up his hopes for renewing his association with Anne. He couldn't give up the only woman who had cared enough about him to cry at his bedside, a woman with her sense of spirit. She had shown more capacity for caring than all his past lovers combined; he was too old to pretend qualities like love and loyalty didn't matter, and he was saddened to learn how much distress he had brought her with their careless act of abandon.

He told himself he would prove how much he'd changed, and that the thoughtless rogue she remembered had come to his senses.

She couldn't resent him forever for a mistake they had made in another life. They were both basically decent people who deserved another chance.

Hell, he thought philosophically, he might as well make the best of a humiliating situation. After all, he'd never get a chance to be this close to her again, not living in the same house.

He stood and sketched a dignified bow in front of the sofa. "Will there be anything else, my lady?"

She looked up at him in alarm. "Is there something seriously wrong with you?"

He put one hand on his hip, brandishing an imaginary tray in the other. "Will her ladyship be taking tea in front of the fire or at her desk?"

She blinked, startled by the sight of the rawboned Highlander mincing about like a May queen. "You look positively ridiculous. Stop it this instant."

"Ridiculous?" He tossed his imaginary tray over his shoulder and bent over her, shedding his masquerade to give her a glimpse of the dangerously determined man beneath. "You just wait, Lady Whitehaven. I will live to please you, aye, in public and in private. Your every whim will be my command, and Society will remark that no woman ever had a more devoted servant. But when I'm through with this charade, when the mystery of Edgar's death is solved, we shall see who ends up giving the orders around here."

She smiled to hide the panic his promise evoked. "I do not think so."

He smiled back to show her the cast-iron confidence of his will. "Wager on it, woman."

7

 few days later they took the train from London to Woolwich and from there embarked on a pleasure steamer to Aberdeen. Nellwyn had arranged for them to travel the rest of the way to Balgeldie House by private coach.

Patrick envisioned intimate moments with Anne at sea on a mist-shrouded deck; the churning of paddle wheels would provide pleasant background for the love words he would whisper in her ear. They would drink champagne in the saloon, and he would soften her resistance.

Instead, he found himself banished to the damp little cabin above the boiler room with two obnoxious footmen who were traveling with the Duke of Glaswell. The footmen looked down their noses at Patrick; as butler to a widowed baroness, he was considered their social inferior.

Patrick did not enjoy his first taste of servitude and he stomped across the upper deck to the sofa where Anne sat to tell her so. "I should like a word with you."

She frowned and put down the book she was pretending to read. "Do lower your voice. A servant does not bellow at his employer in public."

Nellwyn tapped him on the shoulder. "He does not bellow at her in private, either. Nor does he stomp about in such handsomely tailored clothes. It's a good thing I thought to bring you proper attire."

"Proper attire?" He frowned. "I hope I am misunderstanding you, madam."

She patted his arm. "You'll look bonny in knee breeches with those nicely developed calves. Did you know that good legs were a desired trait in one's manservants?"

Patrick caught a glimpse of the grin creeping across Anne's face. "I am not a damned pet monkey to be paraded about, and I'm not wearing any knee breeches."

"Well, I hope you thought to bring your guns," Nellwyn said.

"Guns?" Anne said, arching forward in alarm. "Whatever for?"

"To protect us, of course," Nellwyn replied. "A butler often functions as a bodyguard. Our man sleeps downstairs with a pistol to keep out housebreakers. Honestly, Anne, it is time you came into the century."

"The very thought of guns for personal protection makes me nervous," she said.

"The thought of knee breeches does the same

thing to me," Patrick said. "I've never made my butler wear them."

"You are not the stickler for tradition that David was," Nellwyn retorted. "Nor are you hosting a shooting party in your fashionable Highland home. Besides, if you don't care to wear knee breeches, you may wear a kilt. Gaelic servants in costume are quite the thing."

Anne chuckled, burying her nose in her book again.

"Now take yourself elsewhere, Sutherland," Nellwyn said, sitting on the sofa with a tin of marzipan. "One does not hold intimate conversations on deck with a domestic. Oh, dear, the Duke of Glaswell is coming over to admire Anne again."

Patrick frowned in annoyance at the stocky figure weaving across the deck. "The old lecher does a hell of a lot of admiring for a man who has a wife and six children waiting for him at home."

Nellwyn's fingers stopped halfway to her mouth. "Do you know him?"

"I've met him once at the races," he said, nodding politely at the captain walking on the bridge. "He was drunk at the time and I doubt he even remembers my face."

The captain, who apparently did remember Patrick, but only as a servant, did not nod back.

"Go away," Nellwyn said, swatting his knee with her gloves. "He mustn't recognize you, or my scheming will be for naught. Go."

Patrick turned in reluctance, and was only a few steps from the sofa when he heard the duke greeting Anne. "My dear, is it wise to sit in the sea breeze with as frail a constitution as yours? Come to the saloon and have a wee nip of brandy to warm you."

Cynically, Patrick noted that Nellwyn, who was every bit as frail-boned and fragile as Anne, was excluded from the invitation for a "wee nip." And when he turned to express his disapproval with a scowl, he saw that Anne had indeed strolled off in the duke's company and that Nellwyn sat alone, smiling benignly at the pair of them.

"Do not glare at her like a dragon, Patrick," she said softly, glancing up at him. "She is, after all, an attractive woman."

"Aye." His voice vibrated with irony. "I think I know that."

She subjected him to a steady scrutiny. "I never did learn why you and she dislike each other so intensely."

"I have never disliked Anne. On the contrary."

"All right." She tightened her shawl around her wrinkled throat. "Let me rephrase that. Anne has not told me exactly what happened between the two of you to spark this antagonism."

"And you won't wheedle a word out of me," he said, grinding his jaw as he saw the duke's hand brush Anne's shoulder. The randy old goat.

"I shall ask Anne," Nellwyn said.

"Ask her."

A hint of understanding softened her face. "You must be quite attracted to her to agree to all this."

"Aye." He swallowed and turned his face to the restless water of the sea. "Quite attracted indeed."

* * *

He got into an argument with the two footmen over his bunk when he returned to his room, and the next thing he knew he was engaged in a round of fisticuffs with the pair of them. It didn't take him long to win the fight, a few jabs and a stunning series of lefts to the chin, and in the end all three men shook hands and feigned a civilized forgiveness; his pride intact, Patrick returned to his bunk, where by this time his blood was pumping so hard he couldn't sleep a wink.

He listened to the clamor of the steam engine, the cranks, air pump, and cylinders oscillating. He tried to concentrate on the churning of the paddle wheels with their feathered floats, but it was of no use. He still thought about sex with Anne, how they had gone at each other like pagans in their youthful passion, and it had not been enough. He thought about kissing the length of her spine from her fragile nape to the cleft of her buttocks, and making love to her with a consideration it had taken him years to learn.

He stayed awake until dawn holding imaginary orgies and meaningful conversations with her so that when he actually saw her again the next day, he looked terse and haggard with shadows sculpting hollows in his face. He looked mean and angry and capable of unpredictable behavior, the sort of fellow a vulnerable widow like Lady Whitehaven should avoid.

At least that was what the Duke of Glaswell advised her as they disembarked on the silvery Firth of Tay to buy marmalade in Dundee. His Grace didn't bother lowering his voice to spare

Patrick's feelings either. He hustled Anne along the gangplank with a proprietary air.

"I do not like the looks of your manservant, my dear, I must say. He's got an antagonistic manner about him. Has he been with you long?"

Patrick swore that a spark of genuine evil sprang into Anne's eye when she answered. "Long enough, your grace, but do not worry on my account. The man knows his place, I assure you."

He knew his place, all right, and given the chance it would be in Anne's life as a suitor and in her bed, on top of her or beneath, whichever position she preferred, he wasn't particular as long as he had her to himself. Worshipping at her feet, he would soon restore her self-worth and faith in him.

They spent four days at sea, Patrick playing cards with the pair of footmen, Anne playing the unattainable widow. Another man might have been discouraged by her aloofness, but as he studied Scotland's bold rocky coast from the deck, he took comfort in the knowledge that he would soon fight for her on his own turf. Anything could happen in a wild land of peat bogs where dragons had devoured helpless virgins, and black lochs where monsters lurked. His beloved Grampian Hills gave home to over a hundred fairy-tale castles; it engendered legends of heroes who had been slain in the name of freedom. No invader had ever conquered the fierce Scottish spirit for long. No foreign king could challenge the wizards who cast spells from primitive cairns on the moor.

A rakehell might ruin a young girl, then repent and win her back years later as ancient chieftains had abducted brides and turned them into loving wives.

He could already feel the magical power of the "haars," the sea mist that haunted the wild cliffs and smugglers' coves of the Mearns coast. The conqueror in his soul awakened; the warrior in him rose to forge into battle, the only hitch in the fantasy being that he would carry a silver tea tray as his shield.

8

"*I* don't know what you're up to, Auntie Nellwyn," Anne said as they steamed into the granite city of Aberdeen. "I only want you to know I don't believe you're doing this solely for Uncle Edgar's sake."

Nellwyn snorted, gathering her mantilla and embroidered gloves. "You have a most suspicious mind, my dear."

"If you're hoping to make a match between us, it won't work. Patrick was, and is, a scoundrel."

"Not the Patrick I knew. And know," Nellwyn said staunchly. "He is the heart of kindness."

"Now I know he has deceived you," Anne exclaimed.

"He was a strong, spirited lad," Nellwyn said, stuffing her gloves into her reticule. "He found my dear Richard wandering at the roadside after his stroke and carried him all the way back to the house."

"You should have checked your silver afterward," Anne said. "He probably wanted money for drink and gambling. Have you forgotten he stole the minister's carriage the day of Richard's funeral and crashed it into the crag?"

"Grief does strange things to a person's mind."

"Grief?" Anne said in astonishment. "Are we talking about the same person? Patrick was a veritable demon. He probably wasn't grieving at all—he was probably stone drunk." And Anne ought to know. She had made her own excuses for him at the time, too drawn to his physical presence to acknowledge his flaws.

"Richard taught Patrick how to play chess," Nellwyn said, smiling fondly. "They spent every Sunday morning on the moor moving rocks about as chess pieces. My husband lived for those games. I vow it is what kept him alive that last year."

Anne sighed in frustration. Of course she couldn't very well categorize Patrick's past sins without confessing her own, and she had once been attracted enough to his hellfire ways to compromise herself; he certainly hadn't forced her. But oh, how she resented him for coming back into her life at a time when she should have been free to find peace.

"You have become hard, Anne."

"And you . . . you are a liberal, Auntie Nellwyn."

Nellwyn sniffed. "But we shall both obey the Queen, won't we? And perhaps you will stop playing the prude long enough to enjoy our little adventure."

"It is not an adventure," Anne said hotly. "It is a

private query. Oh, it is absurd, unfair. I have no wish to return to Scotland."

"Make the best of it, Anne," she said unsympathetically. "One must do what is for the highest good."

The next day they struck out from Aberdeen's High Street; their coach clattered over cobbles toward Aboyne, passing Macbeth's cairn at Lumphanan where Nellwyn insisted they take a picnic. They climbed north past Glenshalg and rumbled over the heather-clad hills and uninhabited expanse of Corrennie Moor. In no particular hurry, they detoured through market towns, and spent an hour at a holy well where Nellwyn made a mysterious wish.

On their fifth night together they stopped at a coaching inn to savor smoked haddock soup. The next morning when they awoke, mist covered the ground and wafted through the stone circles that overshadowed the road.

The moment they passed through the mist, magic happened. Anne instantly felt the difference, as if she had stepped through a mirror into another world; she fought an impulse to tear off her tightly laced boots and stockings and run in the pools of rainwater on the moor until her sides ached and she had shed the last vestiges of civilization.

Yet she knew she had to be extremely careful of her own behavior, or she would end up in trouble again.

"I don't think Patrick should ride in the carriage

with us for the rest of the way," she said, out of the blue. "It doesn't seem proper, a butler on equal footing with his mistress. He ought to sit up on the box."

"Hell's bells," he said. "I'm not your butler yet."

"No," she conceded, "but we might be seen together by someone traveling to the village."

"It is misting," he said.

"I'm sorry about that," she said unconvincingly. "Would you like to borrow my veil?"

"I am a not riding on the box like a piece of old luggage." He grinned. "And I don't look good in a veil."

"Hellfire and damnation," Nellwyn said, waking up from her nap. "If the two of you don't stop fighting, I'm sitting up on the box myself to get some quiet."

They crossed a packhorse bridge and heard the distant croaking of ptarmigan on the moor. Anne counted blue hares on the cairns to avoid talking to Patrick. The moorland air was so pure, it almost burned her lungs to breathe it; she felt afraid without knowing why. Then suddenly it began to rain and she couldn't help thinking about their affair, as much as she resented the man. She couldn't help thinking about what they had shared. Rain, like so many things, reminded her of Patrick.

"I can't stay, Patrick. I think my cousin Isobel knows about us. I think she followed me here."

"Isobel is a silly pea hen."

"Aye, but—"

He pressed her against the castle wall, and went down on his knees. Anne was excited; she could not resist him, but she was afraid, too, and even the jackdaws that occupied the castle turrets seemed unnaturally raucous in the afternoon silence. She wanted to tell him what she feared, but they had only a few hours together. Then his head disappeared under her skirts, and his tongue was making a furrow between her flesh; he was loving her with a concentration she dared not interrupt.

It started to rain—that was another bad omen. There hadn't been a cloud in the sky when they had met on the moor, and it was only afterward, after they'd made love and were getting dressed, that Patrick noticed the bruises on her shoulder.

"How the hell did those happen?" he demanded.

She didn't tell him the truth. He had a quick temper; he'd already beaten up half the boys in the village for the hell of it, and she was afraid if she admitted her father had struck her with his walking stick for riding alone, Patrick would confront him. She was starting to believe Papa's assertion that she was a wicked creature, she would never have given herself to Patrick otherwise, but she didn't want him to fight with her papa. The two of them were so different. Patrick had such a liberal view of life, and his father moved in high social circles. Her papa rarely visited town, not since selling his shipping interests. He spent his days praying and judging people. He saw sin everywhere.

"I fell off my horse," she whispered, pulling on her gown before he could question her further. She was shivering with anxiety, relieved that he accepted her explanation. In those days neither she nor Patrick had done much thinking anyway. They had acted on instinct, and they were fortunate their behavior had not brought them more heartache.

Instinct.

Anne wished she had learned to ignore her baser instincts, but obviously where Patrick was concerned she hadn't. Now she was older and supposedly wiser, but it didn't seem as if her experience had done much good. How else had she gotten into this situation?

She lifted the carriage curtain, her skin prickling as she recognized the recumbent stone circle in the distance. Suddenly she knew where she was. She knew that a sleepy hamlet lay just beyond those hills. If the carriage continued past the ruins of a thirteenth-century castle, it would take them to the manor house where she had lived with her parents, until they had married her off in a relief that was almost comical. She'd had little contact with them after her wedding.

Her ailing Aunt Mildred and Mildred's daughter Isobel lived there now. As part of her strict upbringing, Anne had been ordered to spend endless nights at Mildred's house, reading to the woman and keeping her daughter company. But half of the time, after Anne had seen to their needs, she had escaped them to steal a few hours riding her horse on the moor. And once she had stolen away to meet Patrick.

She glanced at him now. "Did you know we were coming this way? Did you know we were passing by my old house?"

He looked annoyed. "Believe it or not, I am not responsible for the fact that the main road, built in Roman times, runs past your family estate."

Nellwyn looked over Anne's shoulder. "Well, bless me, the butler is right. I suppose we shall have to stop."

"Stop?" Anne bit her lip. "Whatever for?"

Nellwyn made an impatient gesture. "One simply doesn't gallop past the home of an aging relative without paying a call. Life is short, Anne. Your aunt may not be alive the next time you come this way, and it's the proper thing to do."

Anne's heart began to pound. Nellwyn knew about Anne's estrangement from her parents and that they had arranged her marriage to David, but she certainly didn't know what an unhappy home theirs had been, or that Anne had vowed never to set foot in that house again.

"It's too late to call on Aunt Mildred," Anne said. "She always retired early, and it would be rude to disturb her. We should have sent word ahead."

"Nonsense," Nellwyn said, hunting for the shawl she was sitting on.

Patrick looked at Anne. "We don't have to stop."

She didn't acknowledge his concern, which came years too late to be of any good. She couldn't blame him for her rigid upbringing that she had fought against with defiance and disobedience. And for which she had paid.

"I don't wish to see Aunt Mildred and Isobel today." Anne's statement was so contrary to her usual nature that Nellwyn dropped the earring she had fished out of her reticule. "They may visit me at Balgeldie House when we've settled in."

Nellwyn and Patrick stared at each other in silence for several seconds. Then Nellwyn said quietly, "You and I will pay a call, Sutherland. Anne may wait in the carriage. We'll say she's feeling sick."

Heartsick, he thought, totally unprepared for the anguish in Anne's eyes, and wondering what was behind it.

9

"Are you certain you want to do this?" Patrick asked his aunt as they stood before the wrought-iron fence that enclosed the estate like a small fortress.

It was a house built in the Scots baronial style on a riverside crag surrounded by bleak moor and peat bog. There were no trees, nowhere a man could withdraw to hide even from himself, and there was a feeling of loneliness that cut to the bone.

"I'm good at patching up quarrels," she said. "If I'd been a man, I would have become an ambassador. My dear father always said that, even when I was little."

"What makes you think Anne and her aunt have quarreled? This is Anne's house, is it not? She is generous to shelter the woman here. It doesn't sound as if she holds any grudge against her."

He looked up at the house, a gray hulking ghost of a thing in the gloaming, and wondered again if it was better not to disturb it. "Perhaps Anne has her reasons."

"If she does, she will not share them."

"Then leave well enough alone."

She primped her silver curls. "It is entirely improper to show up on the doorstep, but I am a woman of rank, so her aunt is bound to receive me in a cordial manner. Go up and announce my arrival, Sutherland. It's time you started to practice a little submission."

"Stop calling me that," he said.

"I like it," she said.

He saw a pale face lurking behind the dark curtains of the house. There was something distasteful about visiting the family of a young girl you had disgraced. And it was too late for him to apologize to her parents, or to make their mistake right. Still, if there was something in Anne's past that would help him to better understand her, he would gladly make the effort.

Nellwyn studied his face. "I was in Kent the summer that Anne married David, but I've always sensed something strange about their courtship. It seemed to happen so fast that I suspected he might have gotten her pregnant, but that wasn't the case at all. What do you know of it?"

He looked out at the hills. "Not much. I was out of the country myself."

She frowned. "Will Anne's aunt remember you?"

"I never met the woman. She might have seen me on the way to church." He smiled without humor. "The one or two times I attended."

"Anne's family was always reclusive," she said thoughtfully. "I don't think I ever actually exchanged more than a passing word with any of them myself. But then I never stayed here long enough to socialize."

"I don't remember," he said vaguely. In those days he had given even less of a damn for social convention than he did now. He'd been furious at his father for pulling him out of school and exiling him to the Scottish Highlands. Actually, he'd been expelled from school, and he had refused to mingle with his unexciting neighbors to please his father.

Until he met Anne. He would never forget the first time he saw her riding a white stallion across the moor, a few days after they had noticed each other in church. He'd thought she was going to kill herself. The wind had dried the tracks of tears on her face, but he had known she'd been crying. To this day he hadn't understood what had made her so sad, but he did know that in the end, he'd probably made her a little sadder, and he was sorry that time and circumstance had conspired against them.

"Are you going to announce me or not, Sutherland?" Nellwyn said, nudging his arm.

He looked back at Anne in the carriage, but he couldn't read her expression through the window.

"I'll go," he said, reluctantly, "but don't call me Sutherland again, Auntie Nellwyn. It's damned annoying."

A flustered housekeeper admitted him to a paneled entrance hall that was striking in its plainness. No portraits, no carpets, not even a clock. His boot heels echoed on bare wood. How had his spirited Anne grown up in this grave of a home, he wondered?

The drawing room was painted in dull green and gold, and he was struck by the cold and oppressive atmosphere, the lack of fire in the marble fireplace. The single globe gaslight hissed, accentuating the shadows and stark quiet of the house.

He was startled to find himself not alone. A young dark-haired woman sat before him on a caned chair, stabbing a needle into a tapestry pillow. She wore the black bombazine gown of a widow, and his unease mounted as she raised her face to his.

"Forgive me for intruding on your grief," he said. "My name is—"

"I know who you are."

He knew who she was too—Isobel of the silly nature who had spied on her own cousin. Yet obviously she had held her tongue; Anne's parents had never discovered her affair with Patrick. It was mildly embarrassing to face another reminder of his misspent youth.

"The Marchioness of Invermont is waiting with Anne to be received," he said. "Is your aunt in the house?"

"My aunt is taking the sea air for a lung condition," she said with a polite smile. "And I am mourning my husband, who died last month." She paused, her needle in the air. "I cannot believe Anne would take up with *you* again. I thought her papa had beaten the willfulness out of her that summer."

So she did recognize him. There was no question of pretending to be a butler, or of Nellwyn's making a polite social call. He released a breath. "Beaten her?" A chill went down his spine. "Is that what you said?"

She nodded hesitantly, perhaps regretting she had revealed such an ugly family secret. One did not expose these things to Polite Society. "He wanted her to go to her husband a submissive wife. Of course poor David was so smitten with her, he would have taken her if she'd come to him on a broomstick." She frowned. "Her father beat her unmercifully that last time, all because Anne would not smile at David during their betrothal ceremony."

Patrick sank into the chair, the image she had invoked so awful he couldn't speak for several moments. The Anne he remembered had smiled at him so easily.

Isobel regarded him shyly. "Sometimes I wondered if Anne did not half hope you would return to rescue her."

"Did she speak of me?" he asked quietly.

"Never. But once or twice after you left, she returned to the castle."

He sighed. "So this house does not hold pleasant memories for her?"

"No," Isobel said. "I suppose not."

"Did Anne's mother never intervene when her father became violent?"

"She was afraid of him too," she whispered. "I do believe he loved Anne in his way. He only meant to rid her of that wild streak before she became a wife. She was a willful girl."

He looked about, envisioning his wee Anne standing up to her father. "Perhaps it is better after all if she does not come in here."

She looked up in surprise. "Does she want to? I should adore—"

"No," he said quickly. "She doesn't."

He rose to leave. The conversation had been as unpleasant as facing enemy fire in the infantry. But at least it answered the question that had nagged at him for years. It told him why Anne had been crying the day they met. It told him what a rare pearl she was, beautiful and unique, formed from a dark atmosphere of criticism and physical intimidation.

It told him why Anne had those bruises on her shoulder, and idiot that he was, he had believed the hellion's story about tumbling from her horse.

It told him why she had given her heart and body to him so unwisely when he had never promised her anything. Desperate for love, she had accepted it from the first man who had shown her any attention, and he too had wounded her.

10

"What did she say?" Nellwyn demanded the instant he returned to the carriage. "Are we invited to tea?"

He glanced at Anne before taking his seat. She refused to meet his gaze, but Nellwyn had put on her elbow-length gloves and a pair of jet earrings.

"It isn't a good time to call. Anne's aunt is away, taking the sea air, and Isobel is in mourning for her husband." He looked at Anne. "I believe she is lonely for your company, Anne."

Her face softened. "Silly Isobel," she said, and all he wanted to do was hold her, to chase away the hurt he and her father had inflicted.

"I am an impulsive old woman," Nellwyn said, watching Anne in concern. "I should have known better than to spring up on the door like a mushroom."

The carriage was circling the drive. The house receded into the purple-gray shadows of the crag, and the hills seemed to engulf it until it vanished. Patrick caught Anne staring back in a combination of longing and dread, shaking her head as if she were denying something inside her own mind. He ached to sit beside her, give comfort, and make everything right.

"I think we'll go a few miles farther before we stop to stretch our legs again," Nellwyn said, apparently sensing something was not well. "Would that be all right with you, Anne?"

She stirred. "Of course. Why wouldn't it be?"

They veered off the main road, skirting a peat-track and a distillery until they came to a path that was nothing more than mossy rocks and heather. Fog engulfed them as they found a burn and ate a snack of ham sandwiches and cranberry tarts on the bank of bracken fern and broom.

"I'm going to offer the coachman something to eat," Nellwyn said, shaking off her skirts. "Can I trust you two to be civil to each other in my absence?"

Anne sprang to her feet. "I'll walk along the water."

She wasn't surprised when Patrick followed her. "Do you remember, Anne, that we skimmed stones on the water and made wishes?"

She tossed a fern frond into the swift-flowing current. She remembered, all right. She remembered wishing they would be together forever and that he would love her the way she ached to be loved. She had wished he would redeem himself and approach her father with a request for her hand.

He pressed a gray-veined stone into the palm of her hand, closing his eyes. "We'll wish together. I know what I want."

She stared down at the stone in her hand as a wicked impulse took hold of her. Then she pulled back her arm and hurled it, hitting him in the chest.

"Hell," he hollered, really upset. "What did you do that for?"

She just chuckled. Odd how an act of physical aggression could make a woman feel so much better.

"Well, hell," he said. "Woman, that was uncalled for."

Nellwyn hurried back toward them, her face alarmed. "A butler cannot walk around hollering obscenities at his mistress. I could hear you from the other side of the hill."

Patrick scowled at the innocent-looking woman beside him. "She hit me with a stone when I was making a wish."

"Well, Patrick," Nellwyn said, "I would have hit you with a stone too if you were swearing at me like that. Goodness gracious, you ought to be ashamed of yourself."

He didn't say another word in his own defense. What would have been the point? Anne was grinning like a she-devil, and for all Auntie Nellwyn claimed he was her favorite, it was clear the two women had formed some sort of ungodly conspiracy against him.

He stared down at the stone he held. Then he threw it into the silvery water, and defiantly, he made his wish.

*　　*　　*

Anne smiled ruefully as she climbed back into the waiting carriage. She remembered the day she'd learned Patrick had left Scotland. The rowan leaves along the wayside had begun to fall, and their red berries looked like pinpricks of blood from a broken heart. Eighteen years old, she wept until she was as empty as a husk. She never understood what David saw in her, why he would want to marry a too-thin woman with haunted eyes who rode like an Amazon and who cried whenever he touched her. He never even asked why she was crying. He just held her hand and told her he understood.

Patrick, she supposed, remembered almost nothing of that time. He was probably carousing with the other young raw recruits, or so dead-drunk he wouldn't even recognize her while she was weeping her heart out.

She had wished him back so hard in the days before her wedding, it was frightening. And now, seven years later, her wish had been granted, and what on earth was she supposed to do with the man?

11

*T*he huntsman raised his rifle and aimed at the hawk perched on the crag. The bird sensed the threat and stared, seemingly transfixed. The man squinted; he was aware of a rush of anticipation, and his finger tightened on the trigger.

Before he could shoot, however, a familiar female voice blasted the silence of the moor with the subtlety of canonfire.

"Papa!" Her voice was petulant and frantic. "Papa, where have you been?" she wailed. "I *need* you."

He lowered the rifle before briefly considering shooting himself in the head. The hawk had taken refuge in a crevice seconds before. "What dire emergency is it this time, Flora? Another pimple on the chin? Another unpaid bill come back to haunt you?"

"Oh, Papa." She clumped up beside him with her hand on her chest to control her breathing. "The most dreadful thing has happened. The most ominous, the most awful—the prediction has come true."

He removed a handkerchief from his tweed jacket and dabbed his upper lip. "Prediction?"

"I told you, but as usual you ignored me. Black Mag predicted that she was coming back, and it's true."

"Black Mag?" His handsome face hardened. "Haven't I warned you to stay away from that old hag?"

"She isn't a hag. She's a genuine Scots-Romany herbwoman and she sees into the future, and she said we have a blot on our souls and that a woman of whiteness is coming back to remove it."

"Woman?" he said, paying attention for the first time. "What woman is the old witch talking about?"

He was awaiting her answer when a pair of ravens burst into flight from a rocky overhang. Their hoarse caws filled the air with ungodly noise. They were evil things, those birds; they brought nothing but trouble, or so weak-minded individuals such as his daughter believed, and even he felt a twinge of anxiety as he faced her and tried to make sense out of what she had said.

"What woman?"

"The English baron's wife, the beautiful one with black hair who was always riding across the moor at all hours."

He blinked. His anxiety had shifted to a different kind of stirring. In his mind he saw Anne cantering through the mist like a pagan queen, her hair tangled, her slim body moving with the animal in the most unladylike, the most arousing manner he could imagine. He had always wondered how a woman of her spirit had ended up with a moth of a man like David, but she had rebuffed any discreet suggestion of a liaison years ago at the last house party she had attended.

"She's a widow now," he said, tucking his handkerchief into his pocket. "I wonder why she's coming back."

"Everyone in the lodge is wondering the same thing." Flora chewed a strand of limp red hair that had escaped her straw hat. "Black Mag is certain she's going to stir up things like the storm witches who live over the mountains."

"Black Mag?" He shook himself. "Is all this based on that crone's prediction?"

"It wasn't just Mag," she said with assurance. "The chambermaid at the lodge said Anne had sent word she was arriving in a few days, and she was sorry for the short notice, but that the staff should be prepared."

"It is her lodge," he said.

"She never liked the lodge. And she never liked shooting, or me for that matter."

"Now Flora, do not start imagining things again. One of these days the wrong person is going to believe you."

"Lord Kingairn was her uncle-in-law." She whispered the realization, watching the ravens circle over some unseen prey on the moor. "She's bound to wonder about his death. It's only been a year."

He gripped her by the shoulders. "There's not much to wonder about. He died of a heart ailment on the loch. He wasn't exactly a young man."

She looked him in the eye, easing away. "Neither are you."

"Thank you for the reminder," he said sourly.

She took a few steps away from him, making a face as her slippers brushed a rain puddle. The hawk flew overhead, as if taunting, certain of its freedom, but suddenly the girl seemed more interested in the mud on her shoes, and her father was definitely more interested in what Anne's visit would mean to him.

Anne had never exactly responded to his subtle attempts at flirtation, but she had not been a widow then either, and he told himself that a woman in her position was going to need a protector, and that such a person should probably be a nobleman with a respectable background and the maturity to take a vulnerable lady in hand. A smile crossed his face as he looked across the moor toward her estate. So Anne was coming back, alone this time. It seemed his hunting urges would have to be redirected toward a gentler type of game.

They traveled for two more days before reaching the hamlet of Glenferg in the Grampian foothills. Patrick remarked that it was about time the railroads ran through this part of the Highlands. Anne disagreed and said she liked her birthplace unspoiled, and who wanted a smelly train chugging over a sacred cairn anyway? Nellwyn told them both to cease their arguing because it was giving her the megrims.

They reached the lodge early on the evening of their eighth day together. Tucked away in a forest of fir trees, a traveler could search for weeks and never find it. David had actually bought the fortified towerhouse with dormer windows and a turret staircase on a whim, claiming he needed a castle for his princess. He had added a white-harled block and four pavilions before his death, but the tower remained the heart of the house.

Nellwyn took Patrick aside in the unlit courtyard after Anne had gone ahead to see if any letters had arrived. "Why are you looking so sour, Sutherland?"

He frowned, watching Anne disappear into the darkened tower. Ever since his confrontation with Isobel he had been obsessed with protecting her. "I didn't know I was looking sour."

Nellwyn shook her head. "Perhaps sour isn't the right word. You look rather wistful whenever you watch Anne, but then again, so does the wolf when he stalks a doe in the woods." She paused. "Something happened back there in her old house, didn't it?"

"Some stones are better left unturned," he said quietly, and he thought of Anne's father beating her, and his entire body tightened in the blackest anger he had ever known.

He stopped, taking a breath. Her father was dead. He was beyond anyone's reach now, and it was left to him to repair the damage, not seek revenge.

"We can't stand here all night," Nellwyn said. "We have work to do."

"Aye," he said quietly. "Lead on, Auntie Nellwyn."

Anne had assembled her small staff in the Great Hall, which smelled of beeswax from a quick cleaning and a lingering hint of must from months of being closed off. The carpet had been swept with wet ashes, and a hasty log fire lit in the vast stone hearth. Billows of smoke began to circulate and curl around the hammer-beam rafters.

"I appreciate your loyalty to both me and my late husband in remaining here during my prolonged absence," Anne began, her slim figure silhouetted by the firelight. "The lodge appears to have been beautifully tended as always."

Patrick leaned up against the rough stone wall as she gave the heartening aristocrat-pats-peasant-on-the-head speech. He wondered where in this gloomy tower she was going to sleep, whether she had slept with David every night, how often they had made love.

He knew that if he had been her husband, he wouldn't have been able to keep his hands off her for an hour straight. They would never have left the bedroom. Weeds would probably have grown high enough to choke the windows. The tower could fall apart, stone by stone, and their finances could be in ruins, but Patrick would be a happy man if he woke up every morning with her in his arms.

He shifted, raising his brooding gaze from the floor to hear her voice ringing across the hall.

"Snap to it, man."

He sighed, his expression bored as he gazed around the room wondering who she was speaking to in such an uncharacteristically rude way.

"Did you hear me, Sutherland?" she said.

Sutherland. Oh, hell.

He straightened, embarrassed, as every eye in the hall turned to observe his reaction to her ladyship's sharp reprimand. Anne was not known for her sarcasm.

"Gathering wool, Sutherland?" she said, with that gloating smile that made him want to spank and kiss her at the same time.

He bowed, his face a mask of dark irony. "Forgive me, madam. I had my mind on other matters."

"A woman, no doubt," she said under her breath.

"How did you guess?"

"I want you to meet my most loyal and dedicated staff, Sutherland," she said, beckoning him forward. And to the curious servants waiting to catch a glimpse of their new leader, she explained, "Sutherland isn't usually this much of a wallflower."

"A wallflower," he said.

"Goodness," she said in mock dismay. "He isn't wearing his knee breeches either."

"Well, good heavens." He looked down at his Bond-Street tailor-made trousers. "I wonder how that happened."

Entranced, the staff of Balgeldie watched this rather unconventional exchange between mistress and servant. Their support would unquestionably go to her ladyship's side. This new butler was an unproven entity in their social equation, and since Anne had always treated her staff with kindness and generosity, any intruder would have to prove himself before being enfolded into the bosom of the domestic family.

"A bit on the stubborn side," whispered Mrs. Forbes the housekeeper, to Gracie, the upper chambermaid.

"A rebel," said Sandy, the head gardener. "I've seen his sort. He willna last the year."

"He's a braw fine-lookin' mannie," said the kitchen maid to Fergus the footman.

The footman grunted, eyeing Patrick's muscular legs and enormous shoulders. "If you like giants waitin' on you."

"I could learn to," the kitchen maid retorted, giggling.

Mrs. Forbes gave the gossiping group a loud harrumph of disapproval and shouldered her way forward. "Welcome to our staff, Mr. Sutherland," she said with dignified warmth. "A good man is hard to find."

"So is a good woman," he said without thinking.

This comment, unexpected from a servant, brought complete silence to the hall. Anne closed her eyes in exasperation and Nellwyn, sitting at the table with a glass of port, let out a chortle of amusement.

"What I meant," Patrick said, "is—"

"Never mind what you meant," Anne said briskly. "See about the supper arrangements. I'm famished."

"Supper?" he said bleakly.

She edged up beside him. "It's your job," she said in an undertone. "They're expecting you to show your mastery."

"Aye, I intend to."

"As my butler, I meant."

"For now." He brushed around her, his blue eyes glittering. "And afterward as your lord and master."

"Sutherland," she said in an imperious voice before he took another step.

He made a mocking bow. "My lady?"

"I will not tolerate insubordination in a servant."

The staff had begun to file from the hall with Nellwyn rising to fire out instructions at the door. Anne and Patrick stood practically alone with the massive pinewood table between them.

"Do you really want to punish me, Anne?" he asked, the creases in his cheeks deepening in amusement.

She pressed her palms down on the table. "Don't tempt me."

"Do I still tempt you?"

"Not in the least."

Their eyes connected in a brief silent battle, and Anne felt more conflicting emotions than she could count. His rugged virility had been her ruin seven years ago, and it was no less potent now.

"Breakfast at eight before I go riding," she said in a dismissive voice.

"Is that a good idea?"

She looked surprised. "Why wouldn't it be?"

"Have you forgotten why we're here?" he asked.

"If Uncle Edgar met with foul play, then there is a chance that his murderer is still in the area. Mrs. Forbes has shifty eyes, do you not think?"

He was mocking her again, making gentle fun of her as he had when they were lovers, and despite herself, she felt another infuriating flurry of anger and attraction.

"No, I do not think her eyes—oh, you are aggravating. Go away. I always ride alone, and we both know Edgar wasn't murdered."

She faced the fire, fuming, her arms clasped across her chest. He came up behind her, his big body both a threat and a comfort.

"Lock your door tonight too," he said.

"Lock my door?" She sounded incredulous. "No one is going to hurt me in the tower, Patrick. It's . . . unthinkable."

He stared at her slender shoulders and reflected on how fragile she was, how ridiculous for someone her size to believe she could defend herself. "Lock your door," he said again.

"If I do," she retorted, half-turning, "it would only be to keep you out."

Mrs. Forbes was a tiny fairy of a woman with gray-streaked red hair and green eyes; she loved people and animals and her position with frightening passion. A spot of grease would not splatter her cast-iron stove for a full second before she blotted it into oblivion. Her scullions were practically trained from birth to swipe, wipe, chop, and clean like an army of furies.

She was as gracious as a duchess. She believed in the order of things, and quite frankly things had not been right since the old butler retired. It was good to have a new man in the house.

"Will you take tea, Mr. Sutherland?" she asked cordially from the hob where a kettle steamed.

"Hell, no." He plopped down onto a stool. "Give me a whiskey."

"Whiskey?" She clapped her hand to her heart, her voice weak. "Whiskey?"

Sandy, the head gardener, who was one of the elite few allowed into her "Pugs Parlour," raised a straggly white eyebrow. "That's what the man said."

Grim-lipped, she darted around the table to throw the latch on the door. Gracie, the upper chambermaid, yanked the Nottingham-lace curtains closed with an air of gravity.

"Are we about to hold one of those séances?" Patrick asked politely.

"The staff only takes spirits on Christmas and Hogmanay," Mrs. Forbes informed Patrick when the parlor was secured against eavesdroppers.

He gave her a charming smile. "Well, I'm not the staff. I'm the butler."

"One must set an example," she replied, not entirely unmoved by his smile.

Sandy shook his head in sympathy. "There are always your days off, Sutherland. A man learns to wait."

"Did her ladyship let you imbibe in London?" Mrs. Forbes asked worriedly.

"She never told me not to," Patrick said.

Mrs. Forbes and Gracie exchanged knowing looks. "It's worse than we thought," the housekeeper whispered.

"We've got our work cut out for us, 'tis certain," the girl agreed.

"It's not hopeless, though," Mrs. Forbes said.

Patrick looked at Sandy. "Do you have any idea what the two of them are talking about?"

The old Highlander propped his tartan-stockinged legs up on the hearth and pulled out his pipe. "Your fate, Sutherland. Resign yourself to it, lad."

Patrick stared through the cloud of fragrant smoke that wreathed the older man's head. He seemed an earnest enough soul. He would probably have a good idea of what, if anything, had happened to Uncle Edgar.

How could you mourn someone you had never really known? Anne sat in bed, staring out the window at the stars. Once she had believed that a new star emerged every time a person died. If her papa were a star though, he was as cold and distant in death as in life.

He had been dead for four years, her mother for three, but it seemed longer, as she hadn't had any contact with them since they sent her away. She believed her mother had loved her, but not enough to protect either of them from her father's constant belittling or his infrequent outbursts of violence. Anne knew a wife was supposed to submit to her husband in all ways, but she would never have let anyone harm her child, should she ever be so fortunate as to become a mother. Still, Anne had always been a rebel, and in that way, she was not at all like her mother.

She jumped, startled, as her hairbrush fell off the bed. The sound briefly disoriented her; she flopped onto her stomach to find it, her mind returning to her troublesome thoughts. It was too late in this life now to please her parents or hope for their forgiveness. She should have accepted that fact the day she married David. She didn't even know why she thought of them now, except for Patrick stopping at the old house and disturbing the ghosts.

He was already stirring up trouble; masses of it were piling up in the air like thunderheads. It seemed to be in his nature, a congenital affliction, just as Anne seemed to be afflicted with an attraction to what would hurt her, and the problem was that even if she could believe Patrick had changed, she wasn't at all sure of herself.

12

$\mathcal{P}$atrick was aware a small audience of servants watched him in secret as he ascended the gloomy slab staircase to Anne's room. Mrs. Forbes had stated in no uncertain terms that the old butler would never have brought up a tray of whiskey to her ladyship. Why, no one had even seen Lady Whitehaven take more than a sip of the powerful drink at one sitting, and the staff worried the grieving widow had lapsed into a state of moral decay with the new butler taking advantage of the situation.

Anne had ignored his order to bolt the door. When he entered she was lying across the bed with her head and arms dangling on the floor, her bum in the air.

"Lovely view," he said, kicking the door shut with his foot. "Do you always sleep like a bat?"

"Hell's bells," she said, struggling around to sit up.

"I believe that is the first obscenity I have ever heard from you."

"Well, give me another week with you, and I'll bet you'll hear them by the bucketful."

He didn't pretend to look away as she pulled on a silk dressing robe. He stared avidly. He could see the shape of her breasts before she covered them, sensual and womanly, the areolas dusky. Her backside was plumper than he remembered; she had always been so thin, but then she had been a young girl when he had known her, and suddenly he was fascinated by the notion of seeing her woman's body ripen with his seed.

"If you tie that robe any tighter, Anne, you're going to cut off the circulation to your lower extremities."

She perched on the end of a Grecian couch, her eyes narrowed in suspicion. "Never mind my lower extremities. I want to know what you're doing in my room. What did you just put down on the night-stand?"

"I have brought her ladyship her evening whiskey."

"I don't take whiskey before bed," she said indignantly.

"You do now." He pulled an extra glass from the pocket of his tight cashmere trousers. "So do I. In fact, it's going to be a nightly ritual between us."

She leaned forward, holding her hairbrush like a hammer. "It is not."

"Yes, it is. For one thing, I need a drink at the end of the day if I'm going to succeed at this masquerade, and we need time alone to plan our strategy in private." He settled his big frame on the massive bedstead. "I have begun to infiltrate the kitchen."

She shot to her feet as he poured himself a drink. "Oh, you are too much. Get off my bed."

He ignored her orders, examining the striped floral curtains, the cabbage-rose carpet, the carved mahogany wardrobe with a mirror on the door. "Did you sleep in this room with David?"

"That is none of your damned business."

He shook his head. "You're swearing again."

"No wonder! What if someone sees you?"

"Anne, I am being the best butler I know how to be." He sat forward with the glass in his hand. "I came all the way upstairs to bring you a drink to settle your nerves. Are you going to repay me with insults?"

"Settle my nerves?" Her voice was rising. "What sort of butler drapes himself across a woman's bed like an old blanket, I ask you?"

"An old blanket?"

"Patrick." She gave the sash of her robe another yank for good measure. "Your duties at the end of the day are to secure the house and make sure the fire grates are in place."

"Your door was not locked, Anne," he pointed out. "You should thank me for catching that oversight."

She drew a breath. "A butler is to concern himself with such things as the arrangements of the dinner table and supervising tea. He is to set an example to the lower servants."

"Did you and David always sleep in separate rooms?"

She paused, giving him a withering look. "I never said we slept apart."

He took a sip of whiskey. "You didn't have to. I took note of the adjoining rooms when I made my inspection of the lodge. I know David was not exactly a man's man, but I doubt even he could stand all the lace and feminine embellishments in this room. My hair is curling into ringlets just sitting here."

She was astonished at his audacity. "David had an artist's eye, and I am disgusted that you would sink to prying out the details of my married life. Even for you that is outrageous behavior."

"I was not snooping to satisfy any prurient curiosity," he said coolly. "I have long suspected you and David did not share a great passion, and contrary to what you think, I was merely exploring the lodge to see if I might unearth any clues to Uncle Edgar's death. That is, after all, why I am in this ludicrous position."

She felt suddenly foolish; there was no one else on earth who could stir her up into such a storm. "Fine. You said you had already spoken with the staff. Did they tell you anything about Edgar?"

He took another swallow. "Yes."

"What?"

"He's dead."

She threw her brush down on the couch. "Brilliant work."

"What did you expect, Anne? I am forced to pretend I am a mere servant, and I could not exactly start asking questions about a man I'm not supposed to know."

The candle on the nightstand went out unexpectedly. She glanced up, shivering a little. "How did his name come up in this conversation? I hope that you were subtle."

He laid his head back on the pillow. "I said that you were planning on giving another party this year and that you hoped to continue in the same tradition."

Another candle expired on the dressing table. Anne looked up again with an uneasy smile. "Do you think we have a ghost?"

"Either that or you might try shutting the window," he said. "Anyway, when I mentioned the party, Gracie said the only tradition she didn't want repeated was another guest turning up dead."

She watched the breeze lift the curtains at the windows, but she didn't intend to shut them, ghost or not. She liked listening to the autumn wind at night and the stags calling to their mates in the morning. She had missed the wilderness more than she realized. "What did you say then?"

He emptied his glass and closed his eyes, so comfortable he looked as if he might fall asleep. "I asked who had died and Mrs. Forbes said it had been Lord Kingairn, and his heart had given out from rowing, but Gracie seemed to think there was more to it than that."

A shiver raised the hair on Anne's nape. "Such as?"

"She didn't offer anything substantial." He yawned loudly. "Said his ghost was seen once or twice since . . ."

His voice drifted off. Anne turned from the window as she realized the scoundrel was dead asleep on her bed. Her lips in a flat line, she marched right up beside him. She plucked the empty glass from his relaxed fingers, set it on the nightstand, and leaned over to shake him.

"Wake—"

He grabbed her before he even opened his eyes and threw her across the bed. Anne landed on her back with the wind knocked out of her. He was sitting on top of her upper thighs, his startled look giving way to a sheepish grin.

"It isn't a good idea to awaken a former soldier that way, Anne. I might have taken you for a rebel and overreacted."

She didn't say anything to that. She was too overwhelmed by his strength and her own weakness. She was aware of his virile scent and the width of his shoulders and his sinfully beautiful blue eyes, not to mention the numbness of her lower body where the blood could not flow.

"This was a very bad idea, Patrick, and it is obvious to me it isn't going to work." She spoke in soft ladylike tones. She was proud of how composed she sounded, how mature and detached even though the arrogant giant was constricting every blood vessel in her body, even if she noticed a certain pleasure tingling through the numbness. "We shall have to tell the Queen that certain circumstances arose over which we had no control. We shall—"

His laughter interrupted her.

She arched her brow, determined to remain calm. "I have made an unwitting joke?"

"Aye." He grinned, resting his palms on his massive thighs. "Although it's true enough. My 'circumstances' are rising uncontrollably as we speak."

Anne made the mistake of glancing downward and seeing for herself exactly what he was talking about. She closed her eyes with a delicate shudder of disapproval. "You have until the count of three to remove your oafish body from this bed," she said in an icy voice. "One—"

His lips grazed hers, and her gray eyes flew open. "What do you think you're doing, Sutherland?"

"Securing her ladyship for the night. Give me a nice kiss before I leave."

"I am not kissing you." She pursed her lips like a prune.

"You kissed me at Windsor Castle."

"Only because you caught me by surprise. Now kindly get up before I lose the sensation in my legs. I can no longer feel my toes."

He glanced around. "They're still there." He turned off to the side, keeping her trapped by throwing his thigh around hers like a shackle. Indignant, she felt him slide his arm under her backside. "What are you doing now?" she whispered.

"I'm holding you."

"Well, don't. No kissing. No holding." She

bounced up and down to dislodge his hand. "The closest contact you may have is handing me a teacup."

He wasn't paying her the slightest attention.

He ran his free hand up and down the curve of her hip, relearning the shape and softness. "Time has done verra nice things to your body," he said quietly. "You would bear strapping bairns."

"That might prove a little difficult without a husband."

"Aye, you need a husband too." He exhaled a whiskey-scented sigh into her hair. He rubbed his chin on her collarbone. "Someone strong enough not to die on you the first time he stubs his toe."

"Patrick."

She hit him in the eye with her elbow at the precise moment he remembered it was always a mistake to bring up David's name. "*Ouch*. That was a bit unkind, Anne."

She wriggled out from beneath him and dropped to her feet, her black curls cascading down her back. "Get out of my room."

He rolled off the bed, resigned but certainly not defeated. "I think I'll leave the whiskey," he said wryly. "You've forgotten how to enjoy yourself."

"I haven't forgotten anything." She had backed into the window, her small shoulders stiff with tension, her silhouette insubstantial against the darkened hills outside.

He picked up his tray to leave, suddenly at a loss for words. "Call me if you need me. Especially if you get lonely in the night."

As he closed the door, he heard her answer in an undertone, "When hell freezes over, Sutherland."

Which wasn't the encouraging reply he had hoped for, but it was only their first night in the house, and it proved that his beloved hellion was still hiding somewhere inside her haughty shell, waiting for him to find the key to unlock her wounded heart.

He walked around David's pinewood-paneled bedchamber and discovered books piled in every available space. Books collecting dust on the walnut davenport. Books on the marble-topped wash-stand, piled on the floridly carved Jacobean bed. The only corner free of literature was occupied by a large easel.

He winced as he lifted the sheet that covered the canvas and stared at an embarrassingly bad portrait of Anne rising from a sea shell. Her breasts were uneven. Her hands had been painted to hang like hamhocks, and her hips could have spanned a continent, let alone the width of the canvas.

"Botticelli you were not, cousin," he murmured. "I imagine her gardener could have done a better job of painting her with a trowel."

But then perhaps David hadn't had anything else to work from but imagination. Patrick deduced from the painting that David might had viewed Anne as a goddess, but he'd hardly demonstrated a realistic perception of her physical charms. Still, they had lived together in apparent harmony for years, they had been faithful to each other, even if they had slept apart. David had been Anne's husband, no matter how unpalatable Patrick found that fact.

And what did all these books mean? He pushed a pile onto the floor to make room for himself on the bed. Such scintillating titles as *Sheep Husbandry in the Highlands* and *The Art of Ciceronian Oratory* stared up at him. Why would any man in his right mind spend his time reading and painting a naked woman when the woman slept only a few feet away in the next room? Why had he not availed himself of her every night?

Perhaps because the man had won her by default, and he knew it? An unassuming man like David would never have attracted a woman like Anne on his own merit in a thousand years. The poor fool must have thought he had died and gone to heaven when their marriage had been arranged. Hell, he'd probably read to her on her honeymoon, not knowing what else to do. The man appeared to have lived like a monk even after marriage.

He closed his eyes, thinking of the time *he'd* made love to Anne, kissing her as he tore off her dress. Why had he not married her the very day he'd laid his big clumsy paws on her? Why couldn't he erase the past and undo the damage? But, oh, she had been so irresistible, so eager to please him. Even as he had deflowered her, taking her virginity in a cruel thrust, she hadn't cried out, and he had seen the shock in her eyes, his invasion of her young body robbing her of breath. Had she given herself so eagerly to her husband?

He hit his fist on the pillow, and the scent of lavender buds filled the air as he collapsed backward on the bed. There was no justice in this world, none at all. Look at David, dead and gone, and here his blackguard of a cousin slept in his bed while the woman they both had loved was sleeping alone. Life wasn't always fair, which was why Patrick believed a man had to make his own luck even if it meant suffering a little humiliation along the way.

13

$\mathcal{P}$atrick took an instant dislike to the distinguished-looking gentleman who banged at the door the following morning and insisted on seeing Anne. The middle-aged caller was bristling with anticipation, practically bursting the seams of his tweed jacket to enter the house. His mustache and thick brown hair, streaked attractively with silver, shone with a light application of Macassar oil.

Patrick was not in a good mood after being awakened before dawn by Gracie so he could get an early start on his duties, and he could smell a wolf when one knocked on the door. God above, he ought to be able to recognize his own kind.

He straightened his impressive shoulders and looked down his nose at the smaller man. It was, after all, a butler's prerogative to intimidate unwelcome callers.

"I will inquire whether her ladyship is receiving visitors," he said with starch in his voice.

The man gave him a smug smile, patting his cravat. "Oh, she'll receive me, all right. Anne and I are close friends."

Patrick frowned at that.

"Her ladyship has not had her breakfast yet," he said, all but closing the door in the man's face. "I believe she has made plans afterward to take her morning ride."

"Yes, yes." The man caught the door with the tip of his highly polished boot. "That is why I'm here. Nobody can outride Lady Whitehaven, and I intend to accompany her on her outing. Now open this door and tell her I am here, or I shall see to it that you get the sack."

Patrick put his hands on his hips. "What did you say your name was?"

The man looked a little startled at a butler assuming such a belligerent attitude. "Wallace. *Sir* Wallace Abermuir. But you may tell her ladyship that Wallie is here to welcome her back. She'll know me."

"Wallie, is it? Well, doesn't that just warm the cockles of your wee heart?" Patrick said to himself as he turned on his heel.

The man blinked and let himself into the hall, commenting under his breath about where one found one's help these days.

Patrick could have given Sir Wallie an earful about where he'd been found. He also could have thrown him out the door, he felt that annoyed as he stalked off down the hall under the unblinking stares of the stags' heads mounted on the wall.

Close friends, were they? And here he'd thought he knew everything there was to know about Anne; he had made discreet inquiries over the years into her personal affairs and was convinced she had never been unfaithful to David; still, he shouldn't be surprised that the local buzzards were already flocking to feast. She was beautiful and well-connected, if not wealthy.

He found her drinking tea in the blue drawing room with Nellwyn. As always, the sight of Anne made his heart beat a little harder, and for a moment he just leaned against the doorjamb, taking pleasure in listening to her talk about her horses. He loved this vivacious side of her character.

Nellwyn noticed him first. "Sutherland, have you brought my digestive biscuits?"

He made a face. "There's an odd fellow at the door to see Anne."

"To see her ladyship," Nellwyn corrected him.

He was staring at Anne's mouth, remembering the taste and texture of her lips. He had never appreciated her innocent kisses before, and now he was starved for them.

Anne frowned at him. "What was this man's name, Sutherland?"

He shrugged. "Walter. William. Hell if I know."

"Walter?" Anne put down her teacup. "I don't know anyone named Walter, and the only William in this area is a bit off in the head."

"Good." Patrick turned before she could stop him. "I'll get rid of him. I didn't like the looks of the walrus anyway."

"Wait a minute." Anne came to her feet. "He might be a friend of David's."

"I don't think he was David's friend," Patrick said, already halfway down the hall. "Anyway, there is something about him that I disliked."

"How intriguing," Nellwyn murmured. She had risen from her chair to follow Anne, although Patrick couldn't imagine what was so interesting about watching him turn away an unwelcome visitor. Bloodthirsty women, he decided. Well-bred but bloodthirsty.

His giant strides ate the distance to the door in no time. In fact, he was rolling up his shirtsleeves for a physical confrontation when Anne arrived and recognized her visitor.

She gasped in surprise. "Wallie, oh, good heavens. It's *you*. He said it was Walter, but I should have guessed. How embarrassing—you'll have to forgive us. After David died, there were so many insufferable men who came to call, claiming to be friends. And—"

She seemed unable to stop talking. In fact, Patrick couldn't remember seeing her so flustered and self-conscious in years, and he was taken aback by the change in her. And jealous. He was actually jealous when Sir Wallace smiled in relief and barreled past him, holding out his arms to Anne.

"Anne, you naughty girl, you should have let me know you were coming. I'd have had a crew of workers busy making this place more comfortable. How long are you staying? Did you ever breed Jocasta to that stallion? Did you hear my bay had foaled and Iolaire took a first?"

Anne was laughing, apparently enjoying the attention. Worse, she was letting the man touch her. Patrick swallowed and felt as if he had been turned to ice, unable to look away. Yet the absurdity of his masquerade made it impossible to express his anger in the usual ways. He couldn't very well pummel Sir Wallace into a pulp, or call him out for embracing Anne. So he did what any butler might do to signal his disapproval. He slammed the front door with a satisfying bang that echoed throughout the lodge. Dust motes danced in the air, and one of the ceremonial swords crossed on the wall dropped to dangle by its foil.

Startled, Anne pulled away from Wallace and turned to see what had caused the resounding crash. She found herself staring up at a very hurt-looking Patrick, who stood glowering back at her with his arms folded across his chest.

She stared at him for a long time. "We shall take fresh tea in the red drawing room. See to it, Sutherland."

Patrick clenched his jaw, not moving as Nellwyn came up to give him in encouraging word. "Don't worry. He doesn't hold a candle to you."

"He tried to kiss her on the mouth."

Nellwyn looked surprised. "She didn't let him, did she?"

"No," he said grudgingly, but who could say what might have happened if she had met Wallace alone—a situation he vowed instantly would never happen.

"Unless I miss my guess, this is all part of your

penance for whatever happened between you and Anne," Nellwyn said thoughtfully. "Have you tried telling her how you feel? Sometimes a woman needs gentle words, a bit of wooing."

He smiled grimly. "She knows I want her back, damn her. I can prove it by squashing that leech who's attached himself to her side."

She touched his arm. "No, you won't do any squashing. You shall better prove it by serving them tea."

§14§

The staff had never seen one of their own in such a pique. Sutherland looked positively forbidding as he left the kitchen shoving his trolley like a plow. Mrs. Forbes held her breath as her best china rattled in rhythm with his thunderous footsteps.

"What's the matter wi' him?" Gracie whispered to the parlormaid as they passed each other in the hall.

"Her ladyship has a visitor," was the reply. "A *male* visitor—Sir Wallace—and Mr. Sutherland is in a snit about it."

They jumped as he practically rammed the tea trolley through the door.

"Tea," he said loudly as he interrupted Wallace in the act of draping a shawl around Anne's shoulders.

Anne looked up from the sofa, her eyes alight with mischief. "There you are, Sutherland. I had just commented on how chilly the lodge is in the morning."

"There should be no need for her ladyship to feel cold," Sir Wallace said in disapproval. "Don't you have a second man, Sutherland, to see to such things as a chilly room?"

Patrick wheeled the trolley into the room with an unearthly clatter. "Her ladyship may complain to me in person if there is a problem. She is perfectly capable of complaining for herself."

The man looked dumbfounded. "Does your butler always speak in such a blunt manner?" he asked Anne.

She gave a helpless shrug. "I'm afraid he does."

"This would not have been allowed were your dear husband alive." Wallace settled back down next to her on the sofa. "It is a sad fact of life that young widows are one of society's most vulnerable members." He gave Patrick a look. "Prone to being taken advantage of by men of every station."

"Isn't that the truth?" Patrick retorted from the tea trolley.

Sir Wallace's eyebrows shot up. "Are you addressing me, Sutherland?"

"Not unless you're an envelope."

Anne shot him a murderous look. "Stop teasing, Sutherland, and pour that tea before it goes cold."

Patrick stared down at the tea trolley, uncertain he could continue with this masquerade and maintain any semblance of dignity whatsoever. And how was he to pour such a sissified beverage into these wee cups with a straight face?

"The tea, Sutherland," Anne said, biting off each word.

He lifted the silver pot and two china cups from the tray. Resentment blatant in his every move, he strode up to the sofa and thrust both cups into Sir Wallace's hands.

"Here. Kindly hold these for a moment."

"What the—"

"Don't move," Patrick warned him. "If you get hot tea dumped in your lap, I shall not accept the blame."

Anne held her breath as Patrick poured from his standing position, and Sir Wallace, speechless, sat as still as death with the cups gripped in his shaking hands.

"This is outrageous," the man sputtered.

"I suppose you both want sugar," Patrick said, turning back to the tray.

"I do," Anne said between her teeth.

"So do I," Sir Wallace said. "However, I do not want it dropped like a bomb into my cup."

Patrick arched his eyebrow. "Fine. Then perhaps you ought to do it yourself." And as Anne watched in disbelief he brought the tea trolley up to the sofa, wedging it as a barrier between her and Sir Wallace.

"There. Now nobody can complain. Drink away."

"Thank you, Sutherland," Anne said tightly. "You may see about your other duties now. Perhaps you could check the flues again. I'm sure Sir Wallace would like to catch me up on the local gossip."

Which meant Lord Kingairn's murder. Patrick didn't need to be hit over the head to get that hint. However, he did not like leaving his Anne alone with this middle-aged Romeo either. Butler or not, he would not tolerate anyone taking advantage of her.

"You know where to find me if you need me, madam," he said. Then he bowed and marched to the door, giving Sir Wallace a man-to-man look that warned him he had better behave himself, or else.

"That is the most aggravating servant I have ever encountered," Sir Wallace said the instant the door closed.

Anne put her hand to her head. It was throbbing. "Yes, I know."

"Why do you tolerate such impudence in an inferior, Anne?"

"I'm not sure." She stared at the door, fighting an urge to laugh. "Perhaps because he and David were once close."

Which wasn't a lie. The two men had been cousins, and David had always admired Patrick from a distance, although to this day Anne wondered how much he had guessed about her past.

David had envied Patrick's confidence and devil-may-care approach to life. David's interests had leaned toward the scholarly, a quiet man who craved hearth and home. Yet more than once he had admitted to Anne that he wished himself strong enough to accompany Patrick to Bermuda, but he didn't have the stamina for fighting. He didn't even have the stamina to ride with his young wife on the moor.

Anne had been secretly relieved. She cherished her time riding alone, even if more often than not she had spent those times thinking about how different her life might have been if she had married another man. But she couldn't complain, could she? Her husband had worshipped her and her reputation was intact.

"Dear, sad Anne."

She gave a start of alarm as she realized Sir Wallace had taken her hand. His knee pressed against hers, and he was looking at her with an indulgent if admonishing smile.

"David and I met during our Oxford days. Do you remember?"

She did, but only vaguely, and what did they say about the kind of wife she'd been? For most of their marriage David had buried himself in the library with his books while she attended the races or rode alone on the heath, a pursuit that had worried her husband half to death.

"David is gone," Sir Wallace said. "Perhaps in your grief for your dear husband, your judgment is not as sound as it should be."

She pried her hand loose on the pretense of reaching for her cup. "Are you saying that my wits are scattered because I have employed Sutherland?"

He watched her carefully. "Let us not discuss your rather eccentric butler. If David was fond of the fellow, then he must have his worthy side."

She took a sip of tea. "Speaking of David, do you remember how he loved his shooting parties? I had thought this year I might resume the tradition, as a tribute to his memory."

He frowned. "It is rather short notice, and I do not wish to sound rude, but the lodge is badly in need of repairs."

"And I am in desperate need of some diversion," she said lightly.

"Perhaps a trip abroad might better do the trick."

"No. No." She smiled, pressing her point. "My heart is set on a party and seeing all of our old friends."

"I see." He smiled back at her. "Then a party you shall have, and I am delighted to offer any help you might need."

She sighed. "Of course it will be sad without David giving his tearful toasts and Uncle Edgar doing that silly sword dance."

"Uncle—Oh, yes, Edgar. Poor fellow. Still, he was fortunate to have lived such a full life, and to die fishing on a loch, well, most men would consider that an ideal end."

Anne set her cup back on its saucer. "I've heard the most distressing rumors about his death."

He took her hand again. "Then do not be distressed, my dear. I was there at the very end when we discovered him gone, and it was a tragic but straightforward affair."

"You were there?" she said in surprise.

"Everyone was there, all the usual guests. The doctor told us his heart probably failed during the excitement of rowing across the loch. He had gone out ahead of us, it seems."

"Alone, you said?"

He looked at her. "Well, yes, he was found by himself, but that is not unusual, is it? Lady Kingairn never attended such affairs." He squeezed her hand. "Now that is entirely enough sadness for one day. Poor Edgar aside, I am delighted that you have come home."

"Home?"

"Yes, home, and I say we celebrate your return with a rousing canter across the moor. Nobody can keep up with me like you—did I mention I was hoping to get a colt-foal out of Carbonel this year? You can come with us to Epsom and—"

Her laughter interrupted him. "That ride does sound tempting, but I'd have to ask Sandy to leave his gardening for an hour and accompany us."

"There's no need to drag the old man from his weeds. Flora will play chaperone to keep everything proper. She's in the stable now."

"Flora?" She tried to keep the distaste out of her voice. "Your daughter did not marry the young painter she met in Dundee?"

"As it turned out, the young painter had a young wife and three young children."

"My goodness," Anne said.

"It's in the blood." He sat forward so unexpectedly that she was forced to lean back against the sofa in self-defense. "We Abermuirs are fools when it comes to affairs of the heart."

"I hardly know what to say, Wallace."

He stared at her intently. He was an attractive man in his fashion, with dark compelling eyes and a solid build. His love of horses was genuine; he bet heavily at the races and employed a private trainer for his thoroughbreds, which he had bought with his pension as a naval officer. Two years ago he'd told Anne he was writing *the* book on the rules of racing; David used to laugh in the background while Wallace and Anne argued heaves and handicaps at the table. "We are a hot-blooded family, Anne. Do you understand what I am saying?"

"Well, not—"

A thunderous crash beside the sofa all but startled her out of her skin. She and Sir Wallace jumped to their feet and found themselves looking up into Patrick's unsmiling face. A load of firewood lay on the carpet where he had dropped it.

"Really, Sutherland." She pressed her hand to her heart. "You might practice a little more grace when you enter a room. You sound like one of the Titans waging war."

His chiseled jaw tightened. "I was concerned that her ladyship might be cold." He cast a withering look at Sir Wallace. "Of course that was before all the talk of hot-blooded hearts began. You probably don't need a fire now."

"Were you eavesdropping on our conversation?" Sir Wallace demanded, incensed.

Patrick took a step forward. "Why? Were you saying something you'd be ashamed to repeat in public?"

Sir Wallace flushed. "Why, you insolent upstart."

"Take that back," Patrick said, his heavy brows drawing into a scowl.

Anne struggled over the firewood to place herself between the two men. "You are overstepping your bounds again, Sutherland," she said in a clipped voice.

"I'll show you overstepping—"

She nudged him away from the sofa. "Make the fire. *Now.*"

They glared at each other, the small angry woman and the powerfully built man who towered over her, with Sir Wallace watching on in utter bewilderment. "Why don't you just give the blighter the sack, Anne?"

"She's keeping me for sentimental reasons," Patrick said as he bent to heft the wood in his arms.

"Do not refer to her ladyship in such a manner," Sir Wallace said.

Patrick unloaded the wood into the huge stone hearth. "What manner is that, sir?"

"Make the fire, Sutherland," Anne said forcefully. She turned to Sir Wallace, deliberately blocking him from Patrick's view. "You must learn to ignore his idiosyncrasies as I have. He can be a wee bit difficult at times, but he does get his job done. And— he's affordable."

"Difficult?" Sir Wallace said in disbelief. "I don't know how you can stand him."

"She cannot live without me," Patrick muttered from his kneeling position at the hearth.

Anne tapped her foot, seriously tempted to give his lean buttocks a hearty kick. "I am going upstairs to change into my habit. Meet me in the stables, Wallace. I think I will accept your offer of that rousing ride, after all."

Patrick stared at the soot on his hands in annoyance. Anne had another thing coming if she thought he was going to sweep ashes while the walrus seduced her. His shoulders squared in determination, he sprang up from the hearth and stalked out of the room. His stormy appearance in the hall startled a gasp out of Gracie, who was on her way upstairs with clean bedding.

Anne had already gone up to her room to change. And Sir Wallace had presumably hurried to the stables in search of a groom before she could change her mind.

"Where were they off to in such a rush?" Gracie asked, her face half-buried behind a hillock of crisply ironed sheets.

"None of your business," he said, debating whether to follow Anne upstairs or not.

"Cheeky bugger—ooh, now where are you going? What about that tea trolley I can see in the drawing room?"

He turned on his heel, walking backward. "Take care of it for me, sweetheart, won't you? I have an important errand to run."

"Sweetheart?" She blushed, almost dropping her sheets on the bottom steps. "You devil—you're up to something naughty, aren't you, Sutherland?"

"Me?" He gave an innocent shrug, hand on his chest. "Why would you think that?"

She shook her head as his tall figure disappeared from sight. "The best-looking ones always bring trouble, God bless 'em."

$\mathcal{E}15\mathcal{S}$

$\mathcal{A}$nne was at a loss for words when she and Wallace reached the stables only to find Patrick waiting for them. Elegant in charcoal riding breeches, jacket, and high-buttoned riding boots, he appeared to be in the process of picking a suitable horse for himself.

Actually, he was looking for a dependable mount for Anne. Her disregard for her personal safety probably frightened him as much as it had her husband, but the difference between the two men was that David would never have dared to intervene when it came to Anne's passion for riding. Patrick dared to intervene, and more, even if he sensed he would have the fight of his life on his hands.

"Her ladyship will take the chestnut gelding, I think," he said to the young groom, turning from the stall.

"No, she will not," Anne said in a curt voice. She wore a cutaway plaid jacket over a green velvet skirt. The veil of her black silk hat hid her agitated expression.

Sir Wallace looked ready to explode. "What the deuce are you doing in her ladyship's stables dressed in—are those Lord Whitehaven's clothes, Sutherland?"

Patrick gave him a perfectly bland look. "I am waiting to accompany her ladyship on her rousing ride, of course."

"Accompany us?" Sir Wallace said, blinking. "A butler?"

Patrick pulled a pair of gray kidskin gloves from his pocket. "Didn't her ladyship tell you? I was a groom before I became a butler, sir."

"Were you indeed?" Sir Wallace said acerbically.

An undergroom led Anne's iron-gray stallion out of the stables. Patrick inserted himself between Anne and Sir Wallace before the older man could huff out a protest.

"Allow me," he said coolly, extending his arm to Anne. "We would not want you to soil that tweed jacket, sir. It does not look as if it has too many years of wear left in it."

Sir Wallace's mouth dropped open, and as there was no predicting what outrageous thing Patrick would say next, Anne hastened to intercede.

"Find out where Flora is, Wallace," she said, glaring down at Patrick's face. "I shall wait for you outside the paddock."

"As you wish, my dear."

"You are the devil incarnate," she whispered to Patrick as Wallace reluctantly wandered off to find his daughter.

"I have no idea what you mean," he said guilelessly.

She grunted and gathered the reins in her left hand. Grinning to himself, Patrick grasped her left leg at the knee, closing his other hand around the ankle, and hoisted her into the air with such force that she practically dove head over horse to the other side.

He chuckled, grabbing hold of her skirts to save her; he caught a glimpse of the chamois drawers she wore to keep from slipping off the saddle. "My goodness, Lady Whitehaven. It appears I don't know my own strength."

"Let go of my behind, you scoundrel," she whispered indignantly.

"What?" He cupped his ear, pretending not to hear. "Speak up, Anne. I cannot understand you when you whisper through that veil. I spent several years in the infantry. Gunfire does something to one's hearing."

"My behind," she hissed.

"Behind whom?" he said, glancing around, his hand slowly easing beneath her bottom, which was positioned at a provocative angle in the air.

"My posterior, you damned fool."

"Your posterior?" Patrick took the opportunity to squeeze her buttocks in both hands before repositioning her in the saddle. "What's wrong with it? It feels verra nice to me. Hmmm. Quite solid. Put on a bit of beef, haven't we?"

"Why, you—"

He backed away, his dark eyes dancing. "The wee

bit of flesh suits you, Anne. I always thought you were too slender. Do you remember how easily I carried you down the hill in the rain? Light as a sprig of heather, you were."

She took a breath. "I don't remember anything of the kind."

"Remember what?" Sir Wallace asked, riding up beside Anne on a lively dun.

"The way to the village," she said carefully.

"No problem there," Sir Wallace said. "I know exactly where to go." He nudged his horse forward, forcing Patrick to step aside. "Advise Lady Invermont that your mistress will probably be home late for supper. I suspect we'll end up dining at the coaching inn. Fancy some grilled salmon, Anne?"

Patrick's lips flattened into a straight line. Sir Wallace was riding the horse he had saddled for himself. It was not unusual for a butler or valet to accompany an employer on a drive or a ride when another servant wasn't available, and he'd had every intention of tagging along on this little outing to make sure the baronet behaved himself.

He looked up mockingly into Anne's veiled face. "I would be remiss in my duties if I did not accompany you, ma'am."

"Her ladyship is an excellent hands," Sir Wallace said smugly. "You may return to your pantry, Sutherland."

Patrick's gaze bore into him with such menace that Sir Wallace's smug look promptly wilted. "I will fetch another horse."

Several seconds passed. Patrick vanished into the stables, and Anne stared straight ahead, her expression inscrutable. Sir Wallace cleared his throat.

"What do you say we lose him, Anne?" he suggested in an undertone. "Between us both, we can surely outride a butler."

"Lead him on a merry chase?"

"Precisely."

She bit her lip and laughed. "I say it's a splendid idea."

Patrick swore aloud as he watched the two riders disappear into the woods, Anne taking the lead. Her spine was perfectly vertical; her right shoulder back and hips square. There was something graceful and suggestive about the way she rocked in rhythm with a massive stallion, and Patrick remembered how he had watched her in fascination years ago on the moor. Was she begging to be caught? Was she running from something even now? Years ago he had not the depth of emotion to understand her.

"Do you want me to chase you?" he said softly. "Aye, I will. Then we'll see who takes revenge."

He spun around, then took a step back to avoid walking into the path of a young red-haired woman who had just emerged from the stables. She looked sleek in a brown riding habit, and her hazel eyes narrowed speculatively when she noticed him.

"Who are you?" she demanded, tapping her riding quirt across her thigh.

He released a sigh. "Sutherland, her ladyship's butler."

"Her—" She looked him up and down. Then she let out a loud hoot of laughter. "Well, we have certainly never had a butler who looked anything like you in our house. Perhaps I need to leave Scotland more often."

He tried to move around her, not in a mood to dally while Anne was beyond his protection. "If you will excuse me, miss, I'm supposed to accompany her ladyship on her ride, and I fear I've lost her."

The quirt poked him in the side. "Take me with you."

He turned and tugged the whip out of her gloved hands, thinking he ought to give her a good swat across her own behind. "I shall get lost if I wait any longer, miss."

"No, you won't. I know a shortcut through the woods." She gave him a knowing grin. "I'll bet my papa will waylay Anne somewhere anyway. He's dying to romance her."

He glanced to the bridle path where Anne and Wallace moved like colorful blurs against the gray September sky. "Show me this shortcut."

"Help me mount first, Sutherland." She wrested the whip from his hand. "And give me this in case I need it. You look as if you could be a very wicked butler indeed."

"Appearances can be deceptive, miss," he said calmly.

An early autumn chill laced the air, and hazelnuts were beginning to drop even though chaffinches still sang from the woods. At the village outskirts the hoddie crows had already claimed the shorn cornfields, rowan hoops were being made to protect the sheep from evil, and Samhain was only a month or so away.

"You truly look nothing like a butler," Flora said thoughtfully as they rode through a grove of alder and mountain ash, following a trail so overgrown it could have been used by the Druids, for all Patrick knew.

"Don't I?" He was barely listening to her; he was staring toward the purple-brown moor at the ruins of a crumbling broch where the ancient Picts had once awaited their enemies. He had caught another glimpse of Anne on the causeway, but now he couldn't see her at all, and that worried him. He knew too well what could happen between a man and a woman in such a setting, and he knew also Anne wanted to punish him.

"You don't act like one, either," she added.

She examined his profile in silence, studying his bladed nose and high-cheekboned face, apparently determined to provoke a reaction. "My papa wants to marry your mistress," she said slyly. "What do you think of that?"

He finally turned his head to glance at her, and Flora caught her breath, regretting what she had said as the thought struck her that if she looked too deeply into his unholy eyes, she might see her own downfall. She did not know exactly who he was, but her instincts suddenly warned her that he brought trouble into her life.

"What should I think of it, miss?" he asked quietly.

She shook her head, unable to answer, but then the faint whickering of Anne's stallion broke the spell of silence, and Patrick turned away.

"What is it?" she whispered.

He drew in his breath; he was unprepared when he saw Anne's horse break into a canter from behind the broch with Sir Wallace at her side. "A race, I think," he said, his body shifting position.

"They're a pair of fools," Flora exclaimed, shaking her head. "Papa is too old to ride like that. The last time—"

He didn't wait for her to finish; his knees gripping the gelding, he thundered hard down the hill to join the race. His male instincts wouldn't allow him to lose, and he felt a savage thrill when Anne glanced over her shoulder and saw him passing Sir Wallace as the moor climbed to a hilly ridge.

He was almost close enough to touch her. He could hear her laughing, and the wind pulled her hat off, the veil tumbling into the rough heather and juniper that flew in tufts from the horses' hooves. When he had first met Anne, he had assumed her penchant for pursuing danger came from a wildness inside her that matched his own rebellious streak. Now he felt like a bastard for never digging deeper into her life, for asking why she tempted fate. His heart ached as he remembered what Isobel had told him. Anne had been trying to run from her own pain, and instead of saving her, he had only made the situation worse.

But Anne didn't look unhappy now. In fact, she was in her element, riding to race the devil, and if he had been paying closer attention, he would have realized she was poised to jump the stallion over a wall of loose-lying stones that had been piled to enclose cattle on the moor.

"Don't." He felt the blood drain from his face, and his shout was lost in the wind. "Damn you, Anne, *don't!*"

Time froze, and he half rose in the stirrups, all his focus on the graceful fury of the woman he realized he had never really known. Was she trying to kill herself? He couldn't stand to watch and he couldn't look away as she took flight, pelvis down, hips straight. His mind stopped for the endless seconds it took for her to soar over the stones and land in a perfect position to canter from his sight.

He reined in his horse at the wall, so shaken and furious that when he heard the other woman's scream behind him, he almost couldn't move at all. He was still paralyzed by the thought of Anne lying in a broken heap before him.

❧16❧

*H*e shook the image off, turning in time to watch Sir Wallace sail over the dun's shoulder, carried by the momentum of the chase.

Apparently, the fall wasn't serious. Sir Wallace was covered in mud and shouting at his daughter, who was making a fuss not because she feared her papa was hurt, but rather because she had splattered mud on her new riding habit, and she had evidently twisted her leg.

"How will I get another skirt in time for the shooting season, that's what I want to know. This red loam will never wash out." She limped through the mud to her father, who was sitting on a rock holding his head in his hands. "Papa, why did you have to chase after her like that? You have made an utter fool of yourself, my clothes are ruined, and my leg is hurt."

Patrick rolled his eyes, then dismounted and walked to the scene of the crime. "Are you all right, sir?" he asked, trying not to laugh.

Sir Wallace looked up at him. True, they were rivals for Anne's affection. In the days of old, they would have battled it out with mace and sword until one of them lay dead or bleeding on the ground. They still might end up in a mortal duel for that matter, the woman was that maddening. And the fact remained that Patrick would not have trusted a man like Wallace under any condition.

But for a moment they were simply two men who had just been made fools of by the woman they desired. Their eyes connected in a flash of shared defeat. They grunted, acknowledging their mutual humiliation and frustration. This bond of male empathy wouldn't last, of course; they'd push each other off a cliff in an instant to be the one to warm Anne's bed.

For this moment, however, they were of one mind. "I'm fine, Sutherland," Sir Wallace said with grudging appreciation. "Thank you for asking."

"Think nothing of it, sir."

Sir Wallace hit his bonnet on his knee. "Damn that woman's hide. I almost had her, Sutherland, and then do you know what happened? I lost my nerve."

"Damn her hide indeed, sir," Patrick said without thinking.

Sir Wallace glanced at him in surprise, but said nothing. They were temporary allies, and a social lapse, a slip of the tongue, could be overlooked considering what had provoked it. "Her husband never kept her in hand," he raged quietly. "That woman has no fear when it comes to personal safety."

"No fear at all," Patrick said, but he was going to put a healthy dose into her the minute he got her alone in the lodge.

"Excuse me," Flora said, tapping her quirt on Patrick's shoulder. "Have we forgotten something? I believe I injured my leg when I jumped down to come to my papa's aid."

"Look at her." Sir Wallace gestured wanly up at the winding road where Anne galloped against the gray shadows of the ridge. "We could be dead for all she cares."

Patrick frowned. "Dead *and* buried."

"She didn't give a damn that I took a fall."

"She didn't even know," Patrick said.

"What about my leg?" Flora bellowed, her voice echoing across the barren landscape.

Her papa lifted his dejected face to look at her. "Just shut the bloody hell up for once," he said, taking the words right out of Patrick's mouth. "We shall see to your leg after we've licked our own wounds."

The servants of Balgeldie House could only shake their heads in consternation. They had been informed via the groom and gardener's boy of every detail of the day's peculiar events, including Mr. Sutherland touching her ladyship on a forbidden area of her anatomy in the stable, and Lady Whitehaven's return alone on her horse.

The staff noted that Lady Whitehaven had positively sprinted up the stairs to her room, the happiest they had seen her since his lordship's death. Humming to herself, she was.

They also noted that, a half-hour later, Mr. Sutherland and Sir Wallace dragged into the stables like two downtrodden warriors returning from an unsuccessful crusade.

What could it all mean?

Sandy, the eldest staff member, who considered himself something of a philosopher because he had read Plato, thought it signified the start of a social rebellion in Scotland. He predicted that a small-scale French Revolution was brewing under their very noses.

Gracie scoffed openly at his theory. "As if the French Terror began with a butler patting an aristocrat on the bum."

"It started wi' something," Sandy said knowingly. "Wars have started over less, lass."

A bell rang on the wall above them, and Mrs. Forbes came bustling into the kitchen. "Her ladyship is wanting a bath, *tout de suite*. Heat some towels and water, and inform Mr. Sutherland that Lady Invermont has requested a plumber here by the end of the week."

"A plumber?" Sandy said in surprise.

Grace nodded. "Aye. She says we're living like primitives and—"

She subsided into silence as Patrick appeared in the doorway, his face a study in dark emotion. Everyone turned to look at him, Maggie the scullery maid quit chopping carrots, and all one could hear was the cheerful bubbling of cock-a-leekie soup on the hearth, and Patrick banging the door against the wall in an entrance that could hardly be ignored.

"Well, well, well." Mrs. Forbes looked him up and down. "Home from our little misadventure, are we?"

"You're quite the man, Sutherland," Sandy said, sitting back in his chair with a wicked grin.

Patrick's eyes burned as hot as smoke. "Where is she?"

Mrs. Forbes shook her head. " 'She' is the family cat who sits by the fire. If by your misusage of the word you are referring to your mistress, then *her ladyship* is upstairs awaiting her bath."

"Is she now?" he said softly, turning on his heel to the door. "Well, let me blister her bum first."

Mrs. Forbes went deathly pale, and Maggie almost stabbed Sandy in the thumb as she dropped her knife in excitement. Never in the history of Balgeldie House had a domestic dared so much, except perhaps centuries ago during the War of the Rough Wooing when a page had dressed up as young Mary Stuart in a game of charades, using a pair of imported grapefruits as breasts.

But even that had been at the request of the laird, and all in fun.

The look on Sutherland's face portended unspeakable evil. It even brought Sandy out of his chair, although it was more from a sense of anticipation than apprehension.

"You're not going to overstep your bounds again, are you, Sutherland?" he asked hopefully.

§17§

$\mathcal{A}$nne was toasting her minor triumph with a small glass of the whiskey Patrick had brought the night before when he entered her room.

She was standing by the window in her smock, drawers, and riding boots, and her smile froze in shock as she recognized his tall figure in the mirror.

She also recognized that black expression. According to Nellwyn, Patrick rarely lost his temper, but when he did it was as if a snowstorm had blown down from the Cairngorms, chilling everything it touched.

The only time Anne had seen that look on his face had been four months after her wedding when they had seen each other at an auction house in London. Patrick had not been home long, and Anne had no idea how he had taken the news of her marriage until that day. David had kissed her in front of all their friends and announced that she was expecting their first child, which she had lost soon after.

For an unspeakable moment, she had feared Patrick was going to kill David on the spot, but instead he had cornered her at the edge of the crowd, not caring that his strange behavior could be watched.

"Is it mine?" he asked in a furious undertone.

She brushed his hand away, shocked by the question. "No, it isn't. Now stop looking at me like that. People can see us. Please, Patrick."

"Why did you marry him?" He was too arrogant and angry at her to care what anyone thought, if anyone overheard them, or if he might ruin the remnants of the life she had salvaged.

And she was too terrified by his reappearance in her settled life to give him any sort of explanation. "He wanted to marry me. I can't believe it would matter to you."

She didn't know what he had said after that but she did remember the way his eyes had raked over her, as if he actually dared to claim as his a child conceived months after their encounter—as if by a simple act he owned her and had the right to destroy her marriage.

And he was looking at her that same way now, only David was gone, and there was nothing to protect her from all that lay unfinished between them; he could not possibly understand how she had struggled to overcome the emotional pain of the past.

She reached for the silk dressing robe on the bed. "I did not summon you, Sutherland."

He slammed the door, and a shudder seemed to

resonate through the soles of her feet. "Are you trying to kill yourself?"

"I am not dressed properly, Patrick."

"I don't give a damn."

"You never did," she said tightly. "I just didn't understand that."

"What were you trying to prove by taking that jump?"

"If my husband didn't try to interfere with my riding, why should I care what you think?"

He was walking her back into the wall, swearing to himself and struggling not to acknowledge that she was beautiful and half-dressed, and that if she were his wife, he'd have locked her in the tower before he let her risk her life.

"David obviously couldn't control you."

"You mean he couldn't dominate me the way you want to."

He backed her into the dressing table, both of them breathing hard as they battled with their emotions. "He was probably afraid to try," he said heartlessly. "Perhaps he knew you'd never loved him."

She closed her eyes and felt the heat of his body invading hers. Her voice broke. "I want you to leave before this goes any further. What I shared with my husband is none of your business."

"It is my business if you ride like a she-demon with no damned concern for your safety. I have not forgotten my promise to Her Majesty to protect you."

She pressed the heels of her hands down on the

table, more trapped by the emotional power he wielded over her than by his show of physical strength. "I did love David. I did." Which was a lie he could never disprove—it was more a half-truth than a lie.

"How did you love him?"

She opened her eyes. His face was unyielding, and for the first time, she realized that either he had truly changed or she had underestimated him all along.

"Did you love him as a father?" he persisted. "Or was he more like an older brother and a good friend? There are many forms of love, Anne."

He was so close to the truth that she felt tears filling her eyes, but anger came to her rescue. "Do you know what's really sad, Patrick?" She pulled back as he put his arms around her shoulders. "It's not what happened to us. The saddest thing is that David was a genuinely good man, and he trusted you. Sometimes I used to think he suspected what had happened between you and me, but he never said a word, and that's just a quality, a maturity neither you nor I can claim. He never hurt a single soul in his life."

"I always will harbor a fondness for David," he admitted. "I confess I was not happy to hear you had wed my own cousin, but I acknowledge a debt of gratitude to him for keeping you safe for me."

"For you?" Resentment surged through all her tender memories, and she was so astonished by his arrogance, she began to laugh. "You are suffering from delusions, Sutherland."

"I'll show you something that is not a delusion, Anne. Something very real."

"You better not—"

"Aye, I will. You have always tempted me beyond my powers of resistance."

His kiss brought an end to the argument, proving again that time had only strengthened their attraction to each other. His large hands cradled her head; she heard him groaning her name into her hair but suddenly he wasn't bullying, he was begging.

"Why can't we simply begin all over again?" he said quietly. "Woman, must I carve out my own heart for you to give me the chance to make amends? I've never forgotten you, Anne."

She couldn't answer, even if she knew what to say. How could she speak when the most basic physical function like breathing was so beyond her? How could she think when his long fingers were walking down her shoulder, slipping inside her smock to make her shiver and hope that he would take her right against the dressing table until the horrible ache of desiring him was appeased?

Her body remembered his mastery. Within a matter of seconds, he had reduced her to nothing. With a kiss he resurrected all the needs and pleasures she had hidden away when she had married a man she did not love. His touch reawakened all the wonder and terror a woman feels when she gives herself to a man she fears will end up hurting her.

"Nothing is different, is it?" he whispered. His mouth lowered to her breast; her head fell back as he untied her smock and nibbled the dusky nipple, and his powerful hands moved over her body, sculpting her curves as if he owned her, as if he could crawl inside her soul, finding his scent and imprint where he had put it years ago.

She lifted her hands to his neck, intending to push him away. Instead, she twisted her fingers in the crisp black hair at his nape, kissing him back with a desire that took them both by surprise.

He lost control—it was Anne who held the power in her delicate lady's hands now even though he knew he could press the point; he could probably make her do anything he wished. But he was too excited to think it through, and he dragged her by her wrists to the bed and decided to let fate take its course. She seemed so fragile and vulnerable when he pulled her down between his legs, and even more than he wanted to make love to her, he wanted to reassure her he would never hurt her again, that his intentions were not to dishonor her.

"Trust me." He ran his strong hands up her belly to her breasts; she was straddling him, trembling uncontrollably as she shook her head, and her long hair fell down around his hips like a mantle.

"I'll never trust you again," she whispered. "This doesn't mean a thing except that I'm weak and lonely and—"

"It does mean something," he said. "Do you really believe it is by accident that we are together again?"

He sat up to wrap his arms around her, but from the hallway came the clamor of voices and footsteps; the footmen Fergus and Allan arguing about which angle to carry the tub into Anne's room. Patrick cursed softly, not willing to let her go.

She pulled her robe on, covering her swollen breasts, and gave him a stricken look before she got off the bed. His glazed eyes traveled over her from head to toe. He was so aroused it was like a physical ache, and his heart was pumping like a piston, but despite his discomfort, he hadn't forgotten why he had come to her room in the first place. He cared for her feelings more than satisfying his own lust.

"Don't ride like that again," he said, rising from the bed at the same time as the knock at the door announced her bath. "I mean it, Anne. So help me God, I will drag you by the hair off your horse if you take another jump like that."

"Thank you so much for your help moving the wardrobe, Sutherland," she said in a clear voice. The two lower manservants bustled between them, their presence defusing the heated threat in the air. "You may see about dinner now. Remember to set a place for Sir Wallace and Miss Flora."

He raised a brow, and their gazes clashed in the mirror as she moved to her desk and began sifting through a pile of old papers, her hands trembling. Without a word he walked up beside her, took a pen, and began to write.

You are mine, Anne.
You always were.
You always will be.

He closed the door with a rueful smile, leaving her alone with his message. She wanted to put her head down and weep, but what good would that do? She could not continue this way—she was fighting something in herself as much as against him, and the most terrifying thing was that even her quarrels with Patrick had a sense of rightness to them. His presence in her room, his anger at her recklessness had seemed so natural, and oh, God, oh, God, she had never forgotten him.

She folded his note in half and stuffed it into the desk, bewildered at how easily she had allowed him to provoke her again. The man did not understand the rules of polite behavior. He refused to understand that he was basically banished from her heart.

Mistress and servant, the balance of power was precarious and liable to shift at any instant if she did not strengthen her guard. Aye, she would have to. She would simply have to work harder to put an emotional distance between them. She would *not* repeat the sins of her past.

❧18❧

$\mathcal{P}$atrick banged into the blue drawing room a few hours later, a man not happy with his position and making no bones about it. "Dinner is served," he shouted, taking great pleasure in the startled way Sir Wallace fell back from Anne.

Anne rose from the sofa where she sat between Flora and her father. "Thank you for that subtle announcement, Sutherland. As soon as the walls stop shaking, we will make our way to the dining room. I trust you've made arrangements for Sir Wallace and his daughter to spend the night."

He frowned. "What for?"

She gave him a look. "It is raining. They cannot possibly ride home in this weather. At least not at night. In fact, I have invited them to stay a few more days if they like."

"Raining?" He strode over to the window and peered out. "Hell, it's barely a drizzle. In the infantry we'd call it midge piss. They—"

"We wouldn't want anything to happen to our neighbors, would we?" she interrupted him in a brittle voice.

Actually, we would, Patrick thought, turning to scowl back at her.

Flora gave a nervous giggle. "The Black Dwarf of the Bog might trap me on the way home. They say he comes out on rainy nights to waylay unwary travelers, and carries them off to his underground lair."

"The Black Dwarf?" Nellwyn glanced up from her game of solitaire. "I believe he only comes out to trap virgins. My goodness, dear, I shouldn't think you'd need to worry on that account."

Patrick shot his aunt an appreciative grin, at which point Anne could have cheerfully throttled the pair of them. There was definitely a streak of wickedness running through that family, and she still wouldn't be surprised to discover that she was the victim of some horrid scheme their two evil minds had invented.

It was Patrick's job as butler to oversee the table setting and to approve of such matters as whether the footmen had polished the nuts to perfection. The first thing he did, however, was to change the seating so that Sir Wallace sat at the opposite end of the table from Anne. Intent on this task, he forgot to trim the wicks and the guests arrived in utter darkness before he figured out how to light the candelabra without burning down the house. He realized suddenly that he had always taken his own servants for granted, not bothering to appreciate the countless tasks they undertook to make his life more comfortable. He had never paid attention to the functions of his aging butler and felt ashamed of himself.

"You make a terrible butler," Nellwyn informed him as she fanned a cloud of smoke from her face. "What are we having for dinner, Sutherland?"

He stared at her from the huge Gothic sideboard. "I can't remember."

"Well, when are we eating?"

He cast a dark glance at Sir Wallace moving his setting next to Anne. "I have no idea. Mrs. Forbes said dinner was ready, and that's all I know."

"Sutherland." She beckoned him over to her chair with her finger. He leaned down to hear her amused whisper. "The butler is supposed to bring up the first course. The footmen are waiting to follow you."

He looked up and saw Fergus and Allan flanking the door, grins on their homely faces. "Hell. What do I do after that?"

"Remove the covers and serve the wine," she whispered. "You may stand behind Anne's chair during the meal to attend her needs if you like. You must certainly remain there while we say grace."

He straightened, watching Sir Wallace scoot his chair closer to Anne's. "Allow me to help you with that, sir," he said, springing forward to wedge Sir Wallace's chair right back where it belonged. "There. Now isn't that better?"

Sir Wallace glared at him. "Hardly."

The meal proceeded quite well in Patrick's opinion, considering the fact that he wasn't paying attention to his butler's duties. His primary objective was to intrude every time Sir Wallace made a questionable move in Anne's direction until finally the dessert course arrived, and the baronet settled back in his chair, thwarted in the romantic overtures he had attempted.

Patrick leaned down next to Nellwyn on the pretext of handing her a fresh napkin. "Can you keep an eye on Anne while I see to something outside?" he said in a quiet voice.

The woman sighed. "You haven't taken to drink again, have you?"

"No, Auntie Nellwyn," he said in irritation. "I haven't, but I don't think anyone could blame me if I did. And by the way, it's nice to know both you and Anne have such great faith in me."

"You were a regular Lucifer in your youth," she whispered behind her napkin, but she didn't sound exactly disapproving. "Will you be back in time for tea?"

"Probably not," he said. "I don't like tea, so it isn't exactly a sacrifice."

"I wasn't asking you to drink it," she said wryly. "It's the butler's job to serve tea and cake a few hours after we dine."

He straightened. "Keep an eye on Anne. I don't trust the walrus."

She caught his hand, her eyes gleaming. "It has something to do with the investigation, doesn't it?"

He backed away from the table. "I'll be back in an hour."

"Do you want me to sneak along to help?" she whispered eagerly. "I've got Richard's dueling pistols in my room."

He winked at her. "I'll send for you if I need you."

Patrick stared through the border of larch trees at the light rain falling on the black waters of the loch. For his own part it seemed plausible that an aging man had suffered a heart attack during a strenuous bout of rowing such a distance, especially after a week of shooting and an excess of rich food.

Still, that did not explain why Uncle Edgar's bank account had been so mysteriously depleted, but neither did that mean he had been murdered. All Patrick had to go on so far was Gracie's unreliable rumors of his ghost, and Sandy mentioning Edgar had seemed distracted the night of the party.

He walked to the end of the pier and back, studying the dozen or so fishing boats that waited on the moon-silvered shore. A few bats flittered across the treetops, but all in all it seemed too peaceful a setting for foul play.

Then a movement on the hill above caught his eye. A lone horseman rode down the stony path toward him, and Patrick thought it strange to find another rider at this hour in such a secluded spot.

The gray-haired man, in a dark coat and trousers, dismounted. Patrick waited. They assessed each other in the silvery drizzle.

"Sir," the man said at last. "I do not know you. Are you lost perhaps? This is a private estate."

"I'm Patrick Sutherland." He hesitated. "I'm staying at Balgeldie House with Lady Whitehaven and Lady Invermont."

"Anne is back?" The older man offered his hand. "Forgive me. I am Doctor Daniel MacDonald, one of the family's physicians and long-time friend. I admit I never thought her ladyship would return after her husband died. David was passionate about this place, but I always thought Anne visited only to please him."

Patrick looked out across the water. It brought him no pleasure to be reminded that she'd shared so much of her life with another man, that she had cared about making David happy. She had created an entire world for herself, and there was no changing that, nor should he waste time wishing it were different.

"Her ladyship is planning the annual shooting party in less than a fortnight," he said. "There is to be a ball at the end of the affair and the torch-lit fishing contest here, which I assume has come to be a tradition."

"It's grand fun," Dr. MacDonald said.

"Except for the unfortunate death last year . . . I assume you were the physician in attendance?"

Dr. MacDonald looked puzzled. "The—ah, you mean poor Lord Kingairn."

Patrick wasn't sure how far he could probe without arousing suspicion. "I would hate for another such accident to befall one of Lady Whitehaven's guests. That is why I am here so late at night, to inspect the loch for potential dangers."

"A man's heart can fail at any time," the doctor answered, "especially during times of high excitement—what did you say your exact relationship was to Lady Whitehaven?"

Patrick hesitated. "I am in her ladyship's employ," he said evasively. "It is my duty to ensure that neither she nor her guests are endangered in any way."

"The new gillie, are you? Well, my good fellow, I did not attend Lord Kingairn myself—Sir Wallace's personal physician did—but I read the report of autopsy. The man died of heart failure. There were no peculiar markings on his body, no sign of internal injury. His shirt was missing a button, which indicates he may have struggled when he felt the crushing pain in his chest. But other than that it is a very classic case."

"So it would seem," Patrick said. "And will this physician also be in attendance should the unfortunate need to call upon him arise?"

"You'll have to make do with me, I'm afraid. I understand he took a position in Aberdeen a few months ago, which is why I am out at this ungodly hour visiting a patient. We could use another doctor in the parish."

There was a pause, the rain barely audible on the trees.

"I see," Patrick said.

MacDonald said, "There is always the risk of drowning when people drink, or an accidental shooting, but as they say, a stitch in time saves nine. I am relieved to see you're a man who takes pride in his position."

Pride in his position?

Patrick had to smile at that.

19

Anne was bidding everyone good night when Gracie burst into the red drawing room like a gunshot.

"Oh, Lord, ma'am, I am sorry I didna warm the sheets, but I saw him with my own eyes tonight. I saw him, and my heart started beating so hard, I almost couldna find my way home."

Gray with fright, the girl reached up to straighten her mobcap. There were leaves and heather twigs on her skirt. Anne stared at her from the sofa, aware that Patrick had also just entered the room and was busy lowering lamps in the background. Was it her imagination, or did his hair look suspiciously damp?

"Calm down, Gracie," she said. "I have no idea what you're talking about."

"Tell us what you saw, girl," Nellwyn said, sitting forward.

Gracie took a breath. "The ghost of Lord Kingairn, my lady, that's what."

"Lord Kingairn?" Flora said in a disbelieving voice. "In the lodge?"

Gracie shook her head. "No, miss. Floating in his ghostly rowboat on the loch, he was."

Anne glanced up at Patrick from the corner of her eye. "What were you doing at the loch at this hour, Gracie?"

"I wasna at the loch, my lady."

"Then how—"

"I was on the hill overlooking the loch." Gracie downed the glass of sherry Nellwyn gave her. "I was walking the dogs wi' Allan, and they took off after a fox. Or perhaps it was a badger. Of course it could—"

"The ghost, Gracie," Nellwyn said.

"Oh, well, I chased them dogs all the way to the hill because Allan lost his shoe, and I was the only one capable of walking." She paused, her eyes misting. "And there he was on the loch, lying dead in the boat wi' a ghostly glow all around him, just like the night last year when we found his body. Only this time, his eyes were red, at least one of them was, and I could have sworn he had a big fang like a banshee."

"Oh," Flora said, looking faint.

Sir Wallace frowned. "How could you tell who he was from the hill?"

"Who else would it be?" Gracie retorted.

"There's an easy way to find out," he said grimly. "Let us go down to the loch."

Gracie collapsed back against the door. "He's gone now. He was gone by the time Allan dragged his helpless self up the hill to see why I was screaming."

"Where did the ghost go?" Anne asked.

"To his grave, I expect," Gracie said. "Isn't that where the undead come from?"

"He'll be back." Patrick's baritone voice broke the silence as he lowered the last lamp; his shadow took on a sinister shape from the dying rose-gold light against the draperies.

Flora put her hand to her throat. "How do you know he'll come back?"

"If his soul is troubled, he might continue his haunting indefinitely," he said.

Sir Wallace frowned. "Stop scaring my daughter, Sutherland. She actually believes in all that supernatural rubbish."

"As well she should," Patrick said, smiling to himself as if he were privy to the secrets of the universe. "For who of us really knows what awaits us beyond this life? Who of us—"

"—is going to bed?" Anne stood up from the sofa. "It is almost eleven and I am getting up early to begin preparing for the party."

Patrick stepped in front of her, his manner faintly mocking. "Her ladyship does not wish to take tea before bed?"

Anne looked at him. Her ladyship wished to know what the troublemaker had been doing at the loch, but that would have to wait. "It is too late for tea, Sutherland."

He smiled slowly. "Very good, madam."

Sir Wallace caught up with Anne in the hallway as she prepared to retire. His face was grave in the darkness. "Did that chit upset you with her silly nonsense, my dear?"

"No. I do not believe in ghosts," she said.

"You look pale, Anne," he murmured. "I fear you are more upset than you will admit. Perhaps I should see you to your room."

"It's all right, honestly."

"Indulge me, Anne," he said. "If only out of respect to David, let me at least pretend to watch over you tonight."

"I do not believe in ghosts, Wallace," she said again.

"Nor do I," he said thoughtfully, guiding her toward the stairs. "Which is why I am wondering if we have a poacher, or even a prankster in our midst. The estate has been without a man's supervision for too long."

She continued up the staircase, annoyed by the way his fingers settled on the curve of her hip. "Your room is in the opposite wing, Wallace."

"Yes," he said, sounding put out. "Your butler had Flora and I removed from the rest of the house."

"I'm sure he was thinking only of your comfort."

"Was he?" Wallace could not suppress the cynicism in his voice.

She firmly removed his hand as they reached her door. "Ah, here we are, and I am safely delivered. Not a specter in sight."

"I want to see you safely inside the room, Anne."

"That is unnecessary." She gave him a discouraging nudge, but he nudged back, forcing them both inside her darkened room.

"If there are poachers or pranksters about, I will not sleep myself without knowing you are safe in your bed." He closed the door. "Is this lock reliable? It does not look so."

She vented a sigh. "Why don't you go outside and test it yourself?"

He turned suddenly and stared at her across the room. "Do not turn me away. Not until I tell you the depth of my feelings."

She closed her eyes. "Oh, no."

He came toward her, oblivious to the dismay in her voice. "Do you have feelings for me, Anne?"

She opened her eyes. "Indeed, I do."

There was a faint rustling from behind the closet door that had connected her room to David's; he had stored his excess books and painting materials there.

"I have kind feelings for you, Wallace," she said. "Friendly feelings."

"Kindly feelings are not exactly what I hoped to inspire in you."

She walked backward into the closet door. "I was afraid of that."

"You're all alone in the world, Anne."

She moistened her lips. "Not exactly alone—I have many close friends and Nellwyn." She raised her voice. "I have *Nellwyn*."

"I meant you do not have a man, in the truest sense of the word."

The closet door began to rattle. Anne wondered if she were shaking against it from apprehension without realizing it. She frowned suspiciously.

"You arouse me, Anne."

She stared at Wallace. The door behind her rattled again, and this time she knew she had not caused it. Nor had she emitted the particular noise that sounded like a deep growl from within. "You mustn't say things like that, Wallace. It is improper."

He went down on his knee. "I worship at your feet. I am feverish for you. Let me kiss the hem of your gown."

"Goodness," she exclaimed, pulling her dress out of his reach. "Get hold of yourself this instant."

He threw his arms around her legs. "Anne, I am—"

He looked up in astonishment as Anne lurched forward, unbalanced by the sudden opening of the closet door from the other side. Patrick stuck his head out, raised his brow, and squeezed around Anne, grasping her arm to reel her away from Wallace.

He straightened the tails of his coat. "I could not find the mouse you complained about, my lady," he said blandly.

Her lips tightened. "Mouse?"

He glanced at Sir Wallace, who had hastily collected himself from the floor. "Or was it a rat?" He peered behind the wardrobe. "I shall have to examine the walls for a hole."

"You might have announced your presence," Sir Wallace said. "You gave her ladyship a scare, popping out like that."

"I am so sorry," Patrick said insincerely. "Did I interrupt a tender moment?"

She drummed her fingers on the dressing table.

"You may conduct your search for mouseholes in the morning, Sutherland. If it is not raining, I intend to arise early for market, and you are accompanying me. If it does rain, we have plenty of work in the house."

"Verra well." He turned from the wall and extended his arm to Sir Wallace. "After you, sir."

Sir Wallace appeared to be in a quandary. There was no socially acceptable way he could explain remaining in Anne's room, and Patrick was perfectly aware of this. He winked slyly over his shoulder at Anne.

"Mouse, indeed," she said under her breath.

Sir Wallace walked reluctantly to the door. "I shall ride with you to market, Anne."

"It will be quite a tedious affair," she said.

He nodded stiffly. "But I shall. A young woman needs protection these days when she ventures abroad."

"Even when she ventures into her own bedroom," Patrick added.

Sir Wallace opened his mouth to respond, then apparently thought the better of it. "Good night, Anne," he said, backing into the hall.

Patrick slammed the door in his face. "Good night, rat."

There was a short moment of silence. Anne gasped, darting forward to the closed door. Then Sir Wallace started to pound from the other side, his voice a restrained roar.

"Just what do you think you're doing, Sutherland? Open this door immediately!"

Patrick threw the bolt home and blocked Anne by

outstretching his arm. "I am testing the safety of the lock, sir. Didn't I hear you mention something about making sure her lock was secure?"

"Only if you were eavesdropping, you scoundrel," Sir Wallace said, his voice rising.

Anne attempted to move Patrick from the door; it was a useless effort. "Calm down, Wallace. Nellwyn will hear you."

"Open this door, Sutherland," Sir Wallace said sternly.

"I cannot do that, sir." Patrick made a pretense of banging at the bolt. "My word, you were right. It appears to be stuck."

"Let me try it," Anne said tightly.

"Go ahead." He held his hand against the bolt, frustrating her attempts. "I need to talk to you," he said quietly. "About Uncle Edgar."

"You might have tried a less dramatic approach," she whispered.

"How was I to know I'd be interrupting a walrus' worship service at your feet?"

"You are incorrigible," she said. "You *were* eavesdropping."

"What is happening in there, Anne?" Sir Wallace asked.

"Sutherland is right," she said in a strained voice. "The bolt appears to be frozen in place."

She turned slowly to find Patrick imprisoning her against the door. "I shall take care of the matter, sir," he said loudly, bending his neck to nuzzle Anne's neck. "It might take an hour or two, though. I seem to be meeting some resistance."

Anne stiffened, pushing forward to escape, but his body wedged her against the door. "Listen to the rain, Anne," he murmured, kissing her nape. "What does it remind you of?"

"Water. Mud." She flattened her shoulder blades against the door panels. "Mildew."

He blew lightly against her ear. "It reminds me of making love in our ruined castle in the summer rain. Have you forgotten?"

"What castle?"

"You were naked, and I knew I ought to make you go home," he murmured. "There were raindrops running down your breasts and buttocks—the tower was riddled with holes. I have never seen anything more erotic than your wet body in my life."

Sir Wallace pounded at the other side of the door. "Shall I send a houseboy up with tools?"

Patrick smiled at Anne. "There's no need, sir. I believe I am well-equipped to handle the situation."

She groaned helplessly. "You are so bad, Patrick," she whispered. "Do you think he's an idiot?"

"What did you say, Anne?" Sir Wallace demanded. "I cannot hear you through the door."

"She was wondering if you were an idiot, sir," Patrick answered.

Anne gasped, trying to shove him away from her. "You beast," she whispered. "You are going to get me into so much trouble."

Sir Wallace raised his voice. "If you are talking to me, Anne, I cannot understand you."

Patrick tossed her over his shoulder without

warning, his arm secured behind her knees. "She said I'm the best, sir."

"The best what?" Sir Wallace asked, sounding aggrieved.

Anne pummeled her fists on Patrick's shoulders as he bore her to bed, dumping her in the middle. "Oh, you—help!"

There was a silence from behind the door. Then Sir Wallace cleared his throat, clearly confused. "Help? Is that what you said? All right. I'll fetch help, but don't expect me to find a decent locksmith at this hour."

20

"You wretch. You demon. You reprobate."

He stared down at her with a shameless grin. "Is her ladyship upset about something?"

She levered herself up on her elbow. Her hair, freed from her chignon, fell in a tumult of black tangled curls across the bed. "I am going to kill you with my bare hands."

"Why?" He put his hand to his chest. "Oh, dear. I have been remiss in my duties again? Did you find a water spot on your spoon?"

She bolted upright as he loosened his cravat and began to unbutton his shirt. "Oh, dear God—what do you think you are doing?"

"Getting ready for my execution. You don't expect me to die dressed as a butler, do you?"

She scooted toward the edge of the bed, but she didn't get far; Patrick dove onto his knees to intercept her, forcing her back into the headboard.

"I did like the part about your bare hands, Lady

Whitehaven," he said wickedly, his shirt hanging open to reveal his muscular torso.

She closed her eyes, praying for strength. One might assume that a woman of her age and experience would not be so affected by the glimpse of a perfectly built man. Unfortunately, one would be assuming wrongly. Anne was horrified at how the sight of his bare chest affected her.

His warm breath flirted with her hair. She felt him cuddling up beside her. "Lord have mercy," she whispered. "What are you doing now?"

"I'm not doing anything. I'm lying here beside you. Having a wee rest after a hard day's work. Is that such a sin?"

She opened her eyes. "Patrick, please remove yourself from my bed. I cannot breathe with you lying against me."

"Let me take off your jacket, Anne. It might help."

"It won't help."

"Of course it will. You can't go to bed buttoned up like a wee pea in a pod."

"I know what you're doing, Patrick. You are so blatantly obvious."

"Good God, Anne, you have the most suspicious mind. There." He helped her out of her snug jacket. "Now unbutton that bodice and draw some deep breaths."

"I will not."

"I'll do it, shall I?"

He brought his hand to her collar, his eyes meeting hers, and even though he knew it was the wrong thing to do, even though he'd promised himself he would behave, he was helpless. Moreover, time wasn't exactly on his side with that moron Sir Wallace about to charge into the room.

He put his hand around her head and kissed her, gently, thoroughly, easing her down until they were rolling across the bed, half undressed, unable to resist each other, like the first time they had been together, but so different.

He pushed his hand under her skirts and rubbed the inside of her thigh. Sexual warmth radiated from her skin, and he groaned; it took every ounce of will power he possessed to stop from sliding his finger into the opening of her drawers. She was wet and inviting, the embodiment of all he desired, and he could feel the faintest pulsebeat beneath her flesh.

She tensed, hiding her face in the pillow. "I'm going to kill you, Patrick."

"You're killing me now," he said, struggling for breath as he imagined stroking between her legs, teasing her, torturing himself. "You know as well as I do we wouldn't be here if we weren't so attracted to each other. Seven years, Anne, and we're back where we started."

Seven years, she thought. How fast the time had gone.

She closed her eyes, amazed that she could recall every bittersweet moment of their encounter when she had fought so hard to forget. How easily it all came back when she allowed it. He had made her feel things she had not dreamed existed, and had not experienced since. So many emotions flooded her, it did not seem possible to wager a defense. Embarrassment underlaid with a languid anticipation. Guilt that she had never shared anything close to this with David followed by the most powerful urge to simply surrender as she had done all those years ago.

"I cannot believe you actually agreed to meet me," he'd said as she ran into his arms. "It was all I could do not to come to your house. I have been insane with wanting you."

She'd been shaking uncontrollably; her heart raced as he lifted her into his arms and kissed her until blackness swam behind her eyes. His body was hard and powerful—Anne could not ever remember being held in such a strong embrace, or perhaps even being held at all. Her parents did not believe in displaying one's affections, but Anne had craved physical warmth with a hunger that made her feel ashamed. Surely it was wicked to want a man to touch her.

In no time at all they were both naked on the castle floor. She remembered fearing she would faint as he suckled the engorged tips of her breasts, the pleasure building upon itself until she begged for release.

"I haven't even begun," he'd whispered, catching her sensitive nipple between his teeth. "I'll stop if you want."

"Yes." She drew a breath, her heart contracting as he dragged his mouth down her belly. "No. Oh, Patrick, I am so afraid of you."

He lifted his head to stare at her, and she stared back, thinking she had never seen anything more beautiful than his rugged face in her life. But her parents had warned her he was the worst sort of trouble, and no decent girl in the village would be caught in his company, no matter how violently she might desire him in secret. But they hadn't seen the gentleness in him that Anne could see. They didn't guess he had a good heart beneath his surly behavior.

"Aye," he said. "What I feel for you frightens me too."

"This is wrong, isn't it?" she whispered in panic.

"I don't know." His mouth brushed the apex of her sex. "So help me God, I don't care."

Her mind froze as she realized what he meant to do. "Patrick," she said in a frantic voice. "We should stop."

"Aye, we should," he said as he parted her thighs to eat at her.

And neither of them moved until he brought her to a climax that reduced her to raw sensation, and she began to cry. Stricken, he kissed her again, and made her put her hands around his neck. When he took her in one deep stroke, she did not even cry, so shocked she could only heed his plea to trust him, that he would pleasure her again. And when the storm broke in his body, he held her so tightly she could barely breathe, absorbing the spasms that went through him. They needed so much more than sex from each other, but were too young to know that.

The minutes ran into hours. They could not tear themselves away from each other's arms, aware they might never be together again. She was exhausted when he finished with her.

"I've never met anyone like you," he said as they parted, but by then she was so frantic to go home, so afraid of what would happen if her father found out, that she barely heard his voice.

It was that same voice that brought her back to reality. Patrick's voice was laden with concern as he regarded her. "Are you all right, Anne? You look as if you are a thousand miles away."

She sat up, hiding her mortified face in her hands as she began the complicated business of rebuttoning herself. She had closed her mind again to the memories. "Not miles, Patrick. Years. I cannot believe we have come to this again."

He lay unmoving on the bed, his voice heavy with a desire for her that went so deeply he thought he might die of it. His body ached to the marrow, but he would not touch her again until she desired it. "I don't quite believe it myself."

"If I were a man," she said, "I would challenge you to a duel and shoot you through the heart."

He closed his eyes. "What a preposterous thought."

"Preposterous?" She slid off the bed, reverting to her prickly self. "I am not the one wearing the breeches and pushing the tea trolley, which you wield with all the grace of a brace of oxen, I might add."

"Did David ever spank you?" he asked softly.

She took a step backward. "Don't you dare."

"Why not? We can categorize it under the list of my duties such as polishing the knives, supervising supper." He came off the bed, his blue eyes narrowing in amusement. "Keeping her ladyship in line."

She picked up a hairbrush. "If you touch me again—"

"What?" He chased her around the chair. "You'll give me a hundred strokes of the hairbrush?"

"We were supposed to be discussing what killed Uncle Edgar."

"A woman with a hairbrush?"

"I'll—"

They both turned at the echo of footsteps outside the door, and then Nellwyn's voice, sounding so slyly amused Anne wanted to pinch her.

"Whatever is the matter, Anne?"

"The lock is stuck, and the door won't open," she answered meekly.

"Well, do not give way to panic," Nellwyn said. "After all, Sutherland is in there to see to your needs, isn't he?"

Patrick dropped back down to the bed, reclining with his arms folded under his head. "I certainly am."

"Shut up," Anne said in an undertone. "Just shut your mouth."

"What was that?" Nellwyn said.

"I wasn't talking to you," Anne said in irritation. "I was talking to the big ape on the bed."

"What did she say?" Sir Wallace asked Nellwyn in a bewildered voice.

"I'm not sure," Nellwyn said dryly. "I believe it was something about big grapes on the bed."

Anne advanced on Patrick. "Are you going to stay there all night?"

"Are you talking to me or the ape?"

"Why don't you go through the damned closet and help them from outside?" she said.

He was pouring himself the whiskey he had brought up the night before. "Because then they'll know we spent almost a half-hour together under false pretenses. I wouldn't want to embarrass her ladyship."

"Is that right?"

"All I am asking is for you to give me another chance."

"Why should I?" she said incredulously.

"Because I want you badly enough to endure the humiliation of being your bloody servant."

She stared at her disheveled reflection in the mirror. "Perhaps you cannot have what you want this time, hard as that might be to believe."

"Aye, I can."

"No. You can't."

He came off the bed to stand behind her. "Aye, Anne. I can. I'm just being polite about waiting, but make no mistake. I do not plan to wait forever."

She smiled coldly. "Good."

"I'll just take you."

"Anne." Nellwyn pounded lightly on the door. "We could use Sutherland's help on our side. We don't want Sandy to use his battle-ax, do we?"

Patrick stared at her for a long moment before he turned in resignation to the door. "Sweet dreams, Anne."

The upper servants called an emergency meeting in Mrs. Forbes's parlor later that same night. Gracie summoned Patrick from his room, and he complied. He was in a good mood because he knew that there was no way in hell Anne would have allowed him to even lay beside her if she did not care for him. There was a chance for them, after all.

The fragrance of her lingered in his mind, so sexual and sweet, so Anne. She hadn't been speaking to him when he left her room; he had looked Sir Wallace straight in the eye for a few seconds after the lock mysteriously unjammed.

"Is Anne all right?" the older man asked tersely.

Patrick suppressed a smile. "She seemed satisfied enough when I left her, sir."

Which Patrick himself was not, nor undoubtedly was she. Undressing Anne had been an exercise in self-torture, and he was probably going to prowl outside her door all night like an animal because he wanted her so badly.

He would have walked right past Mrs. Forbes's parlor, except for the single gaslight glowing in the center of the table, and the three gloomy faces seated around it who watched him worriedly.

He stepped into the room. "All right. Confess. Is this to be another séance, or the Spanish Inquisition?"

"We know your secret, Mr. Sutherland," Gracie said quietly, hanging her head.

He stopped midstride. "Do you?"

"Sit down, lad," Sandy said in a somber voice.

"Have a glass of brandy." Mrs. Forbes pushed a bottle across the table.

"Cooking brandy?" He smiled, taking a seat. "Now, this must be a serious matter indeed."

"We know about you and her ladyship," Gracie blurted out.

"About me and—"

"We know you're in love with the mistress." Mrs. Forbes put her hand over his. "Come clean, lad. Confession is good for the soul, and in the end, you can count on us."

"Fine." Patrick shrugged. "I love her ladyship."

"Oh, my God." Gracie blanched, hand covering her mouth. "It is true."

Patrick put his feet up on the empty chair. He felt very hopeful and in high spirits after his time alone with Anne. "Yes," he said, unable to hide a mischievous smile. "Your suspicions are well-founded. I am irrevocably in love with Lady Whitehaven."

Sandy stared at him. "You poor helpless sod."

Patrick laid his head back against the chair and listened to the steady thrum of rain on the roof. "I have loved that woman from the day I first met her," he said musingly. "Only I didn't have the sense to realize it."

"You dinna have any sense now, lad," Sandy said in a stern voice. "You might as well chase after the Queen for all the chance you have of a happy outcome in this affair."

"This will be the end of your career, Mr. Sutherland," Mrs. Forbes predicted.

"Wouldn't that be a tragedy?" he murmured. Then as he lowered his head to examine the trio of morbid faces that watched him, he realized Anne would throttle him for what he had just admitted. He had hardly proved himself to be discreet.

Mrs. Forbes squeezed his hand. "We have come to care for you, Mr. Sutherland."

He swallowed. "Have you indeed?"

"Aye, lad." Sandy pushed his leathery hand across the table. "Love you like the son I never had, I do."

Gracie frowned. "I thought your son was building the railroad in Aberdeen."

"So he is," Sandy said, "but I only hear from the rascal when he needs a loan, and so he may as well be lost to me."

"We do not want to see you get into trouble," Gracie said shyly. "You're part of our family now. We watch out for one another."

"Do we?" he said softly as he stared down at the small mound of work-worn fingers which claimed his in a stranglehold. He had deceived them. He had used them, and they meant to protect him from sorrow. He was unwillingly touched by their misplaced humanity. Still, he had a job to do, and he wouldn't leave Uncle Edgar's death an unsolved mystery, if there was any mystery to solve.

"Have you done the act of darkness with her ladyship?" Sandy asked him unexpectedly.

"Mr. Guthrie," Mrs. Forbes exclaimed. "Shame on

you. Of course he hasn't—have you, Sutherland?" she asked in horror.

"Do you suppose I would tell you if I had?" Patrick retorted.

"Lad," Sandy said, "life is like a garden. All the wee creatures have their place. Some of us are born to be butterflies and some of us are destined to remain worms."

Patrick took another sip of brandy, reflecting again that discretion might have served him better than blathering like a blasted fool. Such folly, however, was a symptom of a man falling in love, for clearly his long-lived infatuation with Anne had covered a more serious emotion. "What is your point, Sandy?"

Mrs. Forbes looked upon him with motherly reproach. " 'The rich man in his castle. The poor man at the gate.' We all have our place, don't we? Despite your quite convincing air of pretension, Mr. Sutherland, it is quite clear you were born belowstairs."

"It is?" Patrick said, mildly insulted.

She gave a tiny sniff of emotion. "I think this would be a nice moment for some Biblical wisdom. Gracie."

Gracie opened the well-worn book and read in a halting voice. " 'Render unto Caesar the things that are Caesar's.' "

Mrs. Forbes released a long-suffering sigh. "Mr. Guthrie, if you would."

Sandy thumbed through the Good Book. " 'All flesh is as grass, and all the glory of man as the flower of grass. The grass withereth, and the flower falleth away.' "

Which as a Biblical quote did not make much sense to anyone at the table, but at least Sandy had managed to bring the focus back to his allegorical garden where Anne flitted about as elusive as a butterfly and Patrick, at least for the moment, seemed fated to remain a worm.

✏21✏

*H*e had just settled by the fire the following morning to read the newspaper when the butler's bell began to ring. He glanced up darkly at the tarnished bronze apparatus hooked above the kitchen press, an instrument of torture. Anne apparently intended to wield her power. She meant to prove her authority to summon him at will.

He threw down the paper and grabbed his jacket from the back of the chair. Hadn't he agreed to play her game? Her heart, after all, was the prize, and a week or so of small humiliations seemed a fair price to pay for the lady's affection.

At that first bell, which came exactly at six o'clock, he trudged all the way up the steep staircase to her room; leaning against the door, he stood in taut-faced silence as she demanded he warm her room by lighting a fire before she touched one tender white toe to the carpet.

Clenching his jaw, he knelt like an obedient fellow

and took his own revenge by lighting a bonfire big enough to roast a rhinoceros. Anne dove under the covers to escape the smoke. Smiling wickedly, he waved a bilious black-brown cloud between the bed curtains.

At the second ring, which sounded precisely one minute after he had returned to the butler's pantry, he marched back upstairs and found her propped up in bed like some sort of evil empress.

"The floor is still too chilly," she explained at his exasperated look. "Warm my slippers by the fire, won't you?"

By bell three, which tinkled just as he reached the foot of the stairs, he was ready to wring her lovely little neck. "I merely wished to know what the weather was like today so I may dress accordingly." She grinned from the shadows of the bed. "Is it fair or foul? If it's still raining, we shall be forced to stay at home."

He stormed over to the window to wrench the curtains apart. "See for yourself."

"Oh, my," Anne said. "Isn't the butler in a black toad's temper today?"

Bell four rang as he reached the first landing; Anne requested tea, toast, and a three-minute egg. Bell five was a change-of-mind to hard-boiled. Patrick hadn't even made it into the hall when bell six rang madly—her ladyship wanted a pen and crested paper to write invitations to the shooting party as they could not go to the market in the rain.

There was a suspicious lull before bell seven. In fact, Patrick waited outside Anne's room for almost twenty minutes, ready to spring into action at the first malicious ding.

Finally, heaving a sigh, he returned to his pantry and newspaper.

His behind had just hit the chair when bell eight began to peal with a vengeance, and even the uncomplaining Mrs. Forbes could be heard muttering, "Lord Almighty. Sounds like Christmas Eve in this house."

Patrick didn't budge. It was a matter of principle.

Still, that bell kept ringing until all the servants, upper and lower, crowded outside the pantry to see what the butler would do.

"Aren't you going to answer her ladyship?" Gracie shouted, hands clapped over her ears.

"For pity's sake, Mr. Sutherland," Mrs. Forbes said in misery. "We'll all go mad if you don't."

Sandy slapped his hand onto the table. " 'Never send to know for whom the bell tolls.' " he quoted, cackling like a crone. " 'It tolls for thee,' Sutherland."

" 'Rings on her fingers and bells on her toes,' " Gracie added, grinning at Sandy. " 'She shall have Sutherland wherever he goes.' "

"Let her ring," Patrick said, burying his face in the paper.

Then silence. Sudden and profound. The golden peace that poets extol and men climb mountains to find. Gracie lowered her hands. Patrick lowered the paper. Mrs. Forbes scolded him.

"With all due respect, Mr. Sutherland, it would serve you right if her ladyship had experienced a dire emergency, and you had failed her in her hour of need."

Sandy nodded ominously. "Aye. What if that Sir Wallace were forcing his attentions on the helpless lady, and her ringing her wee heart out, and you sitting here reading that paper as if you havena care in the world?"

The bell rang again.

Patrick sprang out of his chair.

Bell nine found Anne sipping tea in bed with one bare foot dangling over the side. "I dropped one of those slippers you warmed for me, Sutherland. Fetch it like a good butler. I think it might be under the bed."

His heart was beating like a war drum. On the way to her room he had envisioned plucking Sir Wallace off her body, and the twenty or so ways he could throw the man. Such as against the wall. On the floor. Down the stairs.

His nostrils flared as he drew a breath, realizing he had been duped not only by the vicious little bellringer, but by his own imagination.

He approached the bed, staring her down in frigid silence. Anne took one look at his face and pulled her foot back under the covers, her teacup clattering to the tray.

"Am I a jack-in-the-box, madam? Am I a lady's maid?"

She blinked innocently. "If you don't hurry, you shall have to warm that slipper all over again."

He leaned down, his freshly shaven face pressed

close to hers. He smelled of juniper shaving soap and starch, and a muscle jumped in his chiseled jaw. "I do not think you want a slipper."

"Of course I do."

He smiled infuriatingly. "I think you want me."

She bit out each word with razorlike precision. "I want my slipper."

"There are easier methods to bring me to your bed, Anne."

"Says the butler from Bedlam."

"I know a better way to warm you up in the morning." He swept her with a heavy-lidded look. "Interested?"

"I'd rather turn on a spit naked."

"Wouldn't that be a sight?" He slid his big hand down her side to massage her knee through the covers. "If you want my personal attention, you do not need to ring that damned bell. And if you want to be naked, we certainly don't have to roast you live as an excuse."

His skilled fingertips were summoning voluptuous sensations inside Anne. She decided the time had come to take firm hold of herself. "Where is my slipper, Sutherland? My foot is freezing."

He gave her a devilish grin. "I'd be happy to share the heat of my body with you."

A fire ignited in the pit of Anne's belly—a very bad sign. She lifted her foot into the air. "Foot. Slipper. Fetch."

He caught her toes in his hand. "Are you sure you want to carry through with this shooting party?"

"Why not?" she asked, suppressing a shiver as he

pressed his thumb into the tender instep of her foot.

"I don't know." He pushed the tray aside and sat down casually on the bed. "People sometimes drown when they drink, or there's an accidental shooting—and think of all the local men who'll hope to court the lovely widow."

"As if anyone has the chance with my butler at my heels like a bloodhound."

"And don't ever forget it." He leaned forward and kissed her gently, drawing her lower lip between his teeth. Anne went still, immobilized by a shiver of sheer lust. "I take my duty to protect you verra seriously," he whispered against her mouth.

For a confusing moment, nothing else existed but him, his virile male scent, his muscular body. "You are crowding the bed," she said, but in truth her complaint went beyond that minor offense. She could not even escape into her private thoughts these days without his presence intruding. He was like the dark horseman on the hill of destiny who waited for the right moment to descend.

He moved his hand up her arm and deepened the kiss while Anne, who knew she should be fighting, sank deeper and deeper into a trance of pleasure.

"I need you so, Anne," he said roughly.

"You don't," she whispered.

"Aye, I do." He lifted his head and gazed at her. "I do."

She glanced away. "You never did find my slipper."

Swearing under his breath, he got down on his knees and began a futile search for the lost slipper.

He hunted under the bed and was on an archeological dig behind the dressing screen when Nellwyn entered the room.

"Don't you ever put anything away after you wear it, Anne?" he muttered. "This place is a disgrace."

"Disgrace is exactly the word for it," Nellwyn said, closing the door behind her. "I see you, Patrick. It's no use hiding. I have eyes like a hawk."

He emerged from behind the screen with a silk stocking over his arm. "I wasn't hiding," he said in annoyance. "I was looking for Anne's slipper in that mess."

Anne sat down at the dressing table. "Come to think of it, that slipper might have fallen out the window."

Patrick frowned. "It *fell?*"

"Really, Anne," Nellwyn said, seating herself on the couch. "Playing fetch with Patrick is hardly helpful to our investigation."

Investigation. Anne sat up straighter, a guilty look on her face. Poor Uncle Edgar's demise had been the last thing on her mind. She gave Patrick a self-righteous scowl.

"You ought to be ashamed of yourself."

"I ought to?" he said. "Listen to Quasimodo of Notre Dame and her bells."

Nellwyn looked at Patrick. "What exactly did you do last night after you left the house?"

"I rode to the loch and met the local physician," he said.

"Doctor MacDonald?" Anne rose from her chair and disappeared behind the screen.

"Aye, and in case you haven't guessed, I was the ghost Gracie saw in the rowboat," he said. "I wanted to get a sense of how Edgar might have died. So I put myself literally in his place."

"Why did the girl claim you had glowing eyes and a fang?" Nellwyn asked.

He grinned. "I was smoking one of David's cigars, which would explain the red eye. I had almost forgotten what it was like to have a minute to myself. The fang was a figment of her imagination."

Anne sighed. "May *I* have some privacy to dress now?"

He leaned against the wardrobe, completely ignoring her. "According to the report of autopsy, Uncle Edgar died of natural causes," he explained to Nellwyn. "Except for the fact his shirt appears to have been missing a button, it seems he expired while rowing his boat."

"A button?" Anne stretched her bare foot out from the screen to feel around the floor. "My stocking is missing."

"Perhaps it jumped out the window to join your slipper," Patrick said.

Her head popped out from behind the screen. "You took it, didn't you—I can see it on your arm. How were you going to explain *that* to the staff?"

He tossed the stocking over the screen. "The same way you were going to explain your slipper in the courtyard."

"Perhaps you could explain them both to the Queen in light of the fact you will have nothing to tell her about Lord Kingairn," Nellwyn said crossly.

"Now my pantalettes of French percale are missing," Anne announced.

Patrick shrugged. "Don't look at me."

Nellwyn rose spryly from the couch. "Instead of intruding on Anne, I suggest that you spend more time belowstairs, Sutherland. I have taken the liberty of advertising for temporary help for our party, and it will be your duty to conduct the interviews."

Anne bumped into something behind the screen. "A most excellent suggestion."

"As for you, Anne," Nellwyn continued, "I do not see how breaking your neck on that horse will do much good either. My suggestion to you is to stay close to Sutherland at all times until the murderer is apprehended."

"Now *that* is excellent advice," Patrick said from the door. "Auntie Nellwyn, I would be obliged if you would make her follow it."

22

Sir Wallace cornered Anne again at the bottom of the stairs early the next morning. She gave a start as he loomed out of the shadows, his cane and bonnet in hand.

"I shall have to forgo our day at the fair, Anne. I'm rather afraid Flora is not feeling quite herself this morning."

She was embarrassed by the scene in her room the night before last. It was a wonder she could still look at the man without blushing in mortification. "Don't worry about me, Wallace. I won't be alone."

He frowned. "You mean your butler is accompanying you?"

"Yes. And Nellwyn. Sutherland is doing the shopping." Which was a sight Anne could hardly wait to see—Patrick haggling over a head of lettuce. "We shall have to work day and night if we're to be ready for the annual party in under a fortnight."

His frown deepened. "Do you really think you

should? It seems rather a load of trouble for a party, and with the fuss—"

She searched his face. "My goodness, Wallace, surely *you* are not thinking of Gracie's raving about a ghost at the loch?"

"Of course not," he said, looking offended as he took her arm, leaning into her. "Be honest with me, Anne. I am a man of the world. There is something going on between the pair of you, isn't there?"

She backed into the balustrade. "Between me and the ghost?"

"Your butler. He's not the bacon-brain he appears to be, is he?"

She paused. "Well, I wouldn't say that."

"Is it blackmail, Anne? Does the scapegrace have some hold over you from a past sin or indiscretion that David committed?"

She reflected briefly on the unintentional irony of his words. Patrick did indeed have a hold over her due to their past indiscretion, but David, poor David, had been entirely innocent of any wrongdoing.

"I know how to deal with blackmailers," he added in a solemn voice. "I've had a bit of experience in that area myself."

She regarded him in surprise. "Have you?"

"Well, not personally; I've met more than a few unsavory characters at the track, though—it is blackmail, isn't it? My God. David was such a shy sort. Still, one can never tell. What was it, Anne, an affair with a chambermaid or minister's daughter?"

"No." She vented a sigh. "It was the Queen."

He blinked in astonishment. "Queen Victoria? David conducted a liaison with Her Majesty?"

She burst into laughter. "David didn't have an affair with anyone, at least not that I know of. I'm talking about my butler, Sutherland."

He frowned in annoyance. "You surely don't expect me to believe that the Queen was carrying on with a servant, a Scotsman at that?"

"Don't be a ninnyhammer, Wallace. I never said the Queen was carrying on with Sutherland. You did. I meant she had given him a sort of personal recommendation." She sighed again. "And of course I was obligated to take it."

"Of course." He looked impressed. "So the Queen recommended him. Old family retainers, and that type of obligation, I suppose. His father probably served the royal family faithfully, and Sutherland, well, he is—"

"—a pain in the neck," she said forcefully.

He raised his brow. "Yes, but one can hardly ignore a royal recommendation, my dear. This puts matters in a rather different light."

"I hate him," she burst out.

"Yes, yes, dear. He does get on the nerves, but if Her Majesty recommended the fellow, he must have his points."

"Two of them," Anne said. "The pair of horns on his head."

"As a butler, he is rather a breath of fresh air, Anne."

"He's a breath of sulfur and brimstone," she said darkly. "As in a genuine devil."

"But the Queen likes him."

"I don't," Anne said.

He gathered her gently into his arms, his head lowering to hers. "Then perhaps you need a husband to manage such matters for you. Perhaps it's time to take—"

"Tea?" Patrick inquired dryly, steering the trolley toward them like a gladiator in a Roman chariot.

Sir Wallace and Anne broke apart, like a pair of children caught in a naughty conspiracy. It was clear by his dark expression that Patrick disapproved of finding them alone together. It was also clear they stood in genuine danger of being mowed down by a breakfast cart.

"Your carriage is waiting," Patrick called over his shoulder to Sir Wallace. "Sorry you won't be staying for breakfast. We're having fresh currant buns, too."

Sir Wallace's lips tightened. "Royal recommendation or not, something has to be done about that man, Anne. He has more gall than an entire army of Highlanders."

Anne could not postpone going to market for her party, even though it rained the entire way to the fair, and the driver had to labor along an old coffin road to keep from getting lost. Patrick complained so loudly about sitting up on the box that Nellwyn overrode Anne's feelings and invited him to travel inside the carriage.

Anne was not happy about the situation. She couldn't believe what appeared to be happening between them, and she was afraid of what it meant. "Your coat is wet," she told him in a crisp tone. "I would appreciate it if you could move to the other side of the seat."

Nellwyn looked at her. "Someone must not be getting enough sleep at night."

"Well, I wonder why," Anne said, staring outside as he settled down beside her, a man who had no intention of being ignored.

They passed fairgoers on shaggy Highland ponies with dogs running alongside them, and stone cottages in which candles burned against the morning gloom. Crows took shelter from the storm in the dripping pine woods and clouds clustered over the Grampians, which stood like ancient gods above the bare hills below.

Patrick stretched his legs on the seat. "That lock certainly took a lot of trouble to open the other night."

"Especially considering the fact that either one of you could have exited through the closet to the connecting room whenever you chose," Nellwyn said.

Anne sat forward. "How could you possibly know that? Were you listening to us the whole time?"

"David gave me a tour of the lodge before he bought it," Nellwyn said bluntly. "And I don't see what all the fuss is about, for that matter. In my day, a man and woman didn't go to such bother to hide their attraction to each other."

Patrick grinned at her. "Your generation will go down in history for its admirable honesty."

Anne narrowed her eyes at him. "Must you encourage her?"

Nellwyn graced him with a smile. "What a nice

boy you are. I can't imagine why she hasn't fallen in love with you."

"Neither can I," he said.

Anne laid her head back against the cushions. "I think the driver is slowing to park, Patrick. Tell him I would like to stop at the dressmaker's shop before we go to the fair."

"Life is short, Anne," Nellwyn said, repeating her favorite theme as Patrick stepped outside. "You and I have lost both husbands and parents. We have no children to indulge and keep us company. Are you going to spend the rest of your days running from my nephew because of some imagined slight in the past? I know he was rather a rogue, but anyone can see he adores you."

"Is that what he told you, that 'some imagined slight' was behind all this?"

Nellwyn frowned. "Actually, he has never said much of anything on the subject. He is obstinately protective of your feelings, but now you've worried me. Was there more to your past association?"

Anne shook her head. "Let the past stay buried, Auntie Nellwyn. Please."

Nellwyn nodded, looking distressed. "As you wish, dear. It's just that I care for you and Patrick both so deeply. If I could bring you together, I believe I could die at peace with the world."

"I'm sorry. It just isn't to be."

" 'To be or not to be,' " Patrick said with a grin as he vaulted back into the carriage. " 'That is—' " He stopped his teasing rendition of the soliloquy the instant he felt the tension between the two women.

"—obviously not the question." He settled down beside Nellwyn. "The atmosphere in here is as thick as the mist outside," he said lightly. "Ladies, the rain has stopped, and this is supposed to be a day of relaxation and enjoyment."

Anne gave him a tight smile. "Not for you, Sutherland. You have to help Mrs. Forbes do the shopping."

"The marketing?" He looked so horrified at the prospect that she started to laugh. "Madam, you have been misinformed. Men do not market."

"Butlers do." Nellwyn said, staring thoughtfully at Anne. "You behave yourself, Sutherland. Do what the mistress tells you."

"She told me the night before last to go to hell."

"And did you?" Nellwyn asked dryly.

"I certainly did," he said. "I spent the rest of that night in an agony of longing for her company. Hades could not have been worse."

"Just wait, you joker," Anne said. "Because when you do die, you're going to find out exactly how bad it can be. You're going to feel just how hot those flames can burn."

Nellwyn looked from Anne to Patrick. "And to think I had envisioned the beginnings of true love between you."

"True love," Anne said, staring out the window, "is kindness, loyalty, and trust."

"It takes a heart to love," Patrick added, his grin fading. "Anne, apparently, doesn't have one."

"She has a heart, all right," Nellwyn said. "But she's keeping it under guard, and I begin to wonder why."

23

Anne jumped out of the carriage the instant it came to a full stop at the village fairgrounds. An elderly piper with a long white beard played the bagpipes on the hill above, an obscure clan tattoo whose magical notes intertwined with the mist. Young people were swirling in kilts on the green, and a band of gypsies hawked unbroken ponies, sealing their sales with a hand-slap. There was a tantalizing odor of an ox roasting in a pit, and everywhere one looked stallholders offered cheeses, gingerbread, and laces.

"I'll leave you to plot your conspiracy in private," she said over her shoulder, and then she slammed the door.

Nellwyn wished now she had kept her thoughts to herself. "I don't know where her spirit comes from, do you? Is it inherited, I wonder."

Patrick watched Anne from the window, his mouth tightening as a crowd of young bucks outside the tavern stopped their conversation to admire her. "I don't know. She does not speak often of her family."

"No wonder," Nellwyn said. "Her parents were unsociable and absolutely puritanical in outlook. Anne's grandmother committed suicide when her mother was only ten, leaving the woman to be raised by her aunt."

His eyes darkened as Anne disappeared into the dressmaker's shop. Even when he was at the height of his hell-making, he had known his father loved him.

"Still," Nellwyn said, "such things are part of life, and somehow Anne has managed to survive. Although—you have never done anything to hurt her, have you?"

There was a spell of silence inside the carriage, broken by the cheer of spectators at a wrestling contest on the common. If there was one person in the world he knew he could trust, it was Nellwyn.

"If you want the truth," he said, slowly turning his face to hers. "I seduced Anne seven years ago before I joined the infantry. I never understood until recently what a beautiful girl like her would see in a rogue like me, and had I known better, I would have found a way to take her from her family until I returned. It was a thoughtless act, Auntie Nellwyn, not heartless. I have always regretted that our affair did not lead to something lasting, but her father would never have let her marry a man like me. Not in those days."

"My, my," Nellwyn said. "And now she's making you pay for your youthful mistake."

"She certainly is. Actually, both of you seem to be enjoying her revenge."

"Believe it or not, I am on your side, Sutherland."

He grunted. "Good. I'm a man who needs all the help he can get."

"I can see that," she said, motioning in amusement out the window at the knot of servants who stood awaiting his company with Mrs. Forbes, who held the basket he would use to carry their purchases.

Patrick escaped Mrs. Forbes when she met another housekeeper and got into a debate over a receipt for haggis. The older woman was driving him mad, a mother hen determined her chick would come to no harm.

He wandered around the fairgrounds until he found Anne, surrounded by a circle of old friends. Still, he was only a butler, and the best he could do was lean against a gingerbread stall, his gaze thoughtful, a basket of eggs over his arm as he waited for her.

He narrowed his eyes as one of the young bucks from the tavern sauntered up to Anne and reintroduced himself, claiming a past acquaintance. He saw her give the man a warm smile, and he wondered what would happen if he hit the charming boy in the face with an egg.

Mrs. Forbes bustled up behind him. "Oh, there you are, Mr. Sutherland. I'll be needing your help selecting a nice goose."

He didn't say anything. He'd just noticed that the

young buck had grasped Anne's hand and was drawing her over to a puppet show. She looked as if she were resisting, but he knew how damned polite she was, and suddenly eggs didn't seem like a strong enough weapon to discourage his suit.

"Have you been drinking, Mr. Sutherland?" Mrs. Forbes asked in a disappointed voice.

He turned to her as Anne managed to shrug off her admirer. "No, but a drink is a good idea, now that you mention it."

"You can't—"

The rest of her reply was lost in the sudden roar that erupted behind them. A fight had broken out at the cheesemonger's stall. A man in a worn jacket and trews writhed on the ground, dodging kicks and blows.

Patrick grabbed a young boy who ran past him. "Why are they beating that man?"

"Stole some cheese."

Patrick handed his basket of eggs to Mrs. Forbes and joined the group of fairgoers rushing to watch the fight. He'd seen that man earlier at the marketplace, looking for work; he belonged to a small group of unemployed crofters from Easter Ross who'd been evicted from their homes by financially desperate landlords.

"Dinna get involved," Sandy called after him.

"They're going to kill him," Patrick said. "Over a piece of cheese."

Mrs. Forbes tugged on his jacket. "I know it isn't right, mister. It breaks my heart, too. But should a shopkeeper have to pay because a greedy landlord somewhere has thrown the poor man from his home? We all suffer hard times, but we don't all steal."

"I'll pay," Patrick said.

"On a butler's wages?" Gracie squeezed in beside him. "Dinna cause trouble, mister. They'll arrest you."

"They'll think we're a band of them Chartists," Mrs. Forbes said with a shudder of fear. "Not that I disagree with their grievances, mind you. But I draw the line at inciting a riot."

Sandy bumped against her. "My brother in Wales got himself put in jail last year. The Rebecca riots, they called 'em, with the men dressing as females."

A gap opened in the crowd, and Patrick dove through it, propelling his way to the man begging for mercy on the ground. He leaned down to shield the man, and a booted foot kicked him in the cheekbone; he looked up into the smirking face of the young buck who had been flirting with Anne.

"Oaf."

Patrick stared at him for a few seconds, trying to remember where he had seen that face before. Perhaps at a gaming club, or a race. Lord Andrew Tynan. Patrick was good at remembering names.

"Get out of the way, clodpate," Tynan said. "The man is a thief and a mental deficient."

Patrick didn't move. He didn't care if Tynan recognized him because then he could challenge him on open ground.

"Are you deaf, giant?"

A housewife was trying to drag the beaten man to

safety, but four or five other fairgoers had scented blood and wanted to fight. As one of them swung at Patrick, he leaped to his feet, aided by Fergus, one of Anne's footmen, who was young enough to fight for a principle he really didn't understand. Then another man in servant's livery joined the fracas, grinning in sympathy at Patrick before he threw a punch.

Patrick hit the man who had swung at him. Then he sent Lord Tynan and two of his friends staggering into a stall of cabbages and turnips at the precise moment Anne reappeared in the crowd.

"Send for the sheriff's deputy," someone shouted. "This big fellow is gone wild."

Anne pushed forward, and she was shaking. "There's no need to send for help. I'll take care of him, and pay for whatever he's damaged."

"He's yours, Lady Whitehaven?" the cabbage vendor said in disbelief, and even Patrick was impressed at how many people knew and liked her.

"Unfortunately, yes." She gave him a prod in the ribs. "Come on, Sutherland."

He bowed mockingly. "Yours to do with as you wish."

They walked away from the hubbub, toward a gypsy fortuneteller's wagon, heading for the grassy knoll. Patrick juggled a pair of turnips in the air; he figured that if Anne had paid for them, he might as well take them home for soup, domestic-minded as he was becoming these days.

She stopped in her tracks and hit the turnips out of his hand. She glanced around; the injured man had been taken under the wing of several good Samaritans. "What I really wish," she said angrily, "is that you would behave yourself for once."

"I'm not going to watch a mob beat a man to death whether he deserves it or not."

She walked away. He watched her skirts swish back and forth for several moments, the movement seemed at once sexual and prudish, inviting and off-putting, the essence of Anne.

He strode up behind her, grinning. "Forgive me?"

She glanced at him from the corner of her eye. "Did it occur to you that you might have gotten injured in that fight?"

"Me? Hell, no. Although I think I might have bruised my tea-pouring hand."

She looked up at him after a long silence. "You have a horrible red mark on your cheek. I cannot believe that I left you unsupervised for a mere two minutes and you got into a brawl."

"There's a solution for that."

"Oh?"

"Don't leave me alone. Obviously I need you." He smiled into her eyes. "Let's have our fortunes read for fun."

She gave him a half smile. "I might be better off not knowing the future, if my past is any indication of what's in store. Anyway, I have to pay for the damage you caused with your fighting. Can you stay out of trouble for a few minutes?"

"I don't know," he said. "You had better hurry back just to make sure."

*   *   *

As it turned out, he wasn't standing there alone for long when the young servant who had come to his rescue during the fight reappeared. The man examined Patrick's bruised face in amusement. "I'm Iain Laing, Lord Murray's valet. You are Lady Whitehaven's man, I take it?"

"Aye," Patrick shook his hand. "Her butler."

"Lucky sod. Did she threaten to skelp you for creating a public disturbance?"

Patrick laughed. "Her mind is preoccupied with the annual party at Balgeldie House."

"There's to be another one?"

Patrick paused. "Why wouldn't there be?"

"I don't know. The peculiar death last year, and all that nonsense about a ghost."

"You mean Lord Kingairn?"

"Aye." Iain glanced around. "Some people called it murder, but my employer does not wish anyone to talk of it. I will tell you this—our gillie thought he saw some odd goings-on that night on the loch."

"Where is this gillie now?"

"Gone back home to Caithness," Iain said. "Lord Murray willna tolerate a gossip. The upper classes dinna want it known they get drunk like the rest of us, and old Kingairn had connections to the Queen."

"Indeed," Patrick said as another door was closed in his face. He could not question the gillie now.

Iain looked up suddenly as Anne reappeared on the green. "Here's her ladyship coming now. What a beauty. Meet me at the inn some evening for a drink, man—or does the woman keep you on a leash?"

Patrick grinned. "Aye, but a loose one."

24

When she returned, he was sitting on the steps of the gypsy wagon, an inscrutable look on his face. The bruise on his cheekbone stood out like a brand. She felt a peculiar sensation in the pit of her stomach as their eyes met. It was partly primal sexual response and something even more threatening and complicated, a softening toward him.

He stood, taking her hand. "Your fortune has been paid for, madam. Destiny awaits."

"Destiny?"

"Aye, destiny, or some such drivel."

"I don't think so, Patrick."

"Come, Anne, I work hard for my money these days. Do not waste it."

She shook her head in resignation and followed him up the rickety steps of the vardo, which was cluttered with such a staggering assortment of herbal potions and remedies, it was a miracle the wagon moved at all.

She recognized the gypsy woman, those alert black eyes in a thin face the color and texture of a walnut shell. It was Black Mag, an herbwoman and charmer, who had been working the fairs since God was in knee breeches. "Sit," the woman said, motioning to a low stool on the other side of her table. She grasped Anne's hand and studied it in the light of a fat tallow candle that burned behind her.

Anne said, "I don't—"

"You are much beloved by a strong, handsome man, lady," the woman broke in. She looked at Anne's wedding ring. "*Two* men, lady," she murmured, glancing quizzically at Patrick, who dressed like a servant but certainly did not act like one.

He held up his index finger.

"One man," the gypsy amended. "One very strong, handsome man with black hair. And blue eyes."

Anne sent Patrick a droll glance over her shoulder. He shrugged, looking as guilty as they came.

"This man's heart is true toward you. He would die to defend you."

Anne sighed.

"He wants to give you many children," the gypsy added, looking to Patrick for confirmation.

He nodded.

"Seven children, at least," Black Mag said.

Anne pried her hand away. "Are you finished?"

The gypsy looked up at Patrick for guidance, but he appeared to be watching a wrestling contest outside. Apparently sensing a dissatisfied customer in

Anne, she reached onto the shelf behind her for an earthenware jar inscribed with mystical symbols.

"Oh, I don't want any love potions," Anne said, holding up her hand in amused horror.

Black Mag leaned forward. "I give you a special reading, my lady."

Anne shook her head. "If you must—what *are* you doing?"

The fortuneteller had emptied the jar onto the black velvet tablecloth. An arrangement of small white bones gleamed weirdly in the semidarkness.

"Sacred bones." Her voice sent a shiver down Anne's neck. "Stolen from the grave of a sorceress who was burned at the stake."

"Charming," Anne said, recoiling, but then the gypsy reclaimed her hand, forcing her to touch the lurid skeletal remains.

"Move your hand over them three times," she said in a voice Anne couldn't seem to resist. "Not for everyone do I bring out my special bones."

"Fortunate me," Anne murmured, and gave a faint shudder as her fingers made contact with a wrist bone. She looked up helplessly at Patrick, who had just turned his attention back to the reading, his cravat loose, his expression slightly bored.

The fortuneteller studied the bones in frowning absorption. Anne made a rude face at Patrick.

"You bribed her," she whispered.

He shook his head and started to deny it when the gypsy's voice broke the silence.

"I see blood on your reflection, my lady."

"Blood?" Patrick stared in alarm. "Is my lady hurt?" he asked anxiously.

The gypsy shrugged. "I do not know, sir." She looked up at Anne. "Beware the stag, my lady."

"She must mean you," Anne whispered to Patrick.

"His horns are sharp," the gypsy added.

Anne smiled faintly. "That's you, all right."

"The stag is dangerous, my lady."

"But I don't hunt," she protested, unable to imagine where this balderdash was leading, or why she was sitting here listening when she had so much to do. "I always stay at home when the men go shooting."

Black Mag didn't blink an eye, and Anne had to give her credit for her acting ability. "The stag will find you at home, lady. Unless you follow your heart, he will hurt you." She glanced up, giving Anne a start. "He could even kill you."

Patrick turned white at that. This wasn't what he'd had in mind. He cleared his throat to catch the woman's attention, to remind her he was paying for an uplifting prediction, not this impending-danger nonsense about homicidal deer.

"Is the reading over?" he said.

Both women ignored him, and even Anne was hunched over the bones now, straining to read her destiny.

"The reading *is* over," he said. "Lady Whitehaven, let us leave."

The Romany woman shook her head. "There is a body . . . and water."

"A body of water?" Anne said hopefully. "Such as a loch or a river?"

"No." The gypsy paused. "A body *in* the water. Or on the water." She glanced up, blinking at Patrick as if she realized that she had strayed from his request.

"And a baby on the way."

"A baby?" Anne sat bolt upright on the stool. "Now I know he paid you."

"The bones have never told a falsehood, my lady," the gypsy said, looking insulted.

Anne rose from the stool. "I can't believe I even sat still for this." She shook her head at Patrick as he helped her down the wagon steps. "Bodies and blood, a baby and stag's horns. It is too much."

"Hell, Anne," he said easily, catching up with her as she marched ahead. "You know it's all nonsense. Except for one part, that is."

She paused, staring at the piper on the hill. She knew she was going to be sorry, it was asking for trouble, but she looked up directly into his eyes. "And that part would be?"

"The baby, of course." He gave her the wickedest grin in the world. "I am destined to get you pregnant by December."

"Destined or determined?" she asked coolly.

He shrugged. "I believe it amounts to the same thing."

Evening had fallen over the hills when the carriage rolled up the drive to the hunting lodge. A horned owl hooted from a yew tree, and a fine mist shrouded the firs that surrounded the stone tower.

The servants lagged a few miles behind; the estate sat in slumbering darkness; the lead-paned lozenge-shaped windows looked like unblinking eyes reflecting the moonlight.

Patrick had remained inside the carriage for the ride, and Anne hadn't complained, partly because they'd shared a bottle of brandy on the way, and she was a tiny bit tipsy, and partly because there was something comforting about being buffeted by a big male body in the dark, even if the man who owned that body had broken your heart.

Besides, he smelled so wonderful, like shaving soap and brandy and man. Anne smiled at the thought of her nose twitching against his jacket as if she were a bunny scenting a mate.

He raised his brow as he helped her out of the carriage. "And what, dare I ask, do you find so amusing?"

"Rabbits," she said, laughing aloud.

Nellwyn wove up behind them. "In my day, a lady could hold her liquor." She walked into a rhododendron bush, looking startled. "Who put that here?"

"I guess times change," Anne said, laughing again. "Don't they, Sutherland?"

He took both women by the arm, wondering if it was the drink that made him feel so absurdly protective of them. "Times change, and so do people."

"He's turning philosophical on us," Anne said in dismay.

"Let's stuff a pair of socks in his mouth to shut him up," Nellwyn said.

He shook his head despairingly. "And this is what the cream of the Scottish aristocracy has come to."

They mounted the mossy stone steps and stepped into the entrance hallway of the lodge.

Silence greeted them, and if they hadn't been drinking they would have sensed the undercurrent of menace that lingered in the air.

A single candle burned low on the hallstand, the flame reflected in the mirror.

Anne frowned. "Who left a candle burning—oh, look, it's not even in a holder. It's going to leave a mark."

Patrick took off his jacket. "It must be the new girl, Janet."

"Perhaps she left it there when she was dusting," Nellwyn said. "I didn't care for her looks myself. Slovenly, that's what I thought to myself."

Anne walked slowly toward the hallstand.

"She might have set the place on fire," Patrick said, following Anne. "I'll have a word with the wee idiot in the morning."

She gestured to the mirror. "Perhaps not."

Nellwyn kicked off her shoes. "Don't be such a tender-hearted ninny, Anne. The girl deserves to be scolded for such carelessness."

"What is it, Anne?" Patrick had just noticed the unnatural way she stood frozen before the mirror. "Did she leave a burn stain on the wood?" he asked, domestic disasters suddenly a part of his world.

"There's writing on the mirror." Her voice sounded distant. She raised her hand to touch the blurry words that were scrawled across the glass. Then she stopped, her hand arrested halfway to the mirror.

He came up behind her, his voice soft with anger.

" 'Go home, Anne,' " he read aloud, " 'or you will be sorry.' "

He touched his forefinger to the smeared message. "It appears to be written in—"

"—blood." Nellwyn pushed his hand away, and ran her own gloved fingertip over the mirror. "Blood or some sort of animal entrail by the smell of it. How disgusting."

"Entrails?" Anne said in restrained horror. "I do not even want to speculate what that could mean."

There was a faint commotion from the back of the house as the servants' cart arrived. Lamps were suddenly lit throughout the house. The clamor of cheerful voices momentarily counteracted the tension in the hall.

"I'll ring for Helen," Nellwyn said. "We'll get to the bottom of this."

" 'Blood on my reflection,' " Anne mused. "Isn't that what your gypsy predicted, Patrick?"

He steered her toward the staircase. He was probably more upset than she was, and trying not to show it. Everything he had done to relax Anne, to put her in a trusting mood, was threatened by something he could not control; the thought of anyone wanting to hurt her brought out vicious impulses in him.

"Black Mag was putting on a show, sweetheart. You know that. Sit here for a minute. Take a breath."

"Someone killed an animal to frighten me?" She shook her head, uncomprehending. "Oh, Patrick. What if we were wrong? What if Uncle Edgar was murdered? What if the murderer is still in the vicinity? What if I find a dead animal in my bed?"

"No one is going to put anything in your bed," he said grimly. "And the message doesn't mean we're dealing with a murderer."

"Not of people perhaps, but isn't an animal bad enough? Who would do such a ghastly thing?"

He wasn't sure, but he could take a guess. He had hired three new servants yesterday morning, two local boys to help Sandy in the garden, and a sullen girl named Janet whose references he had not had time to check. The girl had stayed home from the fair, pleading illness, and Patrick had ignored Mrs. Forbes's warning that this was not a good sign in an under parlormaid.

Mrs. Forbes came hurrying into the hall, her cap askew. "You rang for me, madam?"

He took her by the arm. "Someone has scrawled a nasty message on the mirror, Helen. Do you happen to know if our new parlormaid Janet has gone to bed?"

"She might have gone to hell for all I care," Mrs. Forbes declared with uncharacteristic vehemence. "The wee thief has absconded with the silver and breakfast blood sausage."

"Sausage?" Nellwyn walked out of the library. "Is that what you said, Helen?"

"I did, ma'am," Mrs. Forbes said. "A horrible mistake in judgment to hire that girl, it was."

"For which I take full responsibility," Patrick said in a terse voice.

Nellwyn put her nose to the mirror. "I thought it smelled rather familiar. The message is written in sausage."

"I never even said two words to that girl," Anne said, gazing at the mirror as Helen frantically wiped it clean with her own apron. "Why would she want to threaten me?"

Nellwyn stole a glance at Patrick. "She might have been put up to it. It does seem a peculiar thing to do."

He knelt down on the step in front of Anne. "Do you want me to take you home?"

She looked at him steadily. "Are we going to let a sausage scare us off a royal investigation?"

He smiled reluctantly. "Not when you put it that way."

25

$\mathcal{A}$nne, Patrick, and Nellwyn met for a midnight conference an hour later in the blue drawing room. In order not to arouse the suspicion of the other servants, who already thought Patrick took far too many liberties, he made a show of performing his nightly duties while the two women drank their tea. Actually it wasn't a show at all. He doubled-checked every door and window in the lodge and wrote a complaint to the sheriff's deputy about the incident, even though the girl would probably never be found. Tomorrow he and Sandy would make a thorough search of the village and outlying area. His guess would be that the girl had fled to Glasgow or Aberdeen, a place where she would not easily be found, unless she was being sheltered by family. He blamed himself for not checking more deeply into her history.

"We cannot very well hold an intimate conversation with you halfway across the room," Nellwyn complained from the sofa. "What on earth are you doing down there for so long, Sutherland?"

"Don't tell me you've found body parts in the fireplace," Anne said, still shaken from the message on the mirror.

"I was checking the grate." His voice sounded subdued.

"Are you going to stay in that peculiar position all night?" she asked.

"I just might."

She put down her cup. Something was wrong. His face was contorted in the fading light of the fire. "What is it?"

He gave a grimace that was a combination of pain and embarrassment. "I cannot get up. I appear to be stuck. My knee has locked."

"Stuck?" Nellwyn said. "A man in your superb condition?"

Anne shook her head. "That's what you get for brawling with young bucks at the fair."

He threw her a black look. He'd been a young buck not that long ago himself. "No. That's what I get for pretending to be a damned butler."

"Do you want us to help you up?" she said carefully.

He didn't answer. The two women came to the fireplace, but he waved them off, his pride injured as he got to his feet, limped a few steps, and stretched out on the wide sofa with his legs sprawled over the overstuffed arm.

"This job will be the death of me yet."

"Did you learn anything more about Janet?"

Nellwyn asked, unsympathetically plopping down beside him.

"Only that she disappeared with some silverware and a sizable sausage."

Anne squeezed down on the sofa beside Nellwyn, moving Patrick's legs to make a place for herself. "I still don't understand why a virtual stranger would want to threaten me away. Even if she was a thief, I have not done anything to offend her."

"Perhaps she sensed we were coming close to solving the mystery of Edgar's death," Nellwyn said.

Patrick sat up, frowning at this suggestion. "But we're not close, and why would a serving girl who had never been to the lodge before care anything about Uncle Edgar?"

A long pensive silence fell.

Nellwyn nodded thoughtfully. "My theory is the only one that makes sense. Someone paid the girl to write that message, and Flora is the obvious suspect."

"Flora *was* alone in the house for at least an hour after we left," Patrick said, looking at his aunt in approval.

"I cannot imagine a twit like Flora murdering Uncle Edgar," Anne said. "She goes into hysterics when she pricks her own finger."

"Perhaps she is protecting her father," Patrick said ominously. "Sir Wallace might be our man. Anne, I forbid you to see him again."

She fought a wave of fatigue. It had been an exhausting day, and she was in danger of falling asleep on the sofa beside the rogue. "Do not be absurd." She closed her eyes. "David went to school with Wallace. He is not a killer."

"Perhaps Flora wanted Anne gone for other reasons," Nellwyn speculated. "Perhaps she was enamored with Patrick and decided you were an obstacle, Anne."

"The woman cannot control the passion I arouse in her," Patrick mused, sounding pleased at the notion. "It is a plausible theory."

Anne opened her eyes. "No, it isn't. If I decided to leave, I would take my butler with me, wouldn't I?"

"Not necessarily," Nellwyn said. "You might leave him here with me at the lodge to take care of the needed repairs. Or perhaps she hoped to hire him away. We do know that the girl has no control over her behavior when it comes to men."

"She might be driven by impulse," Patrick said, folding his arms behind his head.

Anne flushed. "If Flora is that determined to have you, I would not stand in her way. She has only to ask me."

He frowned. "I resent being referred to as a piece of property that can be passed from hand to hand. Furthermore, I find it easier to believe Flora would lust after my body than dispose of a dead one in a boat."

"Typical male arrogance," Anne said.

"Poor Edgar," Nellwyn said. "Murdered in his prime."

"Edgar was almost eighty years old," Patrick said.

"Well, somebody does not want Anne in the lodge," Nellwyn said. "We did not imagine that message."

"I'm going to find her," Patrick said. "I'll leave early in the morning."

Anne sat up abruptly. "You're going to leave us alone?"

"Perhaps it's not a good idea," he conceded.

"It most certainly is not," Nellwyn said. "You belong here in this house at Anne's side. And we all belong in bed. We have a busy week ahead preparing for the party."

No one moved. Patrick pretended to close his eyes, studying Anne's silhouette in the darkness. She was the sweetest woman beneath the surface. He could not believe that anyone would want to frighten her. He leaned forward to touch her hand. "Nellwyn is right, you do need to go to bed."

Nellwyn took a final sip of her tea. "Who would not have been shocked, reading that message in one's own bloodied reflection?"

Anne looked at Patrick. "Do you know what part of the prediction comes next?"

"Our baby?" he said hopefully.

Nellwyn nearly dropped her cup on the carpet. "Do my ears deceive me? A baby? Now what—oh, I know I am a matchmaker par excellence, but this exceeds even my expectations. When is the little blessing due?"

Anne's eyes flashed. "It isn't."

"Probably sometime next September," Patrick said confidently, which of course meant that the conception had not yet occurred.

"September?" Nellwyn said in disappointment. "Well, at least I still have time to renovate the nursery."

"And find a nursemaid," Patrick added. "I would not have just anyone raising my child."

"Do you think she ought to go to London for her lying-in?" Nellwyn asked. "Have you decided on a name?"

"I favor Niall for a boy," Patrick said, rubbing his jaw. "Elizabeth is always nice for a girl, rather Biblical and royal, but Anne may venture an opinion."

"I am going to bed." Anne sprang to her feet. "Lord above, the pair of you will have this baby born and christened before it has even been conceived."

"Have you given much thought to a college if it is a boy?" Nellwyn asked Patrick, completely in her element.

"I would not mind Edinburgh, if he shows an interest in medicine," Patrick said. "That way, we could spend some time together during the holidays."

Nellwyn looked up at Anne. "She doesn't show, does she?"

"Lord above!" Anne shouted. "I am not having this man's baby."

Patrick couldn't quite hide a smile at her denial of the inevitable, and Nellwyn gave him a knowing look, a woman of the world who had seen it all before.

"You shall have to get used to this sort of thing, I'm afraid," she said in a stage whisper. "Women tend to throw quite a few tantrums when they are in the family way. And you take her in hand about the horses, Patrick. She cannot go galloping into her *accouche-*

ment." She paused, eyeing his broad frame with a worried frown. "You were a veritable monster when you were born. I should guess this baby will be a wee devil to deliver."

Patrick followed Anne out into the hallway and caught her arm. "Anne, wait. We meant no harm. We were only teasing."

She turned at the stairs, lifting her gaze to his. Shadows played across his bold features, giving a foreboding quality to his face. God had not been in a refined mood when he had created this man; he might have used granite to fashion the model. But even Anne could not mistake the genuine concern in his eyes.

God had slipped a streak of gentleness into the granite. Despite herself, she had to admit that the wildness in Patrick appeared to have been channeled if not conquered. And even though he had never meant to hurt her seven years ago or made any promises for the future, she had half hoped he would burst into the church to claim her as she gave herself in marriage to his cousin. But he hadn't, and now that he was here, asking her to overlook the past, she didn't know what to do.

"What is it, Patrick?"

"Should I walk you up to your room?"

"To protect me from the stalking sausage?"

"I wouldn't let anything hurt you, Anne."

"I'll be fine." She started up the stairs, then paused, smiling mischievously. "Shall I call you if I go into labor early?"

He began to follow her, chuckling softly.

"Patrick, I said I'd be fine by myself."

"You never know, Anne. That sausage could be waiting right around the corner."

She turned without warning, and found herself practically in his arms. "A butler's duty doesn't include putting his mistress to bed."

He leaned into her, lowering his lashes. "But we both know I'm so much more to her ladyship than a butler."

"You're not much of a butler, now that you mention it."

She stumbled down a step, caught off guard as he brushed his mouth against hers. "I want you so badly."

"Hmmm." She didn't respond, backing into the railing, but she was vulnerable, and she would not mind being held for a very short moment.

"Should I carry you upstairs?" he whispered, biting the edge of her ear.

"Don't be silly."

"Should I do this? I—"

For a moment she allowed him to kiss her, deeply, wetly, moaning as he wrapped his arms around her waist. His touch elicited needs inside her that hurt, and she felt herself floating, responding, her blood thickening. She was getting hot, and he sensed it, pressing his groin against her belly. His tongue plundered her mouth like a gentle weapon, weakening her, staking his claim. Another minute of this, and he wouldn't have to work at seducing her—she would be tearing off his jacket and dragging him into her bed.

"Anne." He rubbed his face against hers. "Tell me what to do."

Blood was pounding in her ears, and this was not a good sign. David had never made her blood pound, and not once in almost five years of marriage had she considered tearing off his clothes for the pleasure of looking at his body.

"Will you stop following me?" she said, shaking off the spell.

"Will you have my baby?"

He looked so determined that she started to laugh, climbing a few steps to safety. "Oh, for heaven's sake."

He followed her anyway, even when she opened her door.

"Go. Go to your own room. Patrick, please. I promise I'll call you if I need you."

He stared at her for so long she was afraid she would relent. There was something inside her that hoped he would insist. "All right," he said. "All right. I'll go to my room."

She laid her face against the door as he backed into the hall. "It isn't as if that message on the mirror threatened me in any physical way, Patrick."

He shook his head. "No. No. Sausage blood is a benign enough substance."

"And no one is liable to sneak into my room while I'm asleep either," she said as she closed the door in his face.

26

She took one look at the large figure looming between the bed curtains before she sat up in bed and screamed. She had been asleep for less than twenty minutes.

"Hell, woman," Patrick whispered, diving into bed beside her. "There is no need to scream like that. It's only me."

"I know," she said. "That's why I screamed."

He gave her a reproachful look. "And now everyone in the lodge will probably come running to see what frightened her ladyship into screaming bloody murder."

They both stared through the curtains at the door, awaiting Anne's rescuer. However, after four entire minutes had elapsed, it became evident that no one was coming to investigate her scream in any hurry. Nothing disturbed the heavy silence of the lodge.

"Well, isn't that reassuring?" he said, making himself more comfortable. "You could be lying dead for all anyone in this house pays attention."

"Everyone sleeps belowstairs except Nellwyn, who probably put you up to sneaking in here in the first place," she said testily. "Exactly what are you doing here at this hour?"

He rolled onto his elbow, his half-buttoned shirt revealing the rugged contours of his chest. "I heard a suspicious noise and jumped out of bed to investigate. Aren't you grateful I'm a light sleeper?"

"What noise?" she demanded.

He sat up slowly. "Listen."

She glanced toward the window. "That is the wind on the tree outside, Patrick. Did you think the branch was going to break inside, form a conspiracy with the sausage, and abduct me?"

"Stranger things have happened. This is Scotland, after all, land of devil dogs and body-snatchers."

"Get out of my bed."

"I can't," he said sheepishly.

"Why not?"

"Because Fergus is sleeping in *my* bed for the night. He appears to be coming down with a bad chest cold and Nellwyn said he needs to sleep in a warm bed with no damp air, and it's very damp belowstairs."

"Then go to sleep with him," she said unsympathetically. "You can keep him warm during the night, since you've developed this sudden maternal instinct."

He leaned over and tenderly brushed a strand of hair from her shoulders. "If he sees me sneaking back in from the closet, he'll think that you and I—"

"He's going to notice you aren't there anyway,"

she said. "Now sleep on the couch if you won't leave. I am in no mood for your nonsense."

Sleeping on the Grecian couch on the opposite side of the room wasn't exactly what he had envisioned, but at least they were together, he knew that nothing would happen to her while he stayed here, and he could always hope she would change her mind and invite him to share her bed.

Of course, neither of them could sleep after that. There was enough tension in the air to generate a thunderstorm. Every sound seemed amplified, every creak ominous, and they both remembered the time when they had been together, those stolen hours of high sexual intensity.

They had been as intimate as any two people could dare to be in a single day, probably more intimate than many couples in a lifetime, and Patrick tortured himself with the memory of what a rare treasure he'd had in Anne and how stupid he had been not to realize it.

"I can't resist you. What have you done to me, Patrick."

She whispered the words in his ear while he lay on the stone floor and let the summer wind waft over their naked bodies. She was sweet and uninhibited and wild, and she had given herself, body and soul, to him without a second thought. Seducing her had been too easy, and it wasn't that he couldn't come to love her, he could, but at the time Patrick was not ready for marriage or commitment. He was shattered by his mother's death and angry at the world. He resented the restrictions his father had imposed upon him; he was running on sheer instinct, running from his pain. He had never made Anne any promises about their future; but in the back of his mind he imagined they would be together when he settled down because she had chosen him. He didn't realize then that youthful hopes and promises rarely come to fruition. He didn't understand how determined her parents were to marry her off before she fell into disgrace.

"You're the prettiest girl I've ever met," he murmured. "What do you see in someone like me?"

"You have sadness in your eyes," she whispered shyly.

"Sadness?" He laughed. "You silly girl."

"I have to go, Patrick."

"Not yet."

He didn't like her riding alone across the moor. She was supposed to be visiting her ailing aunt and young cousin, reading the Bible, and being a dutiful niece, but she'd left the old woman dozing after seeing to her needs.

"I don't want to leave you," she whispered, wrapping her hip-length hair around his waist. "I'm going to bind you to me."

He groaned. The contact of her full breasts and belly against his naked body aroused him again, and he turned her on her back and thrust inside her, embedding himself so deeply that she gasped and went still.

It was a dangerous game. He knew he could end

up getting a child on her, and God help them both then. Her parents would kill him, and his own father could barely tolerate him as it was. But from the moment he'd seen Anne, he had wanted her beyond reason.

"Am I hurting you?" he asked in concern, withdrawing from her a few inches to study her face. The knob of his shaft pulsed against her slick flesh.

"No," she whispered.

"No?" He smiled, driving even deeper inside with the next thrust. "Good. Because I don't think I could stop even if you begged me."

Climaxing inside Anne, emptying himself in the depths of her delicate body, had been a primal and powerful experience. Even now he shook just recalling it, and there had never been another woman who had taken him to such a peak or who had left the mark on his soul as she had.

Even now, she was the only woman he could not forget.

As the memory faded, he groaned and turned onto his side, aching to touch her again. Anne had been such a sweet girl, so good, and he'd been so bad, deflowering her without a second thought, selfish in his sexual hunger. Why had he not stayed that summer? Why had he not seen beyond the obvious? Why could she not see what he was trying so hard to prove?

"Sutherland." Her voice snapped him out of his exercise in self-torture. "Would you kindly stop bumping back and forth on that couch? What *is* the matter with you?"

"You don't really want me to answer that question, Anne."

She sat up on her elbow. "Answer the question. You are thrashing about like a landed trout."

"If you really want to know, I was thinking about the time we made love."

"I'm sorry I asked," she said quietly.

"Aye. So am I."

There was a long spell of silence. Anne sank back down onto the bed and finally after another hour, she started to fall asleep only to hear Patrick drag a chair up to her side.

"Now what is it?" she said through her teeth.

He leaned over her, his expression earnest. "Well, you got me thinking about that gypsy's prediction again."

"I did?"

He nodded. "It's true I don't put much stock in superstition, but one doesn't want to take a chance where one's loved one is concerned, does one?"

"Are you staring at my breasts again?"

"I'm sorry." He raised his unapologetic gaze to hers. "I was thinking about the next part of the prediction."

"That isn't what it looks like you were thinking about," she said.

"Are you going to keep interrupting me with your suspicions about my sexual fantasies?" He leaned down even lower. "Unless it's *your* secret fantasies we're really talking about, in which case, I'm all ears."

She snorted rudely.

He drew back, arching his brow. "As I was saying—"

"Do you think a stag is actually going to attack me in bed? That an enormous beast is going to come lumbering across the courtyard, up the stairs and impale me where I lay?"

"Only if he's trying to get a word in edgewise," he said in annoyance. "I am trying to make a point."

"Which is?" she said, tapping her fingers on the quilt. "It's only four o'clock or so in the morning."

"The point," he said irately, "is that a prediction does not have to be taken literally. Omens and such are open to interpretation. The stag could be a heraldic device on someone's shield. Your enemy could be hiding behind a mask of aristocracy."

"You're starting to sound cracked, Sutherland." She thumped onto her side. "And I can feel you staring at my backside."

He grinned, not even bothering to deny it.

She pulled the quilt up and pretended to fall asleep, peeling open one eye to watch him walk across the room.

"What are you doing now?" she asked in exasperation.

"I'm looking in the mirror."

She vaulted out of bed. "Is there another message?"

"No. There is, however, a thick coating of dust. You notice these things when you're in domestic employment. I am going to have to talk to Gracie about it in the morning."

She jumped out of bed and marched up behind him. "Dust? You're looking in the damned mirror for dust when I have to get up in a few hours to survey the forest?"

He squinted. "No. I was looking at my black eye when the dust distracted me. My eyelid is starting to swell shut. Don't worry about it, though. It's only a bruise. It'll have gone down before the shooting party—"

"Don't be such a martyr, Patrick. Let me see it."

"Go back to bed, Anne. It's nothing."

She stood on tiptoe to touch his eyelid. "Everyone will think my butler is a blackguard."

He suppressed a shudder as her fingers brushed his face. "Which he is. At least you seem to think so."

Their bodies were barely touching, but memories of what they had shared magnetized them. Anne fell back a step in self-defense, trying to break the connection.

"I have to ride out early to survey the forest for the shooting," she said quietly. "We'll probably have to remove a few blasted pines from the bridle path."

"I'll go with you," he said, staring at her as she returned to her bed alone.

"No. You have to look for Janet."

"Then I'll make Fergus and Allan go with you."

"Don't you dare."

But he would; they both knew it, so Anne didn't bother to argue further, and they spent the rest of the night apart, lonely and aching, until the ferocious roar of a stag in heat awakened them as dawn broke over the hills.

27

"Dear God." Patrick nearly collided with Anne as they rushed to the window to investigate the agonized bellowing. "What in the name of creation was that?"

She shoved her hair onto her shoulders. Her face was remarkably calm for someone who had been awakened by such an ungodly noise. "A stag. In rut, I think."

"In the courtyard?" he asked, forcing open the window.

"No." She pointed beyond the lodge to the ridge of wooded hills that encircled the estate. "Look," she said softly. "Up there."

Even as she spoke, a guttural roar resounded from the violet shadows of the ridge where a gigantic black stag stood, proclaiming his authority. Below him a hind darted through the trees as if daring the beast to master her.

"The rut begins," Patrick said, leaning across the

windowsill on his elbows. "I'd forgotten what it was like."

Anne was suddenly acutely aware of his presence, of how attractive he looked in his rumpled linen shirt and breeches with his dark hair disheveled and his big feet bare. He was leaning against her on purpose. She should have pushed him away, but the autumn mist made her shiver, and his large body lent her warmth.

Suddenly the stag roared again, a challenge, and the hills echoed with the grunts and answering roars of younger stags who posed no match for his mastery.

"The dominant male," she said in a subdued voice. "Arrogant creature."

"But he'll win," Patrick said, a grin creasing his face. "Look at the size of him. His body is a mass of muscle."

She stole a glance at Patrick from the corner of her eye. "I had noticed. The hind is teasing him."

"So like a woman."

They watched for a few moments as the hind wove through the misty pines toward the black stag who summoned her. The hind rubbed against him in invitation, and the beast began to nuzzle her neck before he mounted her.

Anne turned away. "So there is your stag, Patrick, and he's already found his mate. You can concentrate on Uncle Edgar now instead of on me."

He followed her to the dressing screen. "There are other stags, and I'm still not giving up my theory that the warning had a symbolic element. I might even return to Black Mag for a more detailed reading."

"It's your money to waste," she said. "Would you leave my room now for me to dress?"

He walked back to the window. "The forest is full of stags. I don't like the idea of you riding out while the males are fighting for supremacy."

"If you aren't going to leave, pass me my riding habit."

"I'm a butler, not a lady's maid. Are you listening to me?"

"No," she said. "Not at all."

"That's what I thought." He found her habit in the wardrobe and tossed it over the screen. "I admit it is a rare occurrence, but I have heard of stags charging humans in fatal attacks."

"Did you hear about the noblewoman who shot her butler because he refused to leave her bedroom?" She paused. "Nellwyn is an early riser, Patrick. She's going to hear our voices and assume the worst."

"She'll be breeding after this," he said, closing the window against the subtle invasion of mist.

Anne stepped out from the screen. "Nellwyn?"

He grinned. "The hind."

"Nature will take its course."

"It usually does." He stretched his arms above his head, affording her an uninvited view of his flat abdomen through his unbuttoned shirt. "What a night. Sandy and I are going out ourselves to search for Janet. I shall need a gargantuan breakfast to get through the day."

She gave him a droll smile. "Then see to it, Cinderella. I have quite an appetite myself."

"I came here to protect you, Anne, not to pour tea." His blue eyes searched her face. "You do realize that I am doing this because I love you, not because I have developed a sudden penchant for housework? I've fallen in love with you, Anne—woman, did you hear me?"

She knelt to hunt in the chest of drawers, muttering that she just had to find her riding gloves, but her mind was frozen, and she did not know what to say. *He loved her.* To think of him in those terms, after all the emotional tumult he had caused, well, what did he expect of her? What did he want her to do?

"There," she said, brandishing the gloves. "I found them."

She looked around, but he was gone, and she stood up, holding her gloves, wishing her life could be as uncomplicated as the stag's and its mate. *Nature will take its course. . . .* In the case of her and Patrick, however, she devoutly hoped nature would not interfere, at least not for the second time. She still had not recovered from the first, and judging by the kiss they had shared on the staircase, she had no reason to believe the feelings they aroused in each other would be any easier to control than before.

Nellwyn gave Anne a guileless look over her tea cup at breakfast a few hours later. "I heard you and Sutherland bumping about in your bedroom all night. Am I to assume you were reenacting the events that led up to Lord Kingairn's murder?"

"I have no idea what you're talking about," Anne said, stealing a glance at Patrick, who stood leaning against the drawing room window with his arms folded across his chest.

His expression was remote, unapproachable.

He hadn't spoken to her much since she had refused to acknowledge his confession, or to encourage him. She could imagine his pride had taken a blow, and as it was turning out, there wasn't as much pleasure in her small measure of revenge as she had imagined.

"Do I look stupid, Anne?" Nellwyn said, breaking into her thoughts. "I know what noises in the small wee hours mean."

Anne frowned as she took a sip of scalding tea to cover her disconcertment. "That was probably the stag in rut on the hill you heard."

"Well, it might have been a stag in rut." Nellwyn cast a meaningful look in Patrick's direction. "But it wasn't coming from the hill, it was coming from your room, and I know because at one point I stood right outside your door and I listened."

Anne put down her cup and covered her eyes with her hand.

"You heard the stags in the hills," Patrick said in a dispassionate voice, not turning around. "You can still hear them if you're in the mood to eavesdrop again."

She hesitated. "Does a stag ask, 'Are you staring at my breasts again?' "

"Dear, dear God." Anne lowered her hand, giving Patrick a furious look. "She *was* listening."

He lifted his shoulders in an unconcerned shrug. "Then she knows nothing happened, doesn't she? And she knows you do not return my feelings for you, and I'm making a fool of myself for nothing."

She blinked. Even Nellwyn, for once, was at a loss for words, but only for a moment.

"Stop feeling sorry for yourself, Sutherland," she said. "Anne is entitled to nurse her wounds until she turns into an old crone if she chooses. There are plenty of other women who will jump at the chance to be courted by you. She won't be this attractive forever."

"Thank you," Anne said dryly. "I feel much better about myself now."

"I feel like hell," Patrick said. "While Anne and the footmen were off in the forest, Sandy and I spent two hours knocking at doors and posting notices only to find out Janet and her brother stole two horses during the night and took off to parts unknown. I suppose it's in the sheriff's hands now unless I go after her myself."

"You do look a bit haggard," Nellwyn said. "However, we have already established you must not leave the house until after the party. Did the pair of you come up with any motives for Janet's message?"

Anne hazarded a glance at Patrick. "Well, we didn't actually have much of a discussion about the subject."

Nellwyn's eyebrows shot up. "You spent an entire

night together, and you didn't discuss a death threat?"

Anne sighed. "We did not spend the night together, not in the manner you mean, and I believe Janet was alluded to once or twice, and anyway, it wasn't a death threat at all. It was a vague warning."

"I do not suppose that either of you got around to discussing Edgar's murder while you weren't spending the night together?" Nellwyn asked.

"I have something in mind," Patrick said from the window.

Anne stared down at the floor, not certain she liked the sound of that at all.

"Are you going to share this fascinating plan," Nellwyn asked, "or are you going to stand there sulking forever?"

"Neither." He turned and strode right past the sofa, giving Anne a smile that was smug and pure Sutherland. "I'm going to read the newspaper in the pantry."

28

As a good butler, Patrick was supposed to iron the newspaper and lay it on Anne's breakfast tray. However, since he wasn't speaking to her, and probably never would again, the woman could wait for her wrinkled paper.

Unfortunately, his spell of peace and self-pity did not last long because the neglected noblewomen of Glenferg began to arrive only an hour later to pay a social call on her ladyship.

Actually, their calls on Lady Whitehaven were only a pretense. They had never gone to any great lengths to cultivate her friendship, believing the wild young beauty gave herself airs, owing to her connections at court.

But several of the parish beldames *had* taken the trouble to watch Lady Whitehaven's butler spring to the defense of a beaten man at the autumn fair. His chivalry and pugilistic skill had not gone unadmired. What woman would not wish for such a defender in their employ? And the fact that Miss Flora Abermuir, that brazen light-skirt, had stated the man was a cheeky, irreverent rascal who could not even pour a proper cup of tea had only enhanced his mystique.

What other assets, besides his boxing talents, did the broodingly handsome butler hide? Was he, they speculated wickedly, polishing more than Lady Whitehaven's silver?

The gentlewomen of Glenferg simply had to get to the truth of this alarming matter. Lady White-haven, a tender widow, must be protected from this attractive predator if necessary, and the good, gos-sip-starved ladies of the parish were all too willing to take up her cause.

Lady Murray and Lady Tarbet volunteered to make the first assessment, lest entering the lodge be unsafe for the other women of their group, who had fol-lowed in a separate carriage. They pounded bravely at the heavy oaken door and stood in silence as, after endless minutes, footsteps tramped from within.

Sandy flung open the door, a shovel in hand, his white hair askew under his bonnet. "What do you want?" he shouted.

The two gently bred women stumbled a few feet back, mortified by this muddied gnome of Scottish manhood.

Then Lady Murray cleared her throat. "Where, pray tell, is the new butler?"

He smirked. "Himself is sitting on his behind readin' the paper while the poor sod of a gardener has to interrupt his work to answer the door."

"Fetch him," Lady Murray commanded in a voice that even Sandy dared not ignore. "We will be announced by a butler, not a gardener."

Swearing under his breath, Sandy brought Patrick to the door, where the two women took one look at his bluer than blue eyes and behemoth shoulders, and understood exactly why Lady Whitehaven had strayed from virtue's path.

"We have come to call on Lady Whitehaven," Lady Murray said breathlessly, putting her hand to her throat as she gazed up into Patrick's handsome face.

"I believe Lady Whitehaven has gone back to bed." He winked impudently at the older woman. "She was out riding early, and she had a verra active night."

"Oh, dear. Oh, my. An *active* night."

"Are you well, madam?" Patrick asked, the epitome of the solicitous servant.

"A . . . little . . . faint," she said, leaning against her friend.

"Well, my goodness," he said, reaching down to scoop the flustered women into his arms. "Allow me to carry you into the drawing room to recover. The mistress would have my head if I let one of her dear friends collapse at the door."

After that, it was no longer a question of why Lady Whitehaven had employed her butler, or whether she was in any danger of a moral crisis. It was quite simply a question of how to steal him away from Anne for oneself.

A woman would pay a king's ransom to have a

man wait on her hand and foot, then turn around and master her in private. How delightful to have your butler battle for you in public and bear you bodily to the couch when you felt a swoon coming on.

Mr. Sutherland was suddenly all the talk at the tea tables of this isolated Highland hamlet.

29

*A*nne was amazed when she came downstairs late that same afternoon and found her drawing room abuzz with conversation and the clink of teacups. Several whispered phrases caught her ear, such as "I'll up his pension." "Wouldn't he be the perfect embellishment to our Edinburgh town-house?" And "How long did Anne think she could keep him to herself?"

The center of all this attention stood casually at the sideboard like a treasure being auctioned off at Sotheby's.

Anne nodded distractedly at the greetings called out to her before she confronted the scoundrel.

"What is the meaning of all this?" she whispered.

He reached up to straighten his neckcloth. "They want me."

"Want you for what?"

"I'm not sure, but my price is apparently going up

by the minute, and if you keep whispering in my ear like that, it will certainly enhance my allure."

"Sit down, Anne," someone called out, and she glanced up to see a group of women, Nellwyn in the middle, waving her over to their corner.

"We've been waiting for you for over two hours," Lady Tarbet said. "We thought you might sleep all day."

Anne turned pink as she caught several winks being exchanged at this pronouncement. She sat stiffly at the end of the sofa, remembering that these women had never befriended her before. They had liked David well enough. They'd attended Anne's parties, but never had included her in their silly social circle, and she knew they'd gossiped about her at church when she had arrived on horseback instead of in a carriage or dog-cart.

"I had trouble sleeping last might," she said, accepting the tea that Patrick suddenly appeared to pour her.

"Indeed." Lady Murray arched her eyebrow, and a few envious sighs broke out as he moved between the group.

"An enormous stag in rut woke me up just as I fell asleep," Anne added, annoyed at the way the women kept gawking at Patrick, as if they'd never seen anything like him before.

"Oh, my," Lady Tarbet whispered, lifting her hand to her mouth.

Nellwyn chuckled softly. "That's the same story she told me."

Anne gritted her teeth, well aware that Patrick was

leaning up against the sofa, listening to every word. "There was a stag on the hill," she said emphatically. "A hind was teasing him to distraction."

"As the female of the species tends to do," Patrick said under his breath, and all the ladies except Anne laughed in appreciation, too charmed to care that a butler was crossing class lines to take part in their private conversation. In fact, his cheekiness was part of his charm.

"He was a beautiful animal." Anne had no idea why she felt compelled to explain the situation to a group of women she cared absolutely nothing about, but she couldn't seem to shut her mouth. "Black and muscular with at least an eleven-point rack. The hind was leading him on a chase through the trees."

"It was a sight to behold," Patrick interjected. "Nature taking its course, as it will."

There was a stunned silence; with his comment Patrick had just informed the world that he and Anne had been standing together at her window in the small wee hours, observing the animal in rut.

Once again Anne felt obligated to defend herself. "Sutherland had brought me breakfast in bed when I was watching from the window." She paused, suppressing a shiver at the memory of his body shielding hers. "Fully dressed," she added. "I was fully dressed in my riding habit."

"We were both fully dressed," Patrick said, which of course only made it sound as if the exact opposite was true, which in turn prompted his audience of startled admirers to picture him fully undressed.

The women all took a sip of tea at once, the image of his naked body apparently overwhelming. In fact, it was several minutes before anyone dared speak again. Anne sank down lower into the sofa, her face scrunched into a scowl. Couldn't they see what an imposter he was? Couldn't they tell the man was born to break hearts? Oh, she wanted to strangle him.

"Is it true you were on intimate terms with Her Majesty?" someone asked him.

"I wouldn't exactly call us intimate," Patrick said. "But I wouldn't call us complete strangers either."

"How did you come into her acquaintance?" Miss Cameron inquired avidly.

Dangerous ground. Anne gave Patrick a warning look, which he blithely ignored. The rogue was in his element, women nibbling out of his hand like . . . a herd of deer.

"I fought for the Queen in Bermuda," he said, sitting down on the arm of the sofa next to Anne and totally ignoring her little nudge to get him back on his feet. "In the 71st Light Highland Infantry."

"How brave you are," Miss Cameron's sister said.

"And then you returned to go into domestic service," Lady Murray remarked. "It must have seemed terribly dull in comparison to the infantry."

"Not really." He glanced at Anne, his blue eyes twinkling. "Every day as her ladyship's butler poses an entirely different battle."

"And do you win these battles?" Miss Cameron asked boldly.

Patrick folded his arms across his chest, giving his

famous grin. "No, but as they say it's the war that counts."

Lady Tarbet pulled her chair closer to the sofa. "I have it on good authority that my neighbor Sir Wallace is hoping to court you, Anne. May I encourage his quest?"

Another silence. Anne felt Patrick staring down at her with a chilling expression that sent a shiver down her back. "I really do not care to discuss this."

"Then there is hope for match between the two of you?" Lady Huntly said.

"Anything is possible," Anne answered vaguely. "I—"

"This tea tastes a trifle bitter," Lady Tarbet murmured before Anne could continue. "Sutherland?"

"I don't make it, madam," he said in a tight voice. "I merely pour it."

Anne dared to look up into his face. Naked jealousy burned in his eyes, and she would be lying to herself if she didn't feel a primitive thrill of satisfaction that she had unsettled him. While they both knew that Anne could never feel anything for a man like Sir Wallace, they also knew that their own association was too precarious to take for granted. She could turn around and marry Sir Wallace just to prove her independence, or for companionship, and Patrick would be forced to concede defeat.

He had lost her to another man before. It could happen again, or perhaps he would grow tired of pursuing her. Perhaps he would even turn to one of the women sitting here in this group who so admired him.

She put down her cup and stood decisively. "Ladies, I shall leave you to ponder my romantic destiny in private. I have an appointment in the ballroom with an army of workmen."

He rose, overshadowing her. "I shall accompany you, my lady."

"No." Her lips tightened. "It isn't necessary. See to my guests instead."

And as usual, he completely overrode her request, following her from the room like a bodyguard while a half-dozen women watched in scandalized envy.

He stalked her like a shadow, not saying a single word as she strode briskly to the ballroom to meet the workmen. She'd have to have been stupid not to realize the remark about Sir Wallace courting her had set him off, and she also had to admit his silence was a little intimidating. There was no telling what he might do.

"You are breathing down my neck," she said, turning so suddenly that they collided at the double doorway to the ballroom.

"I thought that was my job." He barred the door with his arm to prevent her from walking away. His voice was angrier than she had ever heard it. " 'Anything is possible.' What was that supposed to mean?"

"You are really getting on my nerves, Sutherland."

"Good. At least I'm getting somewhere."

She wedged herself deeper into the doorjamb to avoid bodily contact. He retaliated by stepping into her, even though he couldn't remember a time when he had used his strength as a weapon against a woman, and they both knew he would never resort to physical force.

"Going somewhere, Lady Whitehaven? Shouldn't you take your butler along with you?"

"Why are you behaving in such an abominable manner, Patrick?"

His smile was humorless. "I'll tell you why I'm behaving like this—because you've brought me about as low as a man can fall without crawling on his belly to prove himself, and if that's what you want, I suppose I'll do that too."

She looked startled, as if she actually thought he would carry out his threat in front of the entire household, and if Patrick believed that getting on his knees would accomplish anything, he would have done so in a second.

"I don't know what I'm going to do with you," she said in dismay.

Just then a carpenter squeezed through the doorway, noticing Anne with a look of relief. "Lady Whitehaven, there you are. We have a worse problem with the roof than I anticipated."

"Dry rot?" Patrick said, stepping a discreet distance away from Anne.

"Aye. It's—" The carpenter glanced at Patrick in hesitation as if he wondered why a butler would speak on her ladyship's behalf. "We'll need to order wood from Edinburgh, and 'twill not arrive in time for the party Lady Whitehaven has planned."

"We can use Glenferg wood," Anne said, deliberately pushing Patrick out of the way. "That's what my husband did in the past."

Patrick pushed her right back. "Which is why we have the problem you've just discovered. The wood wasn't seasoned, and it shrank."

Anne tried to elbow her way back to a prominent position. Patrick guarded his space like a front-line infantryman, refusing to let her through.

"My *butler* doesn't know what he's talking about," she said over Patrick's shoulder to the speechless carpenter, who had probably never witnessed a jostling match such as this between a servant and an employer.

"That roof could cave in on everyone's head if the wood isn't seasoned," Patrick said, sticking out his left leg so that Anne couldn't sneak past.

She darted around to his right side. "He's full of nonsense, as usual. That roof could hold a hillside."

The carpenter scratched his head. "Actually, madam, your man is correct, although I daresay we'd safe to wait another month or so if I make the few temporary repairs."

"What did I tell you?" Patrick practically crowed like a rooster, earning a glare from Anne that could have turned a lesser man to stone. "David didn't have a clue as to how to maintain a house."

She would probably have smacked him silly for his remark if the plasterer hadn't interrupted at that precise moment. Wringing his hands, the workman bemoaned the ruined cornice in the ballroom.

"Please, madam, let me show you some of the newer designs from London," he said as he motioned Anne into the room.

He gestured upward in despair at a moldy plasterwork frieze of Hephaestus and Cyclops fashioning thunderbolts for Zeus.

"It's ruined," he said, "beyond restoration."

"It was undoubtedly as ugly as hell even in the old days," Patrick said behind him. "In fact, this entire room is a mausoleum of bad taste."

Anne's mouth thinned but there wasn't much she could say as she surveyed the cavernous ballroom. The boar and deers' heads mounted on the wall were moth-eaten monstrosities. The tasseled silk curtains smelled of mildew. Every wall panel was embellished with a mythical deity committing a heinous deed; every alcove boasted a marble bust or coat-of-arms. Ceramic urns stuffed with dusty peacock feathers filled the corners, and gilt cherubim shot arrows at unsuspecting guests from a cutglass chandelier the size of an iceberg.

"It just needs a wee bit of attention, that's all," she said meekly.

Patrick grimaced. "It needs to be razed to the ground as a kindness to humanity."

The plasterer turned in confusion to the carpenter, who was trailing along to overhear the conversation. "Who is he?" he whispered, nodding at Patrick.

"The butler, I think," the carpenter whispered back.

"I think plate-glass windows would brighten this room," Patrick said. "Of course, we would not have time to install them before the party."

"Plate-glass windows?" Anne said. "I can't afford to pay for plate-glass with all the debts from the townhouse. Besides, I barely come here once a year."

He moved around her, frowning in consideration. The glazier and his assistant had arrived to consult with Anne, but it was Patrick who had commanded their attention.

"I've been thinking," he said. "We should spend the summers here, away from the congestion of the city. And I'll pay for the plate-glass. Have the glazier make up an estimate."

Anne caught the plasterer glancing at the carpenter, eyebrows raised. Had they chosen the wrong line of work? that look seemed to ask. An aggressive butler might lord it over a household, but to pay for repairs . . .

She spoke to him under her breath. "Stop giving yourself airs, Sutherland."

He ignored her. "I've also been meaning to talk to the masoner about an estimate for the garden wall. And I've sketched a plan for the stables which I would like executed by next spring if possible."

She stood there, flabbergasted and abandoned, while he began to lead the workmen around the room, indicating which outrageously expensive repairs he deemed essential.

A four-inch plasterwork thunderbolt fell at her feet. Patrick glanced back at her, raising his eyebrow. "A sign from the gods?" he said wryly. Then he turned back to the workmen, gesturing expansively. "Also, a sideboard recess in the dining room so that the servants aren't impaled every time a guest pulls back his chair."

"He's going to land me in the poorhouse," she said to herself.

"And," Patrick added, flicking a bit of plaster from his cuff, "I should like the dressing-room doors to her ladyship's bedchamber removed so that the two rooms open onto each other. Her husband should have free access to her, night and day."

And that remark left her entirely speechless. She backed into the wall as he turned to appraise her.

The hammering intensified all around her, the dogs were barking in the kennels, the workmen shouting at one another. Patrick, in complete control, was warning the plasterer to be careful when a thunderbolt broke from the frieze and fell on his head.

He looked up in astonishment. "Hell, man, you're going to give someone a brain contusion if you don't watch what you're doing."

Then he said something to Anne but she didn't hear him because she was laughing too hard. He'd looked so ridiculous with a plaster thunderbolt protruding from his head, and she knew in that instant that it was useless to keep fighting him. She loved him, right or wrong, saint or scoundrel, and she always would, even if it had taken a sign from the gods for her to admit it. But realizing the truth did not help the situation nor did it guarantee a happy ending. She was no longer a giddy young girl who did not think beyond tomorrow.

"It's hopeless," she said, shaking her head.

He looked over at her with a puzzled grin. Perhaps he had an inkling of what she had just realized. Perhaps the truth showed on her face because he took a tentative step toward her, and she could see the glimmer of hope in his eyes. Then all of a sudden someone behind him shouted, and his startled gaze lifted from her face to the wall.

"*Move.*" His grin faded, and a look of panic crossed his face. "Anne, get away from the wall."

He looked so frightened that she instinctively obeyed him, moving forward a second before she felt something hard glance off her shoulder, and heard a crash on the floor behind her. Half turning, she saw an enormous stag's head sitting in the exact spot she had occupied a moment earlier. A cloud of dust settled in the air.

Patrick brushed around her, apparently more shaken than she was by the accident. If he'd lived here longer though, he would have gotten used to the faulty plumbing and insecure fixtures. He was right—David had never paid much attention to maintenance.

"Well," she said. "This really is our stag this time."

"Do you know what would have happened if you hadn't moved at that precise moment?" he demanded, his face gray.

Anne didn't answer; it seemed unlikely that she would have suffered more than a mild concussion. Workmen were crowding around them. The carpenter shouted at the plasterer that he was an idiot. Everyone asked her ladyship if she wanted to sit down, and before she could protest, chairs were shoved at her from all directions. She and Patrick had to brave a covert escape onto the terrace to hold a private conversation.

"A battleground is safer than that ballroom," he said grimly, grasping her hand.

She bit her lip against a smile. "Patrick?"

He frowned, glancing down into her face. "What?"

She stood on tiptoe, extending her free hand. "You still have bits of that thunderbolt in your hair. Hold still."

He smiled into her eyes as she gently brushed a bit of plaster from his face. "It is verra dangerous for you to touch me like that, Lady Whitehaven."

She dropped her hand, deliberately pulling him down the stairs into the garden. "I wasn't thinking."

"Do you remember what Black Mag predicted would happen next?" he asked quietly. The wind was scattering leaves across the flagstones. Something was brewing in the air, although there wasn't a cloud in sight. "The body," he said. "If you believe in such things as bone readings and gypsy prophecies."

Anne looked up at him. "Do you?"

He watched the wind lift her dark curly hair from

her shoulders. "I think it might be a good idea if we acted as though we did."

She shivered. "Whose body do you think she meant?"

"I don't know," he said. "But I believe the time has come to go back and ask her."

30

Autumn spread a brilliant blue sky over the Grampian Hills in the week that followed. Deer foraged for toadstools on the forest carpet, and the heather faded to brown. Fewer and fewer bats flew at night, and it was whispered that the storm witches were starting to collect them to put in their cauldrons for their *geasons,* spells they would cast on All Hallows' Eve.

Anne complained that putting on this party was straining her nerves and her finances. Patrick informed her that she didn't know what nervous strain was until she had been her butler for a week.

And even though neither of them would admit it, they practically lived on pins and needles as they waited for the next part of Black Mag's prediction to come true. The gypsy had vanished from the area by the time Patrick found her family's wagon, and her daughter said Mag had left Scotland days ago to make her annual pilgrimage to France; she didn't have her mother's powers, but she could cure impetigo.

Patrick made himself obnoxious as Anne's personal bodyguard and protector. Every night she caught him creeping around her room, and, unconsciously, they both started to look for bodies in the oddest places, even though the gypsy had said there would be water involved.

Anne dreaded opening her wardrobe and looking in the mirror. She began to awaken with a pounding heart from weird dreams of corpses and ghosts with glowing red eyes. Patrick scoffed at her, but the truth was he thought of skeletons a few times himself when he went to the pantry late at night to take care of his butler's business.

Once he almost gave Mrs. Forbes a genuine heart attack when he found her on the floor with a knife at her side and thought she was dead. She wasn't dead. She was looking for the onion she had dropped, but Patrick had given a shout of alarm that had been heard by the stags fighting in the hills.

Gracie suspected that Lady Whitehaven and her butler were under a strange bewitchment, and Sandy attributed their aberrant behavior to lovesickness, which could only come to a tragic end.

"The servants all think you're a pair of nincompoops," Nellwyn informed them. "Did I ever tell you Black Mag predicted Gracie would marry an Austrian prince and bear him six children?"

"So you're saying that she's a fraud and we shouldn't expect to find a body?" Anne asked anxiously as she walked across the ballroom to open the new brocade draperies in what had become an obsessive daily ritual.

God only knew what she feared she would find outside the window. Perhaps someone impaled on the garden wall with a pair of stag's antlers, or a dead body in the fountain. She did not turn a corner in this house anymore without holding her breath in anticipation of something awful appearing.

"I half hope we do find a body," Nellwyn said. "I'd hate to think I traveled all this way for nothing."

"That is morbid," Anne said. "A woman of your background should have better things to do than hope a murder has been committed."

"What exactly should a woman of my background do to entertain herself?" Nellwyn asked. "I cannot gamble. No one has made me an indecent proposal. You and Patrick, despite my best efforts, obviously haven't made a baby together to enliven the last years of my sad and lonely life and I have no offspring of my own."

Anne arched her brow. "Are you suggesting I bear Patrick's child to alleviate your boredom?"

"Either that or produce a dead body to appease her," Patrick said in a dry voice from the doorway.

Anne rubbed her forearms. "Black Mag said something about the body in water. It's so vague a warning, it could mean anything ... a body in the rain."

"Or a bathtub," Nellwyn said. "My first husband drowned while drinking whiskey in the tub. It happens more often than you'd think."

"He drowned in his bath?" Patrick said in disbelief. "You never told me that."

"You never bothered to ask," Nellwyn retorted. "Now stop trying to change the subject. We shall never solve this mystery if we don't put our brains together."

Anne moved away from the window. She could feel Patrick watching her with that half-menacing, half-protective look that drew her toward him like a magnet even though she knew that, for her, he was the most dangerous man in the world. Oh yes, she could see why all the women in the neighborhood wanted his attention despite the fact they believed him to be a servant. A look like that from Patrick could give a woman wicked dreams for a month.

She paced in front of him. "A body in water. The millpond. A bath. The loch. A burn—"

"Perhaps the murderer is going to kill someone on the loch again this year," Nellwyn said. "Perhaps he hopes to make it an annual occurrence. The question is, who does he intend to rub out next?"

Anne stopped in her tracks. "Now I really shall not be able to sleep tonight."

"Why not?" Nellwyn said. "If my theory is correct, the next victim will be found in another boat, not a bed. Isn't that right, Sutherland?"

He stirred. "Isn't what right?"

"Were you listening to my theory?" Nellwyn said.

"About drinking whiskey in the bathtub?" he asked politely.

"You weren't listening," Nellwyn said.

"Yes, I was," he said, studying Anne through his lowered lids. "You have given me an idea, Auntie Nellwyn."

Anne looked up into his face, which she should have known would be a mistake. She felt a crackle of energy, a force go through her as if she had been sheared in half by lightning, and he obviously felt something too if she were to judge by the way he stiffened his shoulders in reaction and drew back against the door. Ever since that day in the ballroom, their antagonism had alchemized into an even more mysterious and unpredictable element. They stood on the verge of either making a permanent commitment or parting ways forever.

"Well, are you going to share your brilliant idea with us or not?" she asked, half afraid he would do just that.

"No." There was a chilling edge to his voice, and she felt faint for a moment, instinct warning her that if whatever he planned involved a dead body, she really didn't want to know the rest.

His smile never reached his eyes. "I am not telling you anything."

Naturally, she and Nellwyn took his vow of secrecy as a challenge. Yet in the next few days, Patrick did not drop a single clue as to what plan he had devised, no matter how deeply the two women probed. In fact, Anne kept thinking that their quest was rather like digging up a grave. Sooner or later, she knew she was bound to find something and it wasn't going to be a pleasant discovery.

"What is he up to?" she and Nellwyn asked each other twenty times a day, intrigued by the way he would disappear at the oddest times without an explanation.

"Patrick is a grown man," Nellwyn said. "He fought in the infantry, and he knows how to take care of himself."

But on the third night of his mysterious behavior, when he never slept in his bed, Anne felt sick to her stomach and couldn't eat the breakfast he served the next morning, studying the lines of fatigue around his mouth.

"Busy night?" she snapped, burning her tongue on a sip of scalding tea.

"Busy enough." His dark gaze moved over her, curious and amused. "Did you miss me?"

"Why would I miss you?"

"Oh, I don't know."

She wanted to pick a quarrel. She hadn't slept a wink worrying about where he was, who he was with. "What makes you think I missed you?"

He straightened his cravat, studying her through half-closed eyes. "You were in my room looking for me."

"Only because you didn't sleep in your bed all night," she retorted. "Just because I thought you might have been murdered doesn't mean I *missed* you."

"Aye. It does."

"You stayed out all night." Anne hadn't wanted him to know she'd been checking on him, to give him evidence that she cared, but she couldn't stop herself. "Where were you?"

He leaned over the sofa and kissed her on the

nose. "I can't tell you now, but you'll find out in due time. And don't expect me back tonight, either. I do, however, appreciate your concern."

If she had any hopes of following him, she soon found her efforts thwarted. Not only did he sneak out when she wasn't looking, but he had apparently commissioned the other servants to watch over her. Everywhere she went, she sensed a shadow; the staff seemed to have been given certain shifts of duty to cover for Patrick's mysterious comings and goings.

Mrs. Forbes pretended to go on a sewing binge whenever Anne settled in the drawing room. Curtains, tablecloth, napkins. The housekeeper stitched up invisible tears while keeping an eye on Anne all the while.

Sandy attached himself to Anne like a limpet when she attempted to take a brief morning ride. He brought along a fowling-piece "for protection" and made her so nervous that she returned to the house and locked herself in the library.

Even when she went to bed that night, Gracie stood guard at her door with her feather duster.

Anne sighed. "What are you doing, Gracie?"

"Obeying orders, ma'am."

"Obeying orders. May I ask what those orders might be?"

Gracie lowered her voice. "I'm to keep all suspicious persons out of your room while Mr. Sutherland is away. Fergus takes the next shift."

"I see." She paused. "What are you supposed to do if they try to force their way inside, dust them to death?"

Gracie gave a shiver. "I'm to shout for help, ma'am."

"Go about your regular duties, Gracie. The guests will be arriving in three days, and the east wing is still in shambles."

"But Mr. Sutherland said—"

"Am I in charge of this household, Gracie, or is Mr. Sutherland?"

"Well, you are, my lady. Surely you dinna need to ask."

Despite this reassurance, it did not escape Anne's notice how unsure of her answer the girl sounded, and for that matter, Anne wasn't convinced herself that when it came to anything in her life, from her servants to her heart, she wielded more than a superficial control at all.

❧31❧

$\mathcal{F}$lora had not been able to eat more than a few bites of food at a time in days. When she drank tea, she read her doom in the black leaves tragically arranged across the bottom of the cup. When she settled down to sleep, she saw a man's body floating toward her, his eyes frozen in accusation.

You have killed me, Flora. She could hear his voice so clearly, it made her skin crawl. She could feel his fingers tangled in her hair and the dead weight of his body on hers, and sometimes she thought it would smother her in her sleep.

The Sutherland butler was setting a trap for her. She had watched him coming and going on the road at all hours. Hadn't she read her downfall in his ungodly blue eyes? Hadn't she seen a fox in her courtyard the same week he arrived, which everyone knew meant disaster would follow? Worse, she had lost her charmed ring the very day they'd raced on the moor.

She put her head in her hands. Her father was shouting at her again about her dressmaker's bill. He barely heard her whisper of despair.

"Papa, do they hang women for murder nowadays?"

He went absolutely white. "What did you say?"

"The truth is going to come out," she said. "My tears fell on Edgar's dead body, and because of that his spirit can't find rest. You should never cry on the dead."

Sir Wallace put his hands to his chest and felt an invisible fist squeezing his heart. He wasn't a young man anymore, as much as he liked to pretend, and this girl would be the death of him, he'd always known that. Her lusty appetite, of course, she had inherited from him, and he couldn't blame her for finding it difficult to resist sexual temptation. But all her talk of hanging sent a chill straight into his vitals.

"You have chosen a hell of a time to develop a conscience, Flora. Have I not warned you never to speak of what happened to anyone? Including me. Put it from your mind."

"There is a rumor in the village that Black Mag predicted Lord Kingairn's ghost will rise from the grave on the hour of his death and point a finger at his murderer. I won't have to speak a word," she said in anguish.

"Oh, hell," he said, collapsing in his chair with relief. "That old hag's nonsense again. I ought to beat you, Flora, for the fright you gave me. I thought you were going to confess."

She hugged herself, a shiver going through her. "Lady Whitehaven is going to have me hanged for it, and her butler is her henchman. That's what she came here for, not to see you. She came for vengeance. That heartless woman is going to have your only child put to death."

The pain in his chest was a vise now. It made him break out in a sweat; yet despite the agony, he managed to find his voice. "I told you I would take care of everything. You leave Anne to me."

"What are you going to do to her?" she said in fascinated horror.

"That's my concern, and stay away from that butler, do you hear me? We shall behave as if none of this ever happened. We are going to attend the party as we have every year because it will look suspicious if we don't."

There was the briefest hesitation before she spoke again. "Then you don't mind if I order a few gloves and shoes to go with the tea gowns I had made?"

"Dear Jesus," he said, closing his eyes.

Patrick found his newly made friend at the village tavern with a group of other upper servants who had been given that night off. A few of the men recognized Patrick from the fight at the fair, and after giving him a nod of respect, they drifted away to leave him in privacy; presumably they believed him to be a man one did not cross.

Soon enough only Patrick and his valet friend Iain, superior in their status to the other servants, were left alone at a corner table with two tankards of ale.

Patrick did not have time to waste in polite conversation. He liked Iain; at least he thought he could trust him enough to keep his mouth shut for another month. He slid a wad of bank notes across the table and got right to the point. "I need a favor. Can you help me?"

The man's eyes widened in astonishment. "Dinna tell me you've robbed Lady Whitehaven, Sutherland. I'll have none of that nonsense—"

"I haven't robbed anyone," Patrick assured him in ironic amusement. "How are your acting skills?"

"I wait on fat old fobs all day long and keep a straight face," Iain said, flashing a grin. "Is that not acting?"

Patrick smiled grimly. "Do you have a friend, a close relative, someone you can trust, to help you with your 'performance'?"

Iain hesitated, looking over his shoulder. "Is this job illegal?"

"Not in the least. But your secrecy is essential."

Iain took a long drink of ale, wiped his mouth, and nodded. "My brother is always good for a favor. What do you want me to do?"

"Take the bag I have deposited under the table for a start. You will find inside it rice powder and rouge, along with a change of clothes. It is to be used in a few days from now, on the evening of the ball."

Iain nearly choked on his ale. "You're asking me to disguise myself as a woman?"

"No." Patrick chuckled and pushed the money into the man's hand before he could change his mind. "As a corpse."

*   *   *

The Highland doctor pulled the bedsheet over his patient's lower body. The entire house was in chaos with the guests due to start arriving shortly. "You have housemaid's knee," Dr. MacDonald said matter-of-factly. "It is unlikely you will die of it."

"I have what?" Patrick said in shock.

"I believe you heard me correctly," Dr. Mac-Donald said crossly. "You are suffering from an inflammation of the patella, which is a common affliction in your profession."

"Housemaid's knee?" Patrick peered incredulously at his swollen leg under the covers.

"It's a hazard of our occupation, mister," Gracie said in sympathy. "Comes from all those years of kneeling at the hearth keeping your employer warm. It's a tribute to your dedicated service."

Patrick frowned, thinking it was more a tribute to the years spent dropping on his knees in the infantry. He had once received accolades for his speed and accuracy in marksmanship. Now he was lucky to get a pat on the head for checking the grate. Bloody hell. He did feel like Cinderella.

The doctor waited until Gracie had left the room to speak again. "Bad luck with the party beginning today."

Patrick grunted. "Isn't it, though?"

"Will it interfere with your little charade?" the physician asked.

Patrick looked up slowly. "My charade?"

"I know who you are, my lord. We attended Lord Gow's funeral in Edinburgh two years ago, and although we've never formally met, I recall my daughter telling me you were related to Lord Whitehaven. I perceived at the loch you were not being entirely truthful, but now, for Anne's sake, I demand to know why."

"You are mistaken," Patrick said.

"I am not. Lord Tynan mentioned last night that he thought he had seen you before the day of the fair. He did not recall your name, but his comment provoked my memory."

There was a pause. Patrick said, "Can I trust you to keep a secret?"

"Only if there is no mischief involved in this masquerade, and I am satisfied neither Anne nor Nellwyn will come to any harm."

"Sit down," Patrick said in resignation. "But do not interrupt me for details, and mind my knee. Anne's guests will be arriving in two hours, and she'll have my head if I don't answer the damned door."

32

$\mathscr{P}$haetons drawn by prancing ponies pulled up into the drive that afternoon. A duchess in a beribboned bonnet arrived with her own bedstead and a pack of personal attendants. Lavender water and scented washballs had been laid out for the ladies, cigars and smoking-jackets for the gentlemen. Even the billiard balls had been polished.

The five-day party began officially that night with a dinner, and for the next few days guests in tweed jackets trooped off into the black hills to stalk deer. Creeping through brown peat pools and climbing crags, they believed themselves great hunters with their rifles and wicker panniers packed with sandwiches and lemonade.

The fourth day of the affair dawned cool and misty. On that morning, Anne awakened with a knot of foreboding in her throat. She had to admit she'd forgotten how much fun a party could be— the gossip, cards, charades, the bluster of people around the house. Still, she did not look forward to what the night would bring, especially the late-night fishing on the loch. It was during that same event last year that Lord Kingairn had been found dead in his boat. But no one talked of such things in the open. The most pressing issue of the day was the constant wardrobe changes between meals.

Anne was a bundle of nerves, and Patrick, preoccupied with his covert activities, did not allay her fears.

"You do not need to announce dinner like a war shout," she said, catching him alone in the hall. "The next thing I know you'll be throwing raw steaks on the table as if we were a pack of hounds."

"Your guests have not complained about my service."

"Not the women."

"Is this madam's way of asking for more personal attention?"

"No, it is not," she snapped.

Her edginess seemed to echo throughout the house. Mrs. Forbes forgot to make mint sauce for the roast lamb, and Gracie overslept, flying into Patrick on her way upstairs.

"Look at you just standing there with all this work to do," she exclaimed. "Aren't you even a little nervous, mister?"

"Gracie, I am as atwitter as a young debutante coming out for the Season."

"A young debutante." She gave him a grin. "Go on."

Dinner was a festive affair. Anne gathered compliments in a gray taffeta gown with a plaid sash. The servants paraded about in their dress tartans, and even Patrick wore a kilt and black doublet with a dirk in his stockings.

The entire female elite of the parish feasted its eyes upon the sight of Anne's handsome butler. His kilt gave the ladies a fine display of his long muscular legs, and since a manly constitution was a component of a desirable manservant, they indulged their prurient interests with clear conscience.

One or two of the more daring ladies even took a page from Lady Murray's book, falling into swoons for the sheer pleasure of being carried to the sofa in his powerful arms.

Anne was appalled at their behavior. Patrick, she suspected, was encouraging them with his outrageously unconventional conduct. Her lips thinned as she watched him.

Lady Grierson complained that the raspberry sauce on the roast duckling was a wee bit sour. Then Patrick knelt down beside her. All the women at the table stopped talking. Of course the men didn't notice a thing. Being men, they missed Lady Grierson's gasp of delight when she looked up into the bluest eyes she had ever seen.

"Lady Grierson," he said solemnly, "the sauce only tastes sour because it has just passed a pair of the sweetest lips in creation. Yours."

"Oh. Oh, my." She blushed becomingly. She couldn't remember when anyone had paid her such a compliment.

Glancing up, Lord Grierson made a mental note

to attend Anne's parties more often; it was the first meal his wife had allowed him to eat in peace.

Patrick even managed to provoke a favorable reaction from the elderly duchess. "Do you require pepper for that steak, your grace, or are you well-seasoned enough as it is?"

There was silence at the table as the guests awaited her response. "I like your butler's style, Anne," she said at last. "Your parties are usually such dull affairs. It's good to see a breath of life in them."

Anne set her teeth, not returning Patrick's smile when he looked her way. She knew he was up to something; all this banter and playfulness was meant to distract from whatever "plan" he had devised. And she knew that when they parted again, she would miss the scoundrel, for all the trouble he had caused her. He brought so much silly wickedness into her life, and she could be herself with him. He had known her at her worst.

Sighing inwardly, she returned her attention to the conversation. "And I met Lord Elderberry during the war," Sir Wallace was telling everyone.

"That would be the War of the Roses, you ancient relic?" Patrick murmured as he bent to remove Anne's plate.

"I should like to borrow your butler for the weekend, Anne," Lady Tarbet whispered over her wineglass.

Miss Cameron giggled. "Wouldn't we all?"

"Wouldn't we all what, miss?" Patrick asked politely, returning to his place behind Anne's chair.

She forced a smile. "Lady Tarbet wishes to engage your services next week, Sutherland."

He pulled a black leather book from his doublet. "Let me see. Saturday? Ah, I'm afraid not. I have a previous engagement. Lady Glendenning's charity tea."

Anne's mouth tightened. "But *I* have need of you next Saturday, Sutherland. We will be closing the house to return to Hampshire. Remember?"

He snapped the book shut. "Saturday is my day off, madam. However, I shall be here bright and early Sunday morning to lend a helping hand."

She glowered at him over her shoulder. "The salmon trifle is starting to melt. Have it taken away."

He made a formal bow, his lips brushing her neck. "I live only to please you, my lady."

"The hell you do," she whispered.

"Butler," Lord Delaney said, snapping his fingers. "Fetch another bottle of burgundy, would you? The footman seems to be deaf to my requests."

"Fetch it yourself," Patrick said. "My hands are full of salmon trifle."

Lord Delaney turned to his wife, his mouth hanging open. "Did you hear what he said?"

"Yes." She smiled dreamily. "Isn't he a scamp?"

He stared at Patrick as he placed the trifle on the sideboard. "If you say so, dear."

"I dare not eat another bite of lamb," Lady Murray exclaimed. "My husband complains that I crowd him in the carriage as it is."

Patrick brought her a fresh plate. "In ancient Greece, you would have been considered a goddess, madam. Men would have placed offerings at your temple. Cities would have been laid to waste in your name."

Every pair of female eyes was trained on his face. Every woman's heart gave a little flutter at his words, except for Anne's. She was ready to grab him by the scruff and shake the wits out of him. And he claimed he wasn't clever with words?

The men started to drift away from the table for brandy and billiards before the women forced them to dance. Lady Delaney instigated a devilish game of dropping her spoon and asking Patrick to find it. Several women followed suit by letting their napkins flutter to the floor.

Patrick crawled under the table, muttering to himself. "This is degrading. I feel like a sheepdog chasing a stick."

"What is degrading, dear?" Nellwyn ducked her head under the tablecloth to speak to him.

"Do you know what those women are talking about?" he demanded.

"I have no idea," she said innocently. "What are they talking about?"

"What I'm wearing under my kilt."

He crept out from under the table, resurfacing to catch the look of disdain on Anne's face. "I suppose you want me to fetch something for you too?"

She threw her serviette on the table. "I most certainly do not. I do think it's time to light the torches in the ballroom though."

"As madam wishes."

*   *   *

He glanced up at the grandfather clock in the corner. Everything was ready. The horse saddled for him in the stable. The rowboat. Iain's disguise. His plan should go off without any problems. However, Patrick was a man who had learned to leave nothing to chance. He intended to sneak away from the ballroom early on to make sure all his preparations were in place at the loch. The only problem was that he didn't wish to leave Anne alone with Sir Wallace. It seemed he would have to engage Auntie Nellwyn's help again, which meant she would insist on knowing what he was going to do. He would have included Anne in his plans, but he knew she would disapprove and try to stop him.

He made his way into the hallway, deep in thought.

If he rode hard, he should be able to return in time to serve hot toddies and hazelnut torte like a good butler an hour before the fishing party.

He might even be able to steal a few minutes alone with Anne before Lord Kingairn rose from the dead to identify his killer.

❧33❧

*A*nne could not quite shake the feeling that the evening would end in disaster. Apprehension overshadowed her as she excused herself from the party to make a final inspection of the ballroom.

Frosted globe gaslights shone on the flocked wallpaper alongside the iron wall sconces. Four bronze girandoles blazed on marble pedestals in the corners, their glow lost in the brightness of the chandelier. The targes and swords above the fireplace had been draped in tartan, the moth-eaten stag's heads had been removed. No thunderbolts should strike her guests as they danced and drank.

Everything was as it should be. Yet her anxiety persisted, her hands felt like ice; she began to pace without even realizing it, some animal instinct putting her on the alert.

When she heard footsteps behind her, she gave a violent start and turned, her taffeta skirts rustling.

"I did not mean to frighten you, Anne," Sir Wallace said. He looked grave and distinguished in his tweed jacket and gray cloth trousers. "Are we alone?"

"I believe so. Is something wrong?"

He hesitated. "I have to make a confession."

"Oh, dear." She stepped back against one of the Windsor chairs that lined the wall. "This sounds terribly serious."

He put his hand to his vest pocket. "Anne, I—"

The door to the ballroom opened with such force that the flames in the girandoles leaped toward the ceiling. A broad-shouldered giant in a kilt towered before them.

"You rang for assistance, madam?" Patrick asked in the coldest voice Anne had ever heard.

"Of course she didn't ring, you insolent man," Sir Wallace said when he recovered. "Do you even see a bell pull in this room?"

Patrick skewered him with a look. "It is not my job to find the damned bells, sir. Only to answer them."

"We wish to be alone," Sir Wallace stated.

Patrick took a step forward, staring down at Anne with deadly calm. "Is that true, madam? You wish me to leave you alone with this walrus?"

She lifted her hand to her temple. She had an awful feeling that if she said yes, Sir Wallace would not leave the ballroom in one piece. "We'll talk later, Wallace. I believe I hear the pipers climbing the stairs to the gallery."

"Very good, madam." Patrick's heavy-lidded gaze

assured her that she had made the right decision. "Do ring me again if you need anything else."

Her sensed of dread persisted. Her heart pounded as she moved among her guests; sipping a glass of madeira only intensified the tension between her temples.

"What do you think Sir Wallace meant to tell me?" she whispered to Nellwyn as they stood watching a lively Highland reel unfold on the dance floor.

"Perhaps he meant to make you an indecent proposal," Nellwyn replied.

Anne gave her a look. "He mentioned a confession."

"The murder confession?" Nellwyn perked up at the thought.

"I'll probably never know because your nephew came barreling between us with his usual bad manners before Wallace could say another word."

Nellwyn didn't respond. Both women had just looked through the terrace doors to glimpse Patrick hurrying past the fountain in the garden. Lamplight silhouetted his tall form. "Lord above, don't tell me that's a pistol in his hand," Anne whispered in horror. "What does the man intend to do?"

Nellwyn shook her head. "I can't tell you. I'd like to, but I'm sworn to secrecy."

"What do you mean, you can't tell me?" Anne said in disbelief. "Do you actually know what he's planned for tonight?"

"Not only do I know, but as of five minutes ago I

have become an integral part of his plan," Nellwyn said. "My lips are sealed, however, and if I told you, you would probably go into hysterics and spoil everything."

She grasped the woman's wrist. "Tell me this instant, Auntie Nellwyn, or I'll—"

"It's a lovely party, Anne," someone trilled behind them as a small group of guests converged on their hostess.

"I think I see my old friend Lady Finley," Nellwyn said, sneaking away from Anne. "I should ask how the dear old thing is keeping."

Anne clenched her teeth, unable to escape her guests to follow the older woman. When she finally broke free, the musicians were playing a waltz and Nellwyn had disappeared. She almost screamed aloud as a strong arm reached out from an alcove and ensnared her.

"I don't believe I've ever had the pleasure of dancing with you, Anne."

She stared up into Patrick's darkly handsome face; her emotions were in such an uproar she didn't really care that he was guiding her out onto the terrace.

"Lord knows we've done everything else," she blurted out.

He grinned, his arm clamped around her waist to keep her from moving away. "Almost. Just dance with me a spell. I don't have long."

"Dance with you?" she said, her voice rising.

Guests were beginning to look at them through the partially opened doors. Gracie watched them in white-faced shock from the bedroom window where she was supervising the undermaids. The mistress and Sutherland dancing together in the garden? It couldn't be.

"I can just imagine what everyone is thinking," Anne said indignantly. " 'She's dancing with the butler. Has the woman totally lost her mind?' "

He whisked her down the terrace stairs. "How do you know they're not saying, 'Look what a lovely couple they make?' And, 'Isn't he graceful for a giant?' "

She laughed, not wanting to, but he was so arrogant and outrageous, and whenever they were together, she came alive, and she loved the feeling. "We are committing a social sin, Sutherland."

"Well, it wouldn't be the first time." He paused and gripped her hand, bringing it right to his heart. "There—that's something, a point for my side. I've made you laugh."

"You made me cry hard enough," she said, turning her face away from what she saw in his eyes.

"And cry," he conceded. "I've made us both cry, but does that mean I'll have to pay forever? Haven't I proven my devotion yet?"

She stared out into the garden, her voice almost inaudible. "I can't say."

"Then kiss me and I shall know the answer."

"Kiss you—a butler—in front of everyone?"

"Then I'll know."

"Silly man," she said, laying her face against their interlocked hands.

"Anne," he said, holding her so tightly that she

couldn't move. "How was I to know that not staying that summer was the biggest mistake of my life?"

Lightning flashed over the distant mountains, and Anne thought of the legends of the storm witches and wizards who dueled for supremacy from their supernatural abodes.

She too was fighting, not for power or to save the world, but to save her very human heart, which she feared had not belonged to her from the day she'd met this man.

"I'll make it up to you for the rest of our lives." His voice was muffled as he buried his face in her hair. "Do you remember what I promised you in London? When people talk about us, they'll say, 'No man has ever made a woman happier.' And, 'Isn't it wonderful she had the good sense to marry her butler?' "

"For God's sake," she said, laughing again.

"After a few months, you won't even remember the confused boy who took advantage of a pretty girl who was the only one in the world to make him believe in himself. Give me another chance, that's all I ask."

He had guided her out into the heart of the garden, past where the lantern lights reached, and she could barely hear the strains of the music from the ballroom, but it didn't matter. They were moving to their own private rhythm, a dance that was close and sexual and fraught with a danger she knew only too well, but she didn't have it in her to fight him anymore. She had always belonged to

Patrick. And, clever, clever man, he had told her everything she had waited so long to hear. Except that she wished it could have come seven years earlier, when she was open and spontaneous.

She raised her face to his. "Are you telling me that a heart can be healed by the person who broke it?"

He stared down at her, and she sensed he was struggling to find the words. "I hope so, Anne. You broke my heart when you married David, and unlike you, I am not prepared to live my life in this much pain."

She felt light-headed and happy, held a prisoner in his arms. "I don't know. I need more time to adjust to everything."

"Your period of mourning is officially over," he said, refusing to show her any mercy, "and Nellwyn is right. Life is short."

They stopped dancing and stood together for several moments, watching the silver-blue streaks of lightning in the distance.

Anne said, "I hope the storm doesn't move down here. It will ruin the fishing tonight on the loch if it does."

"I want to have children with you," he said. "I want to enjoy my sons and daughters before my housemaid's knee gets any worse."

She had wanted to have his children once too. Stupid girl that she was, she'd half hoped he had gotten her pregnant that bittersweet summer so he could rescue her from an arranged marriage.

But Patrick had rebelled against the conventional; he had infuriated his father with his refusal to conform, and in the end her fairy-tale dreams had died a painful death.

"Patrick—"

"You don't have to say anything now. But don't send me away."

She closed her eyes. She didn't want to cry. She *wasn't* going to cry. "Wouldn't I be a fool to believe you?"

He rubbed his cheek in her hair. "You would be a fool not to believe me. I'll take such good care of you if you allow me."

Somehow she found the strength to break away from him, needing time to think. "It's my guests you should be taking care of. Honestly, if any of this gets back to the Queen, I shall never be able to explain it."

"You're absolutely right." He backed away from her, pain and disappointment etched on his face. She hadn't given him the answer he wanted, and finally he was forced to face the fact that perhaps she never would. Perhaps she would continue to push him away, punishing them both for a past mistake, and in the end they would slip back into lonely and separate lives.

He managed a droll smile. "It would serve you right, however, if I decided to remain your butler."

She tried to smile back; she felt cold and unbearably empty without his arms around her, but that was a feeling she knew too well. "We ought to go back inside," she murmured. "We're almost to the bottom of the garden."

He took a few steps toward the gate. "Go ahead. I have something to do first."

Suddenly she remembered the pistol she had seen in his hand, and her anxiety returned with the impact of an arrow. "Where are you going? I know you have a gun. Nellwyn and I saw you on the terrace. What are you planning to do, Patrick?"

He walked to the gate, answering her over his shoulder. "I'll be back in time to serve the whiskey toddies. Fergus is going to take my place at the party until then. Think about what I said, Anne. I expect your decision tonight."

$\mathscr{P}$atrick tethered his horse in the trees and walked to the boathouse on the hill above the loch. He had visited the loch several times in the past week, but it wasn't until yesterday morning that he had connected the boathouse to his uncle's death, and even now he could not be certain his hunch would prove correct.

It was an isolated spot for two lovers to meet, and Patrick and Anne had taken advantage of such a place themselves. The boathouse also wasn't far off the bridle path, for fast access through the woods to the road, or to the loch.

A dead body could be dragged down the hill and put into a rowboat in a matter of minutes. The ruse wouldn't take much planning or muscle. A woman could accomplish the deed alone if she had enough motivation. A year had passed so there wasn't any point in looking for tracks. Patrick didn't even know what he expected to find in the boathouse, or what he would do with any evidence, but the fact was that he was committed to uncovering the truth, and that meant he had to deal with whatever he discovered.

The boathouse was dark and unwelcoming; the flashes of faraway lightning didn't begin to penetrate the gloom of the trees that overshadowed it. The single room smelled of damp and mouse droppings. With distaste, he lit a candle and examined the musty heather-tick mattress on the dirt floor. He wasn't really surprised when he found several strands of long red hair adhering to the woolen fibers.

"Well," he said aloud, crouching in the dark, "that gives me a good idea what my uncle was doing before he died and who he was doing it with, but it doesn't tell me what I'm supposed to do with the information."

It didn't prove Flora had murdered Edgar either, at least it wasn't evidence enough to sway a Scottish jury. The most any prosecutor could hope for in such a case was a Not Proven verdict, which was neither a conviction of guilt or a statement of innocence.

"Damnation," he muttered. "The Queen is really going to hate—"

He wasn't sure what he noticed first, the low-voiced chanting outside or the explosion of flames at his feet, followed by a spray of dirt that hit him in the face. Something thumped rhythmically against the door.

"What the hell?" he said, lifting his head. It

appeared that some deranged creature was nailing the door shut in order to roast him alive.

He jumped up to stamp out the fire, straining his sore knee in the process. The boathouse erupted in flames that leaped up toward the turf-and-mud roof, and as he struggled to breathe, he realized his assailant must have doused the flimsy exterior in pitch oil, or some other flammable substance. Coughing, he pulled the plaid from the bed and covered his face before he threw himself against the door.

He broke free just as a cloaked figure disappeared through the trees; his attacker had done a terrible job of nailing the door shut. In fact, a flea could have pushed its way outside.

He didn't bother giving chase; he still had the second part of his plan to unfold, and he could hear footsteps shuffling in the underbrush behind him.

It was Sandy, who gawked at the smoking boathouse in disbelief before joining Patrick in his efforts to extinguish the fire. The structure lay in ruins, no more than a stack of turf and twigs to begin with, and its charred remains sketched an eerie tableau on the hillside against the background of bare trees.

"What are you doing here?" Patrick asked in a grim voice, wiping his face with the plaid.

Sandy blinked. "I ought to ask you the same thing. Mrs. Forbes was worried about you and sent me out on a search. She knew you'd taken a flintlock pistol from the pantry. 'Tweren't hard to find you with them flames. Were you sneaking a smoke?"

"Indeed, I was not," Patrick replied. "You didn't happen to recognize the person running away into the woods when you arrived?"

Sandy looked frightened. "God Almighty," he said under his breath. "Do you mean to say someone wanted you dead?"

"I don't think my assailant meant to relight my candle."

Sandy leaned on his staff, staring through the smoke to the trees. "What have you done to deserve this, Sutherland?"

"It isn't what I've done," Patrick said. "It appears to be what I know. However, I cannot afford the time for a detailed explanation. I have something to do at the loch before I return to the house. Help me to clean up this mess before I go, and reassure Mrs. Forbes I am fine."

Sandy studied Patrick's black-streaked face. "If you say so, lad."

35

*A*nne paced on the path at the bottom of the garden. She was so on edge, she jumped every time she saw a glimmer of lightning in the distance. The storm was miles away. It wouldn't move down from the mountains for a day, if at all, but its dark energy had chilled the air, and she couldn't help thinking that it portended something evil.

Her heartbeat accelerated as she spotted Patrick shove open the garden gate, pausing to stare at her from the same spot where they had parted.

Grimly he walked through the shadows, releasing a profound sigh of relief when she stepped into view. Without a word, he gathered her into his arms and pressed her against his chest, absorbing her into the heat of his body, reassuring her with his presence. He was back. He was safe. They were together. He hadn't disappeared from her life this time—she was only fleetingly aware of that fear lurking behind her more logical thoughts.

She savored the bittersweet feelings that flooded
her. Then she tilted back her head and examined his
face, frowning at the streaks of dirt and ash. Her
voice caught. "I don't think I want to know where
you have been or what you've been doing."

He smiled, but she noticed that his facial muscles
didn't relax. "You probably don't."

"Is it all over?"

"I'm afraid not." He held her close, frowning
because she was standing outside without a wrap.
Her skin felt chilled, or perhaps he was still over-
heated from his brush with the fire. "Did anyone
return to the party in a disheveled state?"

"I wouldn't have noticed," she said, angry again
now. "I've been too worried about you."

"What about Sir Wallace?"

"The poor man has been standing on the terrace,
searching for me since I left the ballroom," she said.
"I hid from him in the garden. As far as I know, he
hasn't left the house."

"Good girl. What about Flora—did she behave in
a peculiar manner at all?"

"With Flora it's hard to tell," she replied. "But I
couldn't answer. I haven't dared to show my face in
the house since you left. No doubt everyone thinks
I've lost my mind after dancing in the garden with a
domestic. It is rather embarrassing to have the
neighborhood aware I'm carrying on with my
butler."

"But what a butler he is."

"You ought to ask Nellwyn about Flora's behavior," she said.

He glanced up at the house. "If Nellwyn is following my orders, she's upstairs at this very moment applying cosmetics to a corpse."

She gasped. "What?"

"Not a real corpse, Anne. It's Iain, Lord Murray's valet and a recent acquaintance of mine. He plays a rather crucial part in my plan, which I hope to unravel after I fulfill my duties at the ball."

Her eyes darkened with temper. "Do you mean to tell me you really did include Nellwyn in your scheme and left me completely out? You trusted that featherbrained old troublemaker over me? You left me here, worrying myself into a state?"

"Calm down, Anne, I wouldn't have trusted Nellwyn either if it hadn't been for the doctor's diagnosis. I felt sorry for her. She needed something to take her mind off her worries."

"What doctor?" she said, startled. "What diagnosis?"

He sighed. "The diagnosis that her heart is probably not strong enough to withstand another winter. One of the chambers appears to have some kind of problem."

"Are we talking about the doctor who diagnosed you with housemaid's knee?"

He flushed a little. "Aye. The same one. There is only one doctor in the damned parish."

"Doctor MacDonald did not give Nellwyn that diagnosis," Anne said. "The plumber did."

"The plumber?" he said in surprise.

"Yes. The plumber. He said that the pipes in her bedchamber weren't strong enough to withstand another winter. The doctor told her that, except for a touch of bursitis, she's as healthy as an ox. I know because I stayed in her room while he examined her. She slapped him because his hands were cold, then she complained that she hadn't had a hot bath since she came here, and that was why the bursitis in her shoulder had been acting up."

"So she isn't going to die?"

"Not from bad plumbing," Anne said, and then she turned her head as a group of guests called her name from the terrace.

She ducked behind a hedge. "We have to go inside, but not until we do something about your appearance. You look as if you've just swept a chimney."

He glanced down at the streaks of dirt on her dress. "You don't look as pristine as a snowdrop yourself, Lady Whitehaven. What were you doing while I was gone—digging a grave?"

"No. Pulling up dead foxgloves. Nellwyn said they cast a pall of evil over a house, and with everything that's happened, I didn't want to take any chances."

He straightened his doublet, then brushed off her dress before they fell into step together. "Stay away from Sir Wallace," he said. "I don't trust him."

She swallowed. "Because you think he's a murderer?"

"No. Because I think he's a walrus."

They paused at the circular marble fountain. "I'll go around the house and reenter the ballroom through the kitchen," he said quietly. "And don't expect to get rid of me for the rest of the night. I am not letting you out of my sight."

"Something awful *did* happen to you while I was waiting," she said, the fine hairs rising on her nape. "Does that mean Uncle Edgar really was murdered?"

He steered her back onto the pathway. "It means I met with an unanticipated complication, and someone doesn't want us to know how he died."

"Are you going to tell me what the next part of your plan is?" she called over her shoulder as they parted.

He gave her a wry grin. "I am going to serve tea and whiskey toddies, of course."

She hesitated on the steps of the terrace, afraid again of how this evening would end. She realized Patrick had managed to evade a proper explanation. Especially about what part a corpse would play in her party.

And when the killer, if there was one, would try to strike again.

Flora had seen a gray dog skulking at the bottom of Anne's driveway the night before. She'd known right away the animal had to be a *bochan*, a demon looking for mischief or revenge. She had been afraid to go to bed for fear it would bite her while she was sleeping. Or that she might awaken with cloven hooves.

In desperation she had rushed off to visit that horrible old hag Black Mag, but she had left the country. For an exorbitant fee, Mag's daughter had told

Flora that the only way to put a ghost to rest was to sprinkle soil from a sorcerer's grave on the place of his death. After the soil settled, Flora was to set a small fire to sanctify his spirit.

She had hurried home, digesting this information. The problem was, she didn't know of any sorcerer, dead or alive. The closest she had come to meeting such a powerful being was that Sutherland man.

She had returned to Black Mag's daughter, paid another small fortune, and came away with a pouch of dirt and lucifer matches, which seemed appropriately named for what she had in mind. Then she had sneaked away from Anne's party during the dancing, the social event of the season, and had returned to the boathouse where Lord Kingairn had died in her arms.

Flora had not been back to that disgusting place since his death. She was shaking with fright by the time she began to pitch soil through the doorway— she couldn't bring herself to take one step inside. Lord Kingairn had been kind to her and he had promised to marry her if he outlived his wife, which seemed likely, as her ladyship was in poor health. Flora had even convinced herself she loved him.

But she didn't want his dead body coming back to life as had the lovelorn ghost in that infamous novel by the DeWilde Brothers, *Confessions of a Scottish Corpse*. And when she had tossed the entire box of flaming matches into the boathouse, then nailed the door shut with three nails and her shoe for good measure, she had never expected, not in her worst nightmares, to hear her deceased lover actually coming to life from within.

She had panicked, her muscles paralyzed with a fear so intense she didn't know how she'd managed to run back to her horse.

She didn't know how she rode back to the party either, or why no one had noticed her absence, or the fact that her lips and fingernails had taken a blue tint of fright. She couldn't dance or enjoy the whiskey toddies that Anne's wicked butler served during the final reel.

The chilling thing was, she sensed that somehow he knew what she had been up to, as if he possessed a secret power to see into her soul. She nearly died when she looked into his eyes, and he stared at her until she began to shake.

Her father was absolutely useless too, focusing all his attention on Anne, who only had eyes for her butler. Flora drank two toddies in a row and hid in the draperies in a haze of detached anxiety.

Somehow she allowed herself to be pulled along in the crowd of guests who piled into carts and drove to the loch. Somehow she found herself staring down the little pier, waiting with a fishing rod to embark. But when her turn came, she spotted that most unlucky of omens, a white pebble, at the bottom of her boat.

Her stomach contracted, and she knew this was a sign that the end was near. No one seemed to notice her silent misery. Nor did they notice when she finally turned and sneaked off the pier to cower in the stand of larch trees that bordered the shore.

No one noticed her strange behavior except the man whose giant figure loomed above the others in the torchlight.

36

$\mathcal{S}$ir Wallace mentally rehearsed his speech. He had tucked his late wife's engagement ring into his vest pocket. Despite what Flora believed, he did not think of Anne as a vengeful woman. He saw her as an angel who would restore his social status and sexual life, a companion for his twilight years, someone who shared his passion for horses.

Anne would probably think he was the most romantic man in the world, asking for her hand on a misty torchlit loch, which was a far more memorable setting than the ballroom. The story of their engagement would likely reach the Queen, and Sir Wallace would be acknowledged at court, for all things Scottish seemed to be in favor.

Perhaps he and Anne would even have a child together. They were both young enough, and in good health. Perhaps Anne could take Flora in hand, and—

"Excuse me, Sir Wallace," a dark voice said in his ear. "I do believe you have taken my seat."

Sir Wallace's fantasy deflated as the broad-shouldered figure of Anne's butler climbed into the boat. "What do you think you are doing now?" he asked indignantly.

Patrick settled down in the confined space. "Didn't her ladyship tell you? I was a gamekeeper before I became a butler. I wouldn't consider allowing Lady Whitehaven to fish unassisted for a second. Why, her delicate white fingers could never touch anything as offensive as a trout."

Sir Wallace turned several shades of purple. "You cannot accompany her ladyship and me tonight. I have plans of a personal nature."

"In a rowboat? You sly old devil. But it's a bit cramped for seduction, don't you think?"

"Not those sort of plans, you impertinent bugger," Sir Wallace retorted, patting his vest pocket. "I have *plans*—to make your mistress a permanent part of my family."

"You're going to adopt Anne? Well, well. I hope you're not waiting for me to congratulate you. She'll most likely laugh in your face."

Sir Wallace leaned forward. "Then do me the courtesy of removing yourself from this boat so that she can laugh at me in private."

"Too late." Patrick gestured to Anne waving at them from the end of the pier. "There's our little orphan now."

"Get out," Sir Wallace said, giving Patrick a shove.

Patrick did not budge, except when he half rose to help Anne down the ladder into the boat. "Sir Wallace has special plans for you tonight, my lady," he said under his breath, gripping her arm to steady her.

"Not another plan," she whispered.

The bog-fir torches mounted on the boat procession cast black-gold shadows on the loch. She went still as she felt Patrick's hand slide down her arm to her back in a gesture that was blatantly possessive. The sexual heat of their dance in the garden still shimmered between them; they had shared too many intimacies to forget. They knew too well what their flirtation could lead to.

"Be careful," he said as he handed her down into her seat.

She grasped his hand before they separated. "And you."

"Must he accompany us, Anne?" Sir Wallace said in a disgruntled voice when she greeted him.

"Just pretend I'm not here," Patrick said, and then he rendered such a suggestion impossible by positioning himself directly between them like a human wall.

Anne craned her neck to see around Patrick's shoulders. "He is rather a nuisance, Sir Wallace, I agree. But I find myself at a loss as to how to handle him."

Sir Wallace sighed. "This is most off-putting, Anne. What I have to say requires the utmost privacy."

"It's a rare woman who can keep a secret from her butler," Patrick said.

Anne nudged his foot. "Row, Sutherland. Don't talk. We shall never catch anything if we sit at the pier. Besides, everyone is waiting for our boat to take the lead."

The boat sliced through the still water, soon followed by a string of others. The surface of the loch shone with the radiance of lanterns and torches mounted on each craft. Along the hillside, where the burn spilled into deep stony pools, some of the younger guests had broken tradition to spear fish and to steal kisses in the dark.

Mist drifted across the loch, and the laughter of the young people in the trees gave a fairylike magic to the party. A pair of fiddlers playing on the hill enhanced the ethereal mood.

"Tomorrow is St. Michael's day." Sir Wallace attempted to look around Patrick to Anne. "It would be nice to announce a betrothal during the feast and then celebrate it with a blessing at kirk."

"I believe Lady Whitehaven already has plans for tomorrow afternoon," Patrick said.

"I do?" Anne said, arching her brow.

Dark humor danced in his eyes. "Yes, my lady." Then he mouthed, "In my bed."

"Anne?" Sir Wallace said. "Is that true? Do you have a previous engagement that cannot be put off?"

She shrugged, trailing her fingers in the water, so aware of Patrick she wasn't listening to anything the other man said. She was hopeless. She had fallen in love with her rogue all over again. "I don't know," she answered.

"Then the evening before the horse races," Sir Wallace said, sounding aggrieved. "Will that do, Anne?"

"Will it do what?" she murmured, blinking as if she had been asleep.

Sir Wallace frowned, unable to see through Patrick's shoulders. "What did you say? I cannot hear you over the creaking of those oarlocks and those deuced fiddlers."

"She said that she's busy then too," Patrick replied, leaning harder into the oarlocks to create more noise.

"Why are you splashing so much, Sutherland?" Anne said, looking up in annoyance. "You're getting us wet and frightening off the fish."

"I am talking about holy matrimony," Sir Wallace said in a louder voice. "I am proposing—"

Patrick plunged the oars practically to the bottom of the loch, shooting the small craft forward like a firecracker. Anne gave a squeal of surprise and grabbed her fishing rod before it bounced off her lap.

"You damned idiot!" Sir Wallace said. "Do you not understand the significance of this occasion?" He released a breath and scooted all the way to the end of his seat, attempting to speak to Anne through Patrick. "I want you to be my bride—the circumstances are hardly what I pictured, but one does what one can." He clapped his hand to his heart. "I am asking you to marry me."

"That's very flattering," Patrick said, leaning all the way to the left to block the man's view. "Lurid, but flattering. I, however, have no wish to be your bride. It's bad enough being a butler."

"Not you, you blasted nodcock!" Sir Wallace shouted. "Was I talking to you?"

Patrick shrugged. "It looked as if you were."

"Would you two like to continue this conversation in private?" Anne inquired tartly. "Perhaps you could let me out on the bank where all the trout have probably taken refuge."

Several boats bumped past them. Lord and Lady Grierson. Lord and Lady Murray, and the Misses Cameron, who giggled when they saw Patrick and raised their fishing rods to him in greeting.

"I believe we are causing another scene," Anne said with a sigh.

Patrick half rose from the boat, his hand lifted to signal to the man standing on the hill. "As far as scenes go, you have not seen anything yet, Lady Whitehaven. Watch this."

At first no one thought anything of the unoccupied rowboat that drifted into the stream of traffic. The other guests were intent on catching the big-boned trout that thrived in the loch, and the rowboat looked like all the others, except that it did not carry a torch.

It was Nellwyn who drew attention to the phantom vessel. Emitting a high-pitched shriek from her own boat, she stood and gestured in horror to the ghostlike figure that rose from the empty rowboat. She was determined to play her part with all the energy she could muster.

"It's Edgar!" She had difficulty making herself heard above the fiddlers on the hill, the only flaw in Patrick's plan. "Dear God in heaven, Lord Kingairn's shade has risen from the grave on the anniversary of his murder to avenge his death!"

"What is she saying?" one of the guests asked.

"Something about celebrating her anniversary," another answered.

Then, with dramatic flair, Patrick raised his lantern to illuminate the dead man's spirit, which was actually Iain moaning in the boat and lifting his arm in an accusing circle around the loch. Finally, after an apparent interval of confusion, the spirit gestured to the woman standing alone on the shore. Flora Abermuir. She stared at the apparition, then spun and ran away. Patrick steered the boat back toward the pier. "Ladies and gentlemen, here we go."

Fortunately for Anne, who had no idea how she would explain any of this to her guests, Iain got carried away and tripped over a big bucket in the rowboat. He toppled into the loch before anyone in the fishing party realized he was meant to be a ghost. His rice powder and rouge washed off before he reached the shore. He ended up looking more like an inebriated guest who could not hold his liquor than an avenging phantom.

But the one person who was intended to believe him to be a resurrected spirit did. The person involved in Lord Kingairn's death saw him clearly from her vantage point between the trees, and nothing could convince her he had not risen from the dead to accuse her.

Flora let out a wail of panic and covered her face in her hands. When she finally saw Patrick with Anne and her papa hurrying toward her, she was ready to confess to everything.

"It was my fault," she said, shaking all over. She leaned up against a tree. She had all but collapsed with the burden of guilt she had carried for a year.

Sir Wallace pulled her into his arms and shook her. "Do not say anything, Flora. Do not say another word."

"Why not?" She raised her anguished face to his. "He is haunting me, Papa. I can't live with myself another day. Not with a death on my conscience."

"You almost had two murders to account for," Patrick said behind her. "I might have believed you were genuinely sorry about Edgar if you hadn't tried to burn me to death just a few hours ago."

Anne looked up at him in shock. "She tried to kill you?"

Flora pulled away from her father's arms. "I have no idea what you're talking about," she said in horror. "I've never tried to harm you in any way. Lady Whitehaven, you must believe me."

"I saw you running away from the boathouse after you set a damned bonfire," Patrick exclaimed.

"But I didn't know *you* were inside," Flora said, her face gray as she shook her head. "I had no idea."

Sir Wallace regarded her in despair. "Setting fire to a boathouse is not an act of a normal mind, Flora. What in God's name were you thinking?"

She scrubbed her face with her fist. "Everyone

said that Lord Kingairn's ghost would rise tonight in the very spot where he drew his last breath. Well, the truth, as you know, is that he did not die fishing in a rowboat. He died naked in the boathouse in the act of making passionate love to me. His heart expired from the strain."

Anne closed her eyes. "Dear Lord. I shall never be able to explain *that* to the Queen."

"You did not kill him," Patrick said. "But you did drag his body into the rowboat instead of leaving him where he was."

Flora sniffed. "Papa didn't want the world to know I was engaged in an adulterous affair with a nobleman. He believed it would destroy my chances of making a decent marriage."

"The world certainly knows of it now," Sir Wallace said, motioning to Nellwyn, who had walked up behind Anne.

"I wasn't trying to kill you," Flora told Patrick. "I was trying to purify Lord Kingairn's spirit and lay him to rest once and for all."

"It sounds to me as if you already did lay him to rest," Nellwyn said. "Permanently."

"How did you know Uncle Edgar had died in the boathouse?" Anne asked Patrick.

He shrugged. "I *didn't* know. I deduced that something was not quite right about his death. First, Sandy once mentioned that Uncle Edgar had forgotten his favorite fishing rod, and a man who loves to fish never forgets his best fishing rod."

"He should have left his other rod at home too," Nellwyn observed.

Patrick paused. "Then Iain, my valet friend, recalled gossip that his employer's gillie had seen suspicious activity on the pier an hour or so before the party. A man who was drunk, he thought."

"The drunk being Uncle Edgar," Anne said softly.

"Who wasn't drunk but dead," Nellwyn added. "This was the same rumor I had heard."

Flora gave a moan of grief. "I didn't kill him. I loved him." She looked up at Patrick, her eyes filling with fresh tears. "And even though I hate you, I would not harm you."

"I would," Sir Wallace said.

"I wasn't trying to set Sutherland on fire in the boathouse," Flora insisted. "I was afraid to go inside to confront Edgar's spirit in case he was angry at me. So I stood outside and threw soil from a sorcerer's grave onto the mattress and set a fire to purify his soul. Then I nailed the door shut with my shoe so his ghost couldn't chase me in case I failed to lay him."

"Where did you get soil from a sorcerer's grave?" Nellwyn asked curiously.

"From Black Mag's wagon," Patrick said. "I noticed a jar labeled F.A. a few days after the fair when I returned to question the gypsy about the accuracy of her predictions. Anne was upset and I wanted to reassure her that such predictions are nonsense. Black Mag was not there, her daughter was, but the jar set me to thinking."

"That wasn't soil from a sorcerer's grave," Flora said. "That was teeth-whitening powder. I bought the soil from Mag's daughter after you started spreading the word that Edgar was coming back from the grave. At least, I assume it was you."

"Did the tooth-powder work?" Nellwyn asked.

"I don't know," Flora admitted. "I never got a chance to try it."

"Did you hire Janet to write a threatening message on the mirror with a sausage?" Anne asked.

"A sausage?" Flora blinked in astonishment. "I never told her to use a sausage."

Patrick frowned. "But you did engage her to threaten Anne?"

Flora bit her lip. "To my shame, yes, I did. But I only wanted her to go away. I was afraid she would find out the truth."

Anne glanced at Patrick, wondering if he found it as difficult as she did to condemn Flora.

"It was an ingenious plan, Patrick," Nellwyn said. "I was proud to play a part in it."

"Ingenious?" Anne said. "He might have been burned to death, or he might have shot Flora in self-defense."

"I'm ready to accept my punishment," Flora said. "I saw the warrant for my arrest on your desk this morning, Papa."

"That wasn't a warrant, Flora," he said. "It was an invitation to Anne's party. It came over a week ago."

"I know what will happen," Flora went on, clearly imagining the worst. "A sheriff's officer will seize me during church tomorrow. I shall be arrested and taken to the Justice Clerk. The jury, finding me young, beautiful and in control of my senses, will show no mercy."

Nobody said anything for a long time. Then Sir Wallace walked over to the boathouse and knelt, sifting through the debris. "Good Lord, look at this," he said. "I've found a flintlock pistol. An ebony inlaid piece. If—"

"It belongs to me," Patrick said, holding out his hand. "I dropped it when the fire broke out. Allow me to take it from you, sir."

Sir Wallace pursed his lips, standing to face Patrick. "I do not think that is wise."

"I don't give a damn what you think," Patrick said.

"*Sutherland*," Anne said.

"Sir," Patrick said, softening his manner. "Give me the gun. The fact is that I am the most qualified person in this group to handle a firearm."

"A pistol is hardly a pastry," Sir Wallace retorted.

"Quite so," Patrick said. "I was, however, an officer in the 71st Light Highland Infantry before I became a butler."

Sir Wallace looked stunned. "Bloody hell, Anne, is this man the biggest liar in Christendom?"

"No, Wallace." She vented a sigh. "I regret to say he is telling the truth."

37

A light drizzle began to fall over the loch. Most of the guests were too intent on fishing to think anything of Anne's absence. Sir Wallace located a plaid and a bottle of whiskey to settle Flora against a tree. She was exhausted from her ordeal, and it had been a job to quiet her down.

"Well," Nellwyn said, "whatever are we going to tell the Queen?"

Patrick placed his hand on Anne's shoulder. For once she did not resist. "We shall explain that Lord Kingairn died of natural causes, which is the truth. There is nothing more to add."

Anne looked back at Sir Wallace, gently stroking his daughter's face. "We would never be able to obtain a conviction. Of course, a case could be made that she moved Edgar's body. But I cannot imagine a jury indicting her for murder because a man died during—well, you know."

"In the act, Anne," Nellwyn said, shaking her head.

"There was no wicked intent," Patrick said. "Only greed and stupidity."

"It would be hard to convict her of simple human stupidity," Nellwyn said. "Let her wait until the Great Day of Judgment."

"We shall all be accountable then," Patrick said piously.

Anne looked him in the eye. "Some of us more than others."

Sir Wallace returned to the small group, his face haggard, his manner one of profound dejection. "I suppose everyone in the parish realizes what has occurred by now."

"I doubt it," Patrick said, not pleased when Anne moved away from him. "I made particularly potent toddies for a reason. Everyone is probably too numb to have noticed anything amiss."

"Lady Tarbet noticed that embarrassing business between you and Sir Wallace on the boat," Nellwyn said, as if there hadn't been enough trouble for one night. "A rumor is circulating that Wallace asked you to be his bride."

"Aye, but I didn't accept," Patrick replied, giving the man a fleeting grin, which Sir Wallace patently ignored.

Anne shivered as a thin wind blew up on the loch, dispersing the mist. A few raindrops splattered on the ground. "It looks as if the storm is coming down from the mountains, after all."

"What about Uncle Edgar's missing money?"

Nellwyn asked Sir Wallace. "Were you blackmailing him, Wallace?"

"Indeed not. From what Flora tells me, he lavished her with expensive gifts to prove he intended to set her up in London as his mistress." Sir Wallace's shoulders slumped in defeat. "I shall, of course, make sure that every penny is repaid into his wife's account even if I have to hire myself out as a laborer."

"Well, I certainly hope you'll use more discretion than you did out there on the loch with Sutherland," Nellwyn said. "I do not want one word of this to reach Lady Kingairn. The woman shall mourn her husband in peace."

"You're shivering, Anne," Patrick said. "Let me take you home."

"What about my guests?" she asked. "And the prize for the biggest fish? It really will look peculiar if I disappear in the midst of my own party."

"I shall stay and oversee everything," Nellwyn said, pulling her old-fashioned arasaid around her thin shoulders. "It's not as if I haven't done it before. Wallace—" She turned to the other man, whose lost expression had touched everyone in the group. "Take Flora back to the house and get her into a warm bed. Things will look better in the morning."

He lifted his forlorn gaze to Anne. "Will you ever find it in your heart to forgive us, my dear?"

"Don't say anything more of it," she said. "Just take Flora away before we're forced to explain what is wrong with her."

He took her advice; Anne, Patrick, and Nellwyn walked slowly across the pebbly shore toward the pier. Anne managed to wave at her guests as if all was well, although she felt bone-weary and wanted nothing more than to crawl into bed and fall into a deep dreamless sleep.

"Did you know what had happened all along?" she asked Patrick.

He stared across the loch and waved to Iain, who was on the hill, drying himself off with a plaid. "No, I did not. I was fortunate my hunch paid off. At one point I even suspected Flora might have bought an herbal potion from Black Mag that killed Uncle Edgar."

"Poison?" Anne asked, clearly shaken.

He glanced at her. "Actually, I was thinking more of a love potion. Even seemingly harmless herbs can damage the liver and heart, causing death. The doctor's autopsy, however, did not support this suspicion."

Anne looked back at the charred remains of the boathouse. "What a disgraceful way for Uncle Edgar to expire," she murmured.

Nellwyn stomped her half-boots on the pebbles in an apparent attempt to get warm. "Disgraceful, nothing. I would not mind going in such a manner myself."

"Neither would I, Auntie Nellwyn," Patrick said, grinning in agreement.

Anne and Patrick climbed the winding staircase of Balgeldie House in silence. When they approached the door to Anne's room, she noticed that he was limping. She smiled gently.

"Housemaid's knee acting up again?"

He grimaced. "It's killing me." He didn't try to touch her, which she thought was odd. "Well, your revenge is complete, Anne."

She wondered why he hadn't kissed her. The house was practically empty, although in another hour or so, guests would be parading all about, slamming doors or ordering snacks and hot water for a wash.

"I never wanted revenge," she said, shaking her head. "Not really."

"Then what did you want?" he asked, his eyes sad.

"I'm not sure. Redemption, perhaps."

"For you or me?"

"For us both." She hesitated, leaning back against the door. "I suppose I wanted to go back in time and make peace with my parents."

"I can't give you that," he said quietly. "But you could forgive me—and yourself. If we can find compassion for Flora and Uncle Edgar, surely we can rise above our own mistakes. We were so very young, and—"

He broke off, distracted by what sounded like a muffled gasp behind him. Mrs. Forbes and Gracie stood at the top of the staircase, gawking at them over an armload of fresh linens. There was really no way to explain the situation—so neither he nor Anne tried.

"Oh, no," Anne whispered, ducking inside her room. "This is too embarrassing."

Patrick glanced back at the two female servants, gracing them with his infamous grin. And then, to their scandalized disbelief, he followed Anne right into her bedchamber, chuckling as he closed the door.

Anne did not know where she found the nerve, some of Nellwyn's audacity must have rubbed off on her, but she went about her nightly routine as if Patrick weren't there. She pulled off her rain-spotted taffeta and donned a sturdy flannel nightdress. She brushed her hair one hundred times. She even brushed her teeth and wondered aloud if Black Mag's tooth-whitening powder really worked.

"If you don't agree to be my wife," Patrick said behind her, "I intend to walk out of this room and never return."

She rubbed the washcloth over her face. "This is hardly the time for an ultimatum."

"Nevertheless, that is what this is. Marry me, Anne. It is what you need. Nellwyn knows that."

"Does she indeed?" she said dryly.

He moved to face her, his gaze serious. "I've decided it would be best if I go away. I might write to you in a few months to see if you have reconsidered. I don't know what else to do."

When she did not respond, he turned away, his gigantic figure outlined in the fire's glow. Suddenly Anne wanted to touch him. She ached to feel his powerful arms wrapped around her, to feel his hands in her hair. She knew the texture of his skin, his scent, the unspeakable thrill of sex with him.

And yet she could not move. Something inside her still needed to test his love, even if it meant she might lose him forever.

"I'm leaving," he said, "and I don't hear you asking me to stay. This is your last chance."

He started toward the inner door. Anne put her cloth down on the washstand, not saying anything as the cold fear of never seeing him again began to sink into her awareness.

"Are you serious?" she said.

"This is my final plea. Never again will I serve tea to your friends."

"Now that's a blessing in disguise."

He dredged up a smile. "Farewell, Lady Whitehaven. I hope you'll manage by yourself in the morning. I have to admit it has been a pain in the arse serving you."

The coldness moved through her system, turning her legs into blocks of lead. He was bluffing. He had to be. She watched as he vanished into the closet that adjoined their rooms, expecting him to return. Or perhaps he was waiting for her to go to bed before he sneaked back into her room.

She extinguished the lamp and crawled under the bedcovers, wishing she had asked for a warming pan. Wishing that she could burrow up against Patrick's big body, that she could bring herself to believe him and pick up the pieces of their broken past.

She stayed awake until she heard all her guests settle into their beds. She listened for sounds from the room next to hers. Was that a drawer being pulled out, a wardrobe opened? Was he really packing to leave the next day? Could she live with this cold loneliness if he went away? She would never feel like this about another man again.

The wind banged against the tower, and she huddled into her bed. As a child she had always been afraid of the storm witches in the mountains, of the mischief they might wreak. Her father had threatened to take her to them whenever she misbehaved. But the scare that settled into her bones now had nothing to do with the supernatural, and she realized what she had to do, even if she lived to regret it.

38

$\mathcal{P}$atrick knew he had to be dreaming. There was no way on earth that Anne had crawled into bed beside him and was undulating her nude body around his. He was starting to wake up from the dream, however. Rather, a certain part of his body was starting to rise in alarming degrees as the dream-vision Anne hooked her arms around his hips and sent her fingers on a very risqué exploration of his nether parts.

Her nipples brushed back and forth across his shoulder blades. She cradled his genitals in her small hands. Then the dream-vision Anne nibbled his neck while simultaneously stroking his rod. His stones contracted with a pleasure that was painful. He opened his eyes and stared down at the delicate fingers that were driving him wild.

"Oh, my God," he groaned, rolling over as he came fully awake. "It *is* you."

She smiled into his sleepy face. "You were expect-ing Mrs. Forbes, perhaps?"

"That was last night." He scratched his bare chest and drew an uneven breath. His entire body was burning with excitement.

"Lady Murray then?" she teased, her fingers still manipulating his shaft.

"You were taking advantage of me." Pleasure lit up his face. "You were fondling my sleeping body."

"Are you complaining, Sutherland?"

"Me? Good God, no. Assault me to your heart's content." He stretched back onto the bed, his body a flat plane except for the prominent ridge of mus-cle that rose between her hands.

"Close your eyes," she whispered. "You make me feel self-conscious."

He obeyed, his breathing uneven. He had to bite his tongue to keep from climaxing on the sheets; he hadn't been with a woman in an eter-nity, and Anne's mere touch was enough to melt his bones.

"I knew you wouldn't let me go," he murmured. "However, I will say the way you chose to admit defeat was a nice surprise."

"Defeat." She leaned down, her long curls cover-ing his chest. "You just hadn't given me notice. I demand my money's worth from my servants."

He brought his hands up to her hips and rolled her beneath him. "Admit it." He kissed the tip of her nose. "I won."

"No."

"No?" He arched his brow, nudging her legs apart

as easily as if he was separating the fragile wings of a butterfly.

"Well. No."

He brushed his mouth back and forth across hers, stopping only when she was breathless. "No?" He grinned playfully, his eyes searching her face.

"Hmmm."

She realized suddenly that the tables had turned. Awake and in control, aware of his potent male appeal, he had the upper hand, and he used it to his advantage.

He moved from her mouth to her throat, leaving tiny love bites to mark his territory. He spent endless minutes suckling her breasts. She was aware of a trembling that began somewhere deep in her belly, a sensation she recognized as sexual anticipation.

"Relax, Anne," he said, stroking gently up and down her spine, and if she'd paid closer attention, she would have realized his hand was trembling too. "If I know David, lovemaking was probably an obligation."

She could have hit him for guessing the truth. She had never reached a climax with David, he'd have fainted in her arms if she had even said the word. Still, a woman had to create some mystery about her, she had to keep some secrets, and it wouldn't hurt for Patrick to suffer a few more pangs of jealousy, to wonder what he'd missed all those years.

Yes, lovemaking with David had never been, well, it hadn't been any Guy Fawkes fireworks display. It had been more like two ships that bumped together in the night, and not very often either. In fact, it was not remarkable that their few matings had never produced a child.

But Patrick didn't need to know that. Let him think that she and David held nightly Roman orgies. He hadn't lived as a monk all those years.

"You'd be surprised," she said. "You should have seen some of the positions he found in those books from India."

It was the wrong thing to say, a torch passed under the nose of a sleeping tiger. Over six feet of solid muscle and sinew uncoiled and pinned her to the bed. She could barely twitch a muscle, shackled from wrist to ankle by one fully aroused and angry male.

"Everything about you is my business."

"Well, I'm hardly in a position to argue, am I?"

He grinned slowly. "No, but it's a position you'd better get used to, and you'll have to admit it does have its advantages."

She caught her breath. He had lifted his weight from her body, but she still couldn't move except to give a helpless shiver.

"Anne," he said, lowering his mouth to hers. "My beloved. I don't need a book to make love to you, or have you really forgotten?"

She wound her arms around his neck and brought him down on top of her again. "Show me, Sutherland."

It was the right thing to say.

"This time it really will be different." He kissed her tenderly. "This time sleeping together means an absolute commitment of body and soul. You have a right to expect my protection and fidelity forever."

Her eyes shone with mischief. "And in return I promise I shall never ring for you again."

"At least not before seven o'clock in the morning. But I was expecting more than that, Anne. I was thinking that in return you would be willing to fulfill my deepest, darkest desires."

"I'm not sure I like the sound of that, Sutherland. How deep and dark *are* those desires?"

"Nothing that you couldn't satisfy. More deep than dark."

She thought she should resist to prove a point, but she didn't. Not when his hand brushed the curls at the cleft of her sex, and she wanted more, to show him finally how she felt.

"Now, Anne?"

"Aye, now," she whispered, hiding her face in his chest as his wicked fingers worked their magic, and she gave herself to him.

He accepted her gift, closing his eyes as emotion overcame him. "You won't be sorry. I swear it."

She moaned softly as he concentrated on pleasing her. She had never experienced such enjoyment, not even during their encounter in the past. Her body was ripe for sex, sensations burgeoning, so primal she was almost ashamed of them. She had forgotten how good he could make her feel.

"Anne." He sighed as she climaxed against his hand, tremors running through her small body. "My love," he whispered. "Mine at last."

She thought she would never stop shaking, and

she lay suspended in anticipation as he penetrated her, pressing slowly inside. The sense of fullness, the pressure nearly brought her off the bed again, but he held her down until she relaxed. He kissed her and told her he loved her. Then she felt herself stretching to accept him, and even though she knew he was being careful not to hurt her, she gasped with the power of his entry, surrendering her whole self at last, stronger in her submission than she had even been before.

"Perfect," he whispered.

She didn't move. She was too afraid, too excited, until he began to thrust, and instinct took over. He drove so deeply inside her that they almost fell off the bed. Vaguely she was grateful that the thunderstorm masked the sound of their lovemaking. Someone had to hear the bed hitting the wall. Someone had to hear the soft moans she could not control.

"I want to come inside you," he said roughly.

Her body wasn't her own. It was his, and she felt his invasion to the tip of her womb, she felt him not only taking but giving of himself. Deprived of him for too long, she craved even more, exploring the hard beauty of his body with her hands. She could not seem to get close enough. She gripped his hips, clasping him to her.

He shuddered, kissing her deeply. "Aye, keep touching me like that."

He paused. Then he impaled her to the hilt, and she couldn't remember what he had just said. She couldn't even take a breath, aware of only him and the bond between them that neither time nor circumstance had broken.

"Open your legs wider." he said, and she did, although such a thing seemed impossible. Surely he could not drive any deeper. She was already spread out beneath him like an offering, and he possessed her, making up for all the years lost in one night with such energy he would surely end up killing them both.

"Raise your arms," he instructed her. When she did, he caught her wrists in one hand and imprisoned her, interlacing their fingers so that when they came together, he was holding her, souls connected, soaring toward the sky.

For the longest time they lay joined together, arms and legs entangled as if by moving they would return to the world they had escaped. Then gradually their breathing returned to normal as they listened to the rain batter the old tower. Anne felt cherished and complete, even though the storm witches had won another round, stirring up a wicked love spell in their cauldron, which was said to be a fathomless loch hidden in the mountains.

"I won't be afraid of them ever again," she thought aloud. "They've done their absolute worst."

"Who?" he said idly, stroking her arm. "Wallace and Flora?"

She smiled. "No."

"Are you cold?" he whispered.

"Are you?"

"Hell, no." He wrapped his arms around her hips, smothering her in Sutherland. "I do love you."

"I know."

"Well?"

"Well, what?" she teased.

"Well, how about, 'I love you too, Patrick. I always have. I've been waiting seven lonely years for this night, but you, my lord, you were certainly worth the wait.' "

"All right."

"Damnation, woman, is that the best you can do?"

"I love you, Patrick," she said dutifully. "I always have. I've been waiting seven years—"

"—seven *lonely* years."

"I've been waiting seven lonely years for this night, but you, my lord, well, you certainly throw around your weight."

He frowned at her. "Thank you verra much."

"You're verra welcome."

He glanced up as a gust of wind hit the window. "The cold weather is coming, and we have a wedding to plan. I think we ought to ask Nellwyn to help."

"I agree," Anne said. "It would give her something to do besides meddling in murders."

"We could be married in London, or here, or Hampshire. I don't care where as long as I can call you my wife within a reasonable period. How does the next two hours sound?"

She laughed. "Oh, Patrick. Do you know what I really want?"

"You insatiable woman."

"Not that. I want a pot of tea. Strong and hot and maybe even laced with brandy. I don't think I can face all those guests without something to fortify me."

He nodded vaguely. "Good idea."

"Patrick?"

He had closed his eyes, pretending not to notice the glimmer of gray light creeping into the room. "Hmmm?"

"You have to fetch that tea. You cannot simply quit serving as my butler."

"What?" He sat up, naked, aroused, and indignant. "Why not?"

"Well, we cannot explain the real reason you were posing as a servant without exposing Flora's part in Edgar's death, and we've all agreed that it's pointless to bring his wife unnecessary pain."

"Am I supposed to masquerade as your menial for the rest of that woman's life?"

"Not quite." She burrowed into him like a small animal, not only to seek his body warmth but to cover the enormous grin on her face. "Probably just for another year or so—"

"Another year of sneaking about in the dark?" he said in disbelief. "Are you serious?"

"Oh, aye." She burst into helpless laughter.

"Woman," he said softly, biting her shoulder, "we've wasted so much time."

He touched her face. Tears of joy stung her eyes, and even though she too was sorry for all the time they had lost, she couldn't regret what they had become or the lessons they had learned, or even the tender memories she had shared with another man.

"Patrick," she whispered, stunned by the thought, "what if I get pregnant?"

"Oh, you will." His voice was a confident purr.

"Black Mag stands by the power of her prophecies, or your money returned in full."

They dressed in separate rooms for the last time. Patrick put on his butler's costume for the last time. When they stepped out into the hallway, from separate rooms, they grinned at each other, then went their separate ways, Anne flying down the front staircase, Patrick clumping down the back for his final tour of domestic service, just like any other mistress and servant.

Except that for a moment before they parted, the butler pulled the lady back into his arms and kissed her passionately right in the middle of the hall where anyone could have seen them, then gave her an affectionate pat on the derrière before continuing on his way.

Nellwyn lifted her brow when Anne finally joined the rest of her guests at the breakfast table. "How nice of you to make an appearance, Anne. Another active night?"

Anne heaped her plate at the sideboard with an enormous amount of bacon, eggs, toast, scones, and marmalade, leaving only the sausages. "Indeed, it was," she said, grinning shamelessly.

Nellwyn chuckled. Sir Wallace did not, regarding Anne across the table with resignation. Flora was not present. Anne heard one of the footmen mentioning that Miss Abermuir had gone to church, which was probably where Anne herself should be.

"And where is our big cheeky butler, Anne?" Lady Delaney inquired.

Anne lowered her fork, horrified to feel herself blushing. "He's—"

"Right here. Right here. Hold on to your wig." And Patrick rattled into the room with a fresh urn of tea and pot of coffee, winking boldly at Anne.

She blushed again.

"Is that the Michaelmas cake?" someone asked, pointing to the triangular object on the tray.

"It certainly is," Patrick said, maneuvering to the sideboard.

"Well, I'll have some," Lord Delaney said.

"Then wait your turn," Patrick retorted, shocking everyone present by pouring himself a cup of coffee.

Anne simply shook her head. "How am I ever going to explain that I'm marrying the man? That it is possible I am bearing the butler's child?"

Nellwyn patted her shoulder. "I've already thought of that. We shall simply say that Patrick lost a bet and had to pose as a servant for a month. It's the sort of thing everyone will appreciate. After all, in my day, we used to wager our—"

Anne shook her head. "Do not say it, Auntie Nellwyn."

"When might this wedding take place?" Nellwyn asked.

Anne sighed. "As soon as possible—for propriety's sake. I assume you will want to help in the planning."

"Naturally," Nellwyn murmured, averting her face to hide a triumphant grin. "I hope, however, you arrange to hold it before November. I have plans of my own to travel to France."

"France? How pleasant."

Nellwyn nodded. "With Flora. I have friends among some very well-connected families who are always begging me to visit." She paused as Anne took a sip of tea, then leaned forward to whisper, "We're going on a manhunt. I have already concocted the most brilliant scheme to bring her back into Society."

The staff had taken the news about Sutherland's true identity very well, considering. Mrs. Forbes claimed she had always known, but felt obligated to keep his lordship's secret. Sandy just snorted, then went about his business—the butler could have been Prince Albert for all it affected him. Gracie asked Patrick for a raise, which he agreed she deserved, and life began to return to normal belowstairs at Balgeldie House.

Sir Wallace waited until everyone else left the room before he cornered Patrick at the sideboard. "I should like a word with you, Sutherland."

Patrick looked down into the older man's face. This could not be an easy time for him. "There's no need to apologize for your daughter's actions, sir. Nor to ask me to keep the affair a secret. Discretion is my password."

"I realize that, Sutherland," Sir Wallace said gruffly. "It's one of the things I admire about you. In fact, I have come to admire quite a few things about you. That is why I'm about to make you a proposition."

Patrick nearly fell into the fire. "Oh, hell. You aren't going to ask me to be your bride again, are you?"

Sir Wallace burst into laughter. "You incorrigible rogue. I do love that wicked wit."

"You do?"

"Indeed, I do," Sir Wallace said heartily, "and that's why I'm making you this offer. You see, I may have lost Anne, but the fact is, she's only a woman, and there's plenty of them to be had, if you know what I mean. Do you?"

"Not exactly," Patrick said politely, wondering what the devil he had gotten himself into now.

"Well, it's like this, Sutherland. You were a soldier, and a damned fine one before you became a butler, if I take my guess, so a man can feel protected in your presence. You were a gamekeeper and a groom, which means you'd make a knowledgeable partner for shooting, or even if a man chose to travel to China, for that matter."

"China?" Patrick said in a startled voice.

"Or Siam," Sir Wallace continued. "And you have connections at court, which can't hurt either of us. Now we both know the bit about being a viscount is pure balderdash, but you're obviously well-versed in the social graces."

Patrick crossed his arms over his chest. "What the bloody hell are you saying, Wallace?"

"I'm saying if I can't have Anne, I'll go one better," Sir Wallace retorted. "I'll have her butler. How much, Sutherland? Just name your price. I shall double whatever she is paying you. I've stayed up all night thinking about this. You give new meaning to the phrase 'gentleman's gentleman.' "

"I'm very honored, sir," Patrick said. "However—"

"—he's not to be stolen," Anne said from the doorway, a devilish sparkle in her eyes. "I lost him once before, you see, Wallace, and I am not letting him go again."

Epilogue

*A*nne sat in bed nursing her newborn daughter Mary Nellwyn while Patrick read aloud letters of congratulations from his desk. The window of their gray-stone residence was opened to the salty summer air of the Portobello sea, a posh watering resort near Edinburgh. They could hear the cheerful sounds of Sandy digging in the garden, the murmuring of gentle waves, and Gracie singing down the hall as she worked.

"Auntie Nellwyn sends her love," he said, his chiseled face amused. "And she brags that her hunt has been an unparalleled success."

Anne nuzzled the top of the baby's head. "She's found a husband for Flora?"

"No. For herself. A count from a very old Norman family." He chuckled, leaving his chair to join Anne on the bed, and for several minutes, he held her, happier than he had ever been. "I do believe I owe that plucky old woman an enormous debt."

Emotion deepened his voice. He kissed his wife with a protective tenderness that was almost painful, and he knew that nothing would ever separate them again. They brought to their marriage a wealth of experience and deep appreciation of each other, which made their second chance all the sweeter.

"Isn't the baby beautiful?" Anne said, shaking her head in wonder at her daughter's fragile perfection.

"Aye." His eyes shone with affection. "Like her mother." And in his child he saw the best of their love, all the hopes and dreams and innocence that God must envision when He sends a new soul out into the world.

"She has black hair like us too, the wee gypsy," Anne said.

"Speaking of gypsies," he said, breaking into a grin, "you do remember the next part of Black Mag's prediction?"

"Next part? Was there something else?"

"Babies," he said, stroking his daughter's cheek with his forefinger. "One down. Only six of the wee angels to go."

She laughed. "I do not believe in such nonsense, Patrick."

He looked into her eyes. "Believe in us then."

She smiled up at him. "With all my heart."

Lose yourself in the passion...
Lose yourself in the past...
Lose yourself in a Pocket Book!

The School for Heiresses ❦ Sabrina Jeffries

Experience unforgettable lessons in love for
daring young ladies in this anthology featuring
sizzling stories by Sabrina Jeffries, Liz Carlyle, Julia
London, and Renee Bernard.

Emma and the Outlaw ❦ Linda Lael Miller

Loving a man with a mysterious past can force you
to risk your heart...and your future.

His Boots Under Her Bed ❦ Ana Leigh

Will he be hers forever...or just for one night?

Relive the romance of days gone by
with Pocket Books!

Only a Duke Will Do ❧ Sabrina Jeffries
The School for Heiresses Series
A duke was the only man who could ever capture her heart—
and the only man who could ever break it.

Fairy Tale ❧ Jillian Hunter
To regain control of his castle, a Highlander must fight
the battle of his life...and surrender his heart.

A Woman Scorned ❧ Liz Carlyle
Forget fury—hell hath no passion like a woman scorned.

Lily and the Major ❧ Linda Lael Miller
In the major's arms she discovered how tender—
and how bold—true love could be.